THE
HAUNTED
LIBRARY

THE
HAUNTED
LIBRARY

Tales of Cursed Books and
Forbidden Shelves

Edited by

TANYA KIRK

This collection first published in 2025 by
The British Library
96 Euston Road
London NWI 2DB
bl.uk

I 3 5 7 9 IO 8 6 4 2

Represented in the EU by Authorised Rep Compliance Ltd., Ground Floor,
71 Lower Baggot Street, Dublin, D02 P593, Ireland. arccompliance.com

Cataloguing in Publication Data
A catalogue record for this publication is available from the British Library

ISBN 978 0 7123 5529 2
e-ISBN 978 0 7123 6215 3

Frontispiece illustration by Sandra Gómez. Illustration on page 256 is the chapter
opener for "The Spiritual Sciences" in *Eene Halve Eeuw, 1848–1898* (1898), edited
by Dr. P. H. Ritter. From the British Library Collections, shelfmark 9406.i.5.

Cover design by Mauricio Villamayor with illustration by Sandra Gómez
Text design and typesetting by Tetragon, London
Printed in England by CPI Group (UK) Ltd, Croydon, CRO 4YY

CONTENTS

INTRODUCTION

In 2016, when I was a curator at the British Library, I edited a volume of classic ghost stories set in and around libraries and other bookish places. I'd often thought about the strange contrast between the bustling public spaces of the Library's building on Euston Road in London, and the eeriness of the basement stores in the evening. Checking references in those virtually silent halls, with rows of volumes on glossy white shelves receding into the distance, it always seemed to me as if the books had an almost sentient presence. All those hundreds of years of people's voices, their lives and experiences, recorded in books that have passed through so many hands—the impressions they leave behind mean you never feel totally alone.

This feeling of the uncanny nature of books and libraries has proved rich subject matter for authors. This is in part thanks to Montague Rhodes James, a Cambridge academic who (almost by chance) established what became known as "the antiquarian tradition" in ghost stories. For a meeting of the Chitchat Society, a group who met to read their compositions and offer each other constructive criticism, James produced two entertainments: "Canon Alberic's Scrapbook" and "Lost Hearts". The success of these stories encouraged him to write more, and he established a Christmas tradition that was later described by Oliffe Legh Richmond:

> Monty disappeared into his bedroom. We sat and waited in
> the candlelight. Perhaps someone played a few bars on the
> piano, and desisted, for good reason... Monty emerged from

the bedroom, manuscript in hand, at last, and blew out all the candles but one, by which he seated himself. He then began to read, with more confidence than anyone else could have mustered, his well-nigh illegible script in the dim light. It was the ghost story of the year, begun that morning.

James's stories are distinctive in a number of ways. The iconic horror actor Christopher Lee observed:

> He wrote his stories so that we might feel just as if we were reading a newspaper, and his characters seemed at first impression to be the kind you could meet on any street. Then by dint of one phrase or sentence a very different picture would emerge from such an apparently normal situation. To me, that is the very essence of terror.

James himself explained this technique in his introduction to *Ghosts and Marvels* (1924):

> On the whole (though not a few instances might be quoted against me) I think that a setting so modern that the ordinary reader can judge of its naturalness for himself is preferable to anything antique. For some degree of actuality is the charm of the best ghost stories; not a very insistent actuality, but one strong enough to allow the reader to identify himself with the patient; while it is almost inevitable that the reader of an antique story should fall into the position of the mere spectator.

So James himself felt that to be effective, a ghost story should be rendered believable due to its closeness to the reader in some key ways. This perhaps goes some way towards explaining the background of the protagonists in his stories—antiquarian scholars; art historians; experts in medieval manuscripts or ancient runes; librarians and archivists; and archaeologists. These are people close to James himself, who was an expert in manuscript studies of the medieval period, and had catalogued most of the relevant collections across Cambridge. They are also figures that would be immediately recognisable and empathetic to his original audience; scholars who had stayed in Cambridge over Christmas when the majority of students had gone down for the holiday. And perhaps many of them would see themselves in the stories, and feel a sense of unease about their own research and what they might uncover.

Reticence is also an important element in James's style. He despised blatancy, feeling it diminished stories to the level of penny dreadfuls, and instead he demonstrated skilfully that withholding information and giving mere glimpses of monsters can be far more chilling than a detailed description. James seeds subtle details to allow the reader to anticipate the horror which is never directly shown to them. "A face of crumpled linen", "something crawling", "a hand where no hand should be"—all these are effective at conjuring indescribable and unknowable horror.

Given James's strong assertion that ghost stories should be set in a time reasonably contemporary, should feature details that people could recognise from their own surroundings, and should avoid graphic horror of the kind we are much more used to today, why is it that well over a hundred years later his stories are still so effective, and read by a far wider audience than his original Cambridge coterie? This speaks to the quality of his writing, but it also says something about how compelling an antiquarian past is for us in an age of encroaching modernism and technology. We have an aesthetic nostalgia for a slower time. In addition, the antiquarian ghost story incorporates elements of detective fiction, with the protagonist delving into the past in search of answers that perhaps should not be disturbed.

In this collection, the stories all take up a theme popularised by M. R. James's work: cursed or haunted books, manuscripts and libraries. I have revisited the 2016 edition of *The Haunted Library*, enlarged it, and selected some alternative stories that I've discovered in the intervening years.* I'm now lucky enough to be part of the historic world that M. R. James inhabited, as since 2024 I've been Librarian of St. John's College, Cambridge, and I'm more aware than ever of the heritage these stories draw on, and the way they continue to fascinate. Some of the writers in this book, such as A. N. L. Munby, William Croft Dickinson, and C. J. Faraday, were very directly inspired by James, and even came from similar scholarly backgrounds. Whereas James told his stories to friends around a cheerfully blazing fire on Christmas Eve, Munby wrote his to entertain his fellow POWs at a camp in Germany during the Second World War: evidence of the different kinds of escape a scary story might offer.

Although the subjects of the stories are similar, they exhibit a wide range of styles and speak to the concerns of the times in which they were written. One of the tales—Mary Webb's "Mr. Tallent's Ghost"—is comic in tone. H. D. Everett's "Fingers of a Hand", which deals with automatic writing, demonstrates an early twentieth century interest in psychical research. "Revenant as Typewriter" by

---

* Two of the stories which have been replaced may be read in other Tales of the Weird collections: "The Nature of the Evidence" by May Sinclair in *Queens of the Abyss* (2018), and "Bone to His Bone" by E. G. Swain in *Haunters at the Hearth* (2022).

Penelope Lively is a fascinating and effective inversion in which it is the trashy and the modern that threaten the scholarly and historic. The dangers of publishing, bookselling, and writing are all explored in addition to the Jamesian theme of research. Several stories deal with evil books which have the ability to control people, inviting us to consider who has the power—the reader, or the text.

Writers are always haunted by the ghosts of books—their books and those of others. No wonder the haunted library motif has proved so tempting. "The Whisperers" by Algernon Blackwood best evokes the uncanny feeling I get in the library stacks after dark. Some of you will know exactly what I mean.

TANYA KIRK
Librarian and Fellow
St. John's College, University of Cambridge

A NOTE FROM THE PUBLISHER

The original short stories reprinted in the British Library Tales of the Weird series were written and published in a period ranging across the nineteenth and twentieth centuries. There are many elements of these stories which continue to entertain modern readers; however, in some cases there are also uses of language, instances of stereotyping and some attitudes expressed by narrators or characters which may not be endorsed by the publishing standards of today. We acknowledge therefore that some elements in the stories selected for reprinting may continue to make uncomfortable reading for some of our audience. With this series British Library Publishing aims to offer a new readership a chance to read some of the rare material of the British Library's collections in an affordable paperback format, to enjoy their merits and to look back into the worlds of the past two centuries as portrayed by their writers. It is not possible to separate these stories from the history of their writing and therefore the following short stories are presented as they were originally published with one edit to the text, and minor edits made for consistency of style and sense. We welcome feedback from our readers, which can be sent to the following address:

British Library Publishing
The British Library
96 Euston Road
London, NW1 2DB
United Kingdom

1895

THE DEVIL'S MANUSCRIPT

S. Levett-Yeats

Sidney Kilner Levett-Yeats (1858–1916) was born in India during the British Raj, the son of the Under-Secretary to the Government of Bombay. He served as a lieutenant in the British Indian Army, and later in the Indian civil service. Having established himself as a commercial novelist of historic melodramas, he relocated to England.

This story was published in *Cassell's Magazine* in December 1895, in Levett-Yeats's very early days as a writer. It was reprinted in his collection *The Heart of Denise* in 1899. Written before M. R. James established and honed the tradition of the antiquarian ghost story, this focuses on a publisher rather than a scholar. It is an indictment of the unscrupulous nature of capitalism and the corrupting power of money at the end of the nineteenth century.

CHAPTER I
The Black Packet

"M. De Bac? De Bac? I do not know the name."

"Gentleman says he knows you, sir, and has called on urgent business."

There was no answer, and John Brown, the ruined publisher, looked about him in a dazed manner. He knew he was ruined; tomorrow the world would know it also, and then—beggary stared him in the face, and infamy too. For this the world would not care. Brown was not a great man in "the trade," and his name in the *Gazette* would not attract notice; but his name, as he stood in the felon's dock, and the ugly history a cross-examination might disclose would probably arouse a fleeting interest, and then the world would go on with a pitiless shrug of its shoulders. What does it matter to the moving wave of humanity if one little drop of spray from its crest is blown into nothing by the wind? Not a jot. But it was a terrible business for the drop of spray, otherwise John Brown, publisher. He was at his best not a good-looking man, rather mean-looking than otherwise, with a thin, angular face, eyes as shifty as a jackal's, and shoulders shaped like a champagne-bottle. As the shadow of coming ruin darkened over him, he seemed to shrink and look meaner than ever. He had almost forgotten the presence of his clerk. He could think of nothing but the morrow, when Simmonds' voice again broke the stillness.

"Shall I say you will see him, sir?"

The question cut sharply into the silence, and brought Brown to himself. He had half a mind to say "No." In the face of the coming tomorrow, business, urgent or otherwise, was nothing to him. Yet, after all, there could be no harm done in receiving the man. It would, at any rate, be a distraction, and, lifting his head, Brown answered:

"Yes, I will see him, Simmonds."

Simmonds went out, closing the green baize door behind him. There was a delay of a moment, and M. De Bac entered—a tall, thin figure, bearing an oblong parcel, packed in shiny, black paper, and sealed with flame-coloured wax.

"Good-day, Mr. Brown;" and M. De Bac, who, for all his foreign name, spoke perfect English, extended his hand.

Brown rose, put his own cold fingers into the warm grasp of his visitor, and offered him a seat.

"With your permission, Mr. Brown, I will take this other chair. It is nearer the fire. I am accustomed to warm climates, as you doubtless perceive;" and De Bac, suiting his action to his words, placed his packet on the table, and began to slowly rub his long, lean fingers together. The publisher glanced at him with some curiosity. M. De Bac was as dark as an Italian, with clear, resolute features, and a moustache, curled at the ends, thick enough to hide the sarcastic curve of his thin lips. He was strongly if sparely built, and his fiery black eyes met Brown's gaze with a look that ran through him like a needle.

"You do not appear to recognise me, Mr. Brown?"—De Bac's voice was very quiet and deep-toned.

"I have not the honour—" began the publisher; but his visitor interrupted him.

"You mistake. We are quite old friends; and in time will always be very near each other. I have a minute or two to spare"—he glanced at a repeater—"and will prove to you that I know you. You are John Brown, that very religious young man of Battersea, who, twelve years ago, behaved like a blackguard to a girl at Homerton, and sent her to—but no matter. You attracted my attention then; but, unfortunately, I had no time to devote to you. Subsequently, you effected a pretty little swindle—don't be angry, Mr. Brown—it *was* very clever. Then you started in business on your own account, and married. Things went well with you; you know the art of getting at a low price, and selling at a high one. You are a born 'sweater.' Pardon the word. You know how to keep men down like beasts, and go up yourself. In doing this, you did me yeoman's service, although you are even now not aware of this. You had one fault, you have it still, and had you not been a gambler you might have been a rich man. Speculation is a bad thing, Brown—I mean gambling speculation."

Brown was an Englishman, and it goes without saying that he had courage. But there was something in De Bac's manner, some strange power in the steady stare of those black eyes, that held him to his seat as if pinned there.

As De Bac stopped, however, Brown's anger gave him strength. Every word that was said was true, and stung like the lash of a whip. He rose, white with anger.

"Sir!" he began with quivering lips, and made a step forwards. Then he stopped. It was as if the sombre fire in De Bac's gaze withered his strength. An invisible hand seemed to drag him back into his seat and hold him there.

"You are hasty, Mr. Brown;" and De Bac's even voice continued: "you are really very rash. I was about to tell you a little more of your history, to tell you you are ruined, and tomorrow every one in London—it is the world for you, Brown—will know you are a beggar, and many will know you are a cheat."

The publisher swore bitterly under his breath.

"You see, Mr. Brown," continued his strange visitor, "I know all about you, and you will be surprised, perhaps, to hear that you deserve help from me. You are too useful to let drift. I have therefore come to save you."

"Save me?"

"Yes. By means of this manuscript here," he pointed to the packet, "which you are going to publish."

Brown now realised that he was dealing with a lunatic. He tried to stretch out his arm to touch the bell on the table; but found that he had no power to do so. He made an attempt to shout to Simmonds; but his tongue moved inaudibly in his mouth. He seemed only to have the faculty of following De Bac's words, and of answering them. He gasped out:

"It is impossible!"

"My friend"—and De Bac smiled mirthlessly—"you will publish that manuscript. I will pay. The profits will be yours. It will make your name, and you will be rich. You will even be able to build a church."

"Rich!" Brown's voice was very bitter. "M. De Bac, you said rightly. I am a ruined man. Even if you were to pay for the publication of that manuscript I could not do it now. It is too late. There are other houses. Go to them."

"But not other John Browns. You are peculiarly adapted for my purpose. Enough of this! I know what business is, and I have many things to attend to. You are a small man, Mr. Brown, and it will take little to remove your difficulties. See! Here are a thousand pounds. They will free you from your present troubles," and De Bac tossed a pocket-book on the table before Brown. "I do not want a receipt," he went on. "I will call tomorrow for your final answer, and to settle details. If you need it I will give you more money. This hour—twelve—will suit me. *Adieu!*" He was gone like a flash, and

Brown looked around in blank amazement. He was as if suddenly aroused from a dream. He could hardly believe the evidence of his senses, although he could see the black packet, and the neat leather pocket-book with the initials "L. De B." let in in silver on the outside. He rang his bell violently, and Simmonds appeared.

"Has M. De Bac gone?"

"I don't know, sir. He didn't pass out through the door."

"There is no other way. You must have been asleep."

"Indeed I was not, sir."

Brown felt a chill as of cold fingers running down his backbone, but pulled himself together with an effort. "It does not matter, Simmonds. You may go."

Simmonds went out scratching his head. "How the demon did he get out?" he asked himself. "Must have been sleeping after all. The guv'nor seems a bit dotty today. It's the smash coming—sure."

He wrote a letter or two, and then taking his hat, sallied forth to an aërated bread-shop for his cheap and wholesome lunch, for Simmonds was a saving young man, engaged to a young lady living out Camden Town way. Simmonds perfectly understood the state of affairs, and was not a little anxious about matters, for the mother of his *fiancée*, a widow who let lodgings, had only agreed to his engagement after much persuasion; and if he had to announce the fact that, instead of "thirty bob a week," as he put it, his income was nothing at all, there would be an end of everything.

"M'ria's all right," he said to his friend Wilkes, in trustful confidence as they sat over their lunch; "but that old torpedo"—by which name he designated his mother-in-law-elect—"she'll raise Cain if there's a smash-up."

In the meantime, John Brown tore open the pocket-book with shaking hands, and, with a crisp rustling, a number of new bank-notes fell out, and lay in a heap before him. He counted them one by one. They totalled to a thousand pounds exactly. He was a small man. M. De Bac had said so truly, if a little rudely, and the money was more than enough to stave off ruin. De Bac had said, too, that if needed he would give him more, and then Brown fell to trembling all over. He was like a man snatched from the very jaws of death. At Battersea he wore a blue ribbon; but now he went to a cabinet, filled a glass with raw brandy, and drained it at a gulp. In a minute or so the generous cordial warmed his chilled blood, and picking up the notes, he counted them again, and thrust them into his breast-pocket. After this he paced the room up and down in a feverish manner, longing for the morrow when he could settle up the most urgent demands against him. Then, on a sudden, a thought struck him. It was almost as if it had been whispered in his ear. Why trouble at all about matters? He had a clear thousand with him, and in an hour he could be out of the country! He hesitated, but prudence prevailed. Extradition laws stretched everywhere; and there was another thing—that extraordinary madman, De Bac, had promised more money on the morrow. After all, it was better to stay.

As he made this resolve his eyes fell on the black packet on the table. The peculiar colour of the seals attracted his attention. He bent over them, and saw that the wax bore an impress of a V-shaped shield, within which was set a trident. He noticed also that the packet was tied with a silver thread. His curiosity was excited. He sat down, snipped the threads with a penknife, tore off the black paper covering, flung it into the fire, and saw before him a bulky manuscript exquisitely written on very fine paper. A closer examination showed that they were a number of short stories. Now Brown was in no mood to read; but the title of the first tale caught his eye, and the writing was so legible that he had glanced over half a dozen lines before he was aware of the fact. Those first half-dozen lines were sufficient to make him read the page, and when he had read the page the publisher felt he was before the work of a genius.

He was unable to stop now; and, with his head resting between his hands, he read on tirelessly. Simmonds came in once or twice and left papers on the table, but his master took no notice of him. Brown forgot all about his lunch, and turning over page after page read as if spellbound. He was a business man, and was certain the book would sell in thousands. He read as one inspired to look into the author's thoughts and see his design. Short as the stories were, they were Titanic fragments, and every one of them taught a hideous lesson of corruption. Some of them cloaked in a religious garb, breathed a spirit of pitiless ferocity; others were rich with the sensuous odours of an Eastern garden; others, again, were as the tender green of moss hiding the treacherous deeps of a quicksand; and all of them bore the hall-mark of genius. They moved the man sitting there to tears, they shook him with laughter, they seemed to rock his very soul asleep; but through it all he saw, as the mariner views the beacon fire on a rocky coast, the deadly plan of the writer. There was money in them—thousands—and all was to be his. Brown's sluggish blood was running to flame, a strange strength glowed in his face, and an uncontrollable admiration for De Bac's evil power filled him. The book, when published, might corrupt generations yet unborn; but that was nothing to Brown. It meant thousands for him, and an eternal fame to De Bac. He did not grudge the writer the fame as long as he kept the thousands.

"By Heaven!" and he brought his fist down on the table with a crash, "the man may be a lunatic; but he is the greatest genius the world ever saw—or he is the devil incarnate."

And somebody laughed softly in the room.

The publisher looked up with a start, and saw Simmonds standing before him.

"Did you laugh, Simmonds?"

"No, sir!" replied the clerk with a surprised look.

"Who laughed then?"

"There is no one here but ourselves, sir—and I didn't laugh."

"Did you hear nothing?"

"Nothing, sir."

"Strange!" and Brown began to feel chill again. "What time is it?" he asked with an effort.

"It is half-past six, sir."

"So late as that? You may go, Simmonds. Leave me the keys. I will be here for some time. Good-evening."

"Mad as a coot," muttered Simmonds to himself; "must break the news to M'ria tonight. Oh, Lor'!" and his eyes were very wet as he went out into the Strand, and got into a blue omnibus.

When he was gone, Brown turned to the fire, poker in hand. To his surprise he saw that the black paper was still there, burning red hot, and the wax of the seals was still intact—the seals themselves shining like orange glow-lights. He beat at the paper with the poker; but instead of crumbling to ashes it yielded passively to the stroke, and came back to its original shape. Then a fury came on Brown. He raked at the fire, threw more coals over the paper, and blew at the flames with his bellows until they roared up the chimney; but still the coppery glare of the packet-cover never turned to the grey of ashes. Finally, he could endure it no longer, and, putting the manuscript into the safe, turned off the electric light, and stole out of his office like a thief.

CHAPTER II
The Red Trident

When Beggarman, Bowles & Co., of Providence Passage, Lombard Street, called at eleven o'clock on the morning following De Bac's visit, their representative was not a little surprised to find the firm's bills met in hard cash, and Simmonds paid him with a radiant face. When the affair was settled, the clerk leaned back in his chair, saying half-aloud to himself, "By George! I am glad after all M'ria did not keep our appointment in the Camden Road last night." Then his face began to darken. "Wonder where she could have been, though?" his thoughts ran on; "half sorry I introduced her to Wilkes last Sunday at Victoria Park. Wilkes ain't half the man I am though," and he tried to look at himself in the window-pane, "but he has two pound ten a week—Lord! There's the guv'nor ringing." He hurried into Brown's room, received a brief order, and was about to go back when the publisher spoke again.

"Simmonds!"

"Sir."

"If M. De Bac calls, show him in at once."

"Sir," and the clerk went out.

Left to himself, Brown tried to go on with the manuscript; but was not able to do so. He was impatient for the coming of De Bac, and kept watching the hands of the clock as they slowly travelled towards twelve. When he came to the office in the morning Brown had looked with a nervous fear in the fireplace, half expecting to find the black paper still there; and it was a considerable relief to his mind to find it was not. He could do nothing, not even open the envelopes of the letters that lay on his table. He made an effort to find occupation in the morning's paper. It was full of some absurd correspondence on a trivial subject, and he wondered at the thousands of fools who could waste time in writing and in reading yards of print on the theme of "Whether women should wear neckties." The ticking of the clock irritated him. He flung the paper aside, just as the door opened and Simmonds came in. For a moment Brown thought he had come to announce De Bac's arrival; but no—Simmonds simply placed a square envelope on the table before Brown.

"Pass-book from Bransom's, sir, just come in;" and he went out.

Brown took it up mechanically, and opened the envelope. A type-written letter fell out with the pass-book. He ran his eyes over it with astonishment. It was briefly to inform him that M. De Bac had paid into Brown's account yesterday afternoon the sum of five thousand pounds, and that, adjusting overdrafts, the balance at his credit was four thousand seven hundred and twenty pounds thirteen shillings and three pence. Brown rubbed his eyes. Then he hurriedly glanced at the pass-book. The figures tallied—there was no error, no mistake. He pricked himself with his penknife to see if he was awake, and finally shouted to Simmonds:

"Read this letter aloud to me, Simmonds," he said.

Simmonds' eyes opened, but he did as he was bidden, and there was no mistake about the account.

"Anything else, sir?" asked Simmonds when he had finished.

"No—nothing," and Brown was once more alone. He sat staring at the figures before him in silence, almost mesmerising himself with the intentness of his gaze.

"My God!" he burst out at last, in absolute wonder.

"Who is your God, Brown?" answered a deep voice.

"I—I—M. De Bac! How did you come?"

"I did not drop down the chimney," said De Bac with a grin; "your clerk announced me in the ordinary way, but you were so absorbed

you did not hear. So I took the liberty of sitting in this chair, and awaiting your return to earthly matters. You were dreaming, Brown—by
the way, who is your God?" he repeated with a low laugh.

"I—I do not understand, sir."

"Possibly not, possibly not. I wouldn't bother about the matter.
Ah! I see Bransom's have sent you your pass-book! Sit down, Brown.
I hate to see a man fidgeting about—I paid in that amount yesterday
on a second thought. It is enough—eh?"

Brown's jackal eyes contracted. Perhaps he could get more out
of De Bac? But a look at the strong impassive face before him frightened him.

"More than enough, sir," he stammered; and then, with a rush,
"I am grateful—anything I can do for you?"

"Oh! I know, I know, Brown—by the way, you do not object to
smoke?"

"Certainly not. I do not smoke myself."

"In Battersea, eh?" And De Bac pulling out a silver cheroot case
held it out to Brown. But the publisher declined.

"Money wouldn't buy a smoke like that in England," remarked De
Bac, "but as you will. I wouldn't smoke if I were you. Such abstinence
looks respectable and means nothing." He put a cigar between his
lips, and pointed his forefinger at the end. To Brown's amazement
an orange-flame licked out from under the fingernail, and vanished
like a flash of lightning; but the cigar was alight, and its fragrant
odour filled the room. It reached even Simmonds, who sniffed at it
like a buck scenting the morning air. "By George!" he exclaimed in
wonder, "what baccy!"

M. De Bac settled himself comfortably in his chair, and spoke
with the cigar between his teeth. "Now you have recovered a little
from your surprise, Brown, I may as well tell you that I never carry

matches. This little scientific discovery I have made is very convenient, is it not?"

"I have never seen anything like it."

"There are a good many things you have not seen, Brown—but to work. Take a pencil and paper and note down what I say. You can tell me when I have done if you agree or not."

Brown did as he was told, and De Bac spoke slowly and carefully.

"The money I have given you is absolutely your own on the following terms. You will publish the manuscript I left with you, enlarge your business, and work as you have hitherto worked—as a 'sweater.' You may speculate as much as you like. You will not lose. You need not avoid the publication of religious books, but you must never give in charity secretly. I do not object to a big cheque for a public object, and your name in all the papers. It will be well for you to hound down the vicious. Never give them a chance to recover themselves. You will be a legislator. Strongly uphold all those measures which, under a moral cloak, will do harm to mankind. I do not mention them. I do not seek to hamper you with detailed instructions. Work on these general lines, and you will do what I want. A word more. It will be advisable whenever you have a chance to call public attention to a great evil which is also a vice. Thousands who have never heard of it before will hear of it then—and human nature is very frail. You have noted all this down?"

"I have. You are a strange man, M. De Bac."

M. De Bac frowned, and Brown began to tremble.

"I do not permit you to make observations about me, Mr. Brown."

"I beg your pardon, sir."

"Do not do so again. Will you agree to all this? I promise you unexampled prosperity for ten years. At the end of that time I shall want you elsewhere. And you must agree to take a journey with me."

"A long one, sir?" Brown's voice was just a shade satirical.

M. De Bac smiled oddly. "No—in your case I promise a quick passage. These are all the conditions I attach to my gift of six thousand pounds to you."

Brown's amazement did not blind him to the fact of the advantage he had, as he thought, over his visitor. The six thousand pounds were already his, and he had given no promise. With a sudden boldness he spoke out.

"And if I decline?"

"You will return me my money, and my book, and I will go elsewhere."

"The manuscript, yes—but if I refuse to give back the money?"

"Ha! ha! ha!" M. De Bac's mirthless laugh chilled Brown to the bone. "Very good, Brown—but you won't refuse. Sign that like a good fellow," and he flung a piece of paper towards Brown, who saw that it was a promissory note, drawn up in his name, agreeing to pay M. De Bac the sum of six thousand pounds on demand.

"I shall do no such thing," said Brown stoutly.

M. De Bac made no answer, but calmly touched the bell. In a half-minute Simmonds appeared.

"Be good enough to witness Mr. Brown's signature to that document," said De Bac to him, and then fixed his gaze on Brown. There was a moment of hesitation, and then—the publisher signed his name, and Simmonds did likewise as a witness. When the latter had gone, De Bac carefully put the paper by in a letter-case he drew from his vest pocket.

"Your scientific people would call this an exhibition of odic force, Brown—eh?"

Brown made no answer. He was shaking in every limb, and great pearls of sweat rolled down his forehead.

"You see, Brown," continued De Bac, "after all you are a free agent. Either agree to my terms and keep the money, or say you will not, pay me back, receive your note-of-hand, and I go elsewhere with my book. Come—time is precious."

And from Brown's lips there hissed a low "I agree."

"Then that is settled," and De Bac rose from his chair. "There is a little thing more—stretch out your arm like a good fellow—the right arm."

Brown did so; and De Bac placed his forefinger on his wrist, just between what palmists call "the lines of life." The touch was as that of a red-hot iron, and with a quick cry Brown drew back his hand and looked at it. On his wrist was a small red trident, as cleanly marked as if it had been tattooed into the skin. The pain was but momentary; and, as he looked at the mark, he heard De Bac say, "*Adieu* once more, Brown. I will find my way out—don't trouble to rise." Brown heard him wish Simmonds an affable "Good-day," and he was gone.

CHAPTER III
"The Mark of the Beast"

It was early in the spring that Brown published "The Yellow Dragon"—as the collection of tales left with him by De Bac was called—and the success of the book surpassed his wildest expectations. It became the rage. There were the strangest rumours afloat as to its authorship, for no one knew De Bac, and the name of the writer was supposed to be an assumed one. It was written by a clergyman; it was penned by a schoolgirl; it had employed the leisure of a distinguished statesman during his retirement; it was the work of an ex-crowned head. These, and such-like statements, were poured forth one day to be contradicted the next. Wherever the book was noticed it was either with the most extravagant praise or the bitterest rancour. But friend and foe were alike united on one thing—that of ascribing to its unknown author a princely genius. The greatest of the reviews, after pouring on "The Yellow Dragon" the vials of its wrath, concluded with these words of unwilling praise: "There is not a sentence of this book which should ever have been written, still less published; but we do not hesitate to say that, having been written and given to the world, there is hardly a line of this terrible work which will not become immortal—to the misery of mankind."

Be this as it may, the book sold in tens of thousands, and Brown's fortune was assured. In ten years a man may do many things; but during the ten years that followed the publication of "The Yellow Dragon," Brown did so many things that he astonished "the city," and it takes not a little to do that. It was not alone the marvellous growth of his business—although that advanced by leaps and bounds until it overshadowed all others—it was his wonderful luck on the Stock Exchange. Whatever he touched turned to gold. He was looked upon as the Napoleon of finance. His connection with "The Yellow Dragon" was forgotten when his connection with the yellow sovereign was remembered. He had a palace in Berkshire; another huge pile owned by him overlooked Hyde Park. He was a county member and a cabinet-minister. He had refused a peerage and built a church. Could ambition want more? He had clean forgotten De Bac. From him he had heard no word, received no sign, and he looked upon him as dead. At first, when his eyes fell on the red trident on his wrist, he was wont to shudder all over; but as years went on he became accustomed to the mark, and thought no more of it than if it had been a mole. In personal appearance he was but little changed, except that his hair was thin and grey, and there was a bald patch on the top of his head. His wife had died four years ago, and he was now contemplating another marriage—a marriage that would ally him with a family dating from the Confessor.

Such was John Brown, when we meet him again ten years after De Bac's visit, seated at a large writing-table in his luxurious office. A clerk standing beside him was cutting open the envelopes of the morning's post, and placing the letters one by one before his master. It is our friend Simmonds—still a young man, but bent and old beyond his years, and still on "thirty bob" a week. And the history of Simmonds will show how Brown carried out De Bac's instructions.

When "The Yellow Dragon" came out and business began to expand, Simmonds, having increased work, was ambitious enough to expect a rise in his salary, and addressed his chief on the subject. He was put off with a promise, and on the strength of that promise Simmonds, being no wiser than many of his fellows, married M'ria; and husband and wife managed to exist somehow with the help of the mother-in-law. Then the mother-in-law died, and there was only the bare thirty shillings a week on which to live, to dress, to pay Simmonds' way daily to the city and back, and to feed more than two mouths—for Simmonds was amongst the blessed who have their quivers full. Still the expected increase of pay did not come. Other men came into the business and passed over Simmonds. Brown said they had special qualifications. They had; and John Brown knew Simmonds better than he knew himself. The other men were paid for doing things Simmonds could not have done to save his life; but he was more than useful in his way. A hundred times it was in the mind of the wretched clerk to resign his post and seek to better himself elsewhere. But he had given hostages to fortune. There was M'ria and her children, and M'ria set her face resolutely against risk. They had no reserve upon which to fall back, and it was an option between partial and total starvation. So "Sim," as M'ria called him, held on and battled with the wolf at the door, the wolf gaining ground inch by inch. Then illness came, and debt, and then—temptation. "Sim" fell, as many a better man than he has fallen.

Brown found it out, and saw his opportunity to behave generously, and make his generosity pay. He got a written confession of his guilt from Simmonds, and retained him in his service forever on thirty shillings a week. And Simmonds' life became such as made him envy the lot of a Russian serf, of a Siberian exile, of an enslaved worker in the old days of the sugar plantations. He became a slave, a living machine who ground out his daily hours of work; he became mean and sordid in soul, as one does become when hope is extinct. Such was Simmonds as he cut open the envelopes of Brown's letters, and the great man, reading them quickly, endorsed them with terse remarks in blue pencil, for subsequent disposal by his secretary. A sudden exclamation from the clerk, and Brown looked up.

"What is it?" he asked sharply.

"Only this, sir," and Simmonds held before Brown's eyes a jet black envelope; and as he gazed at it, his mind travelled back ten years, to that day when he stood on the brink of public infamy and ruin, and De Bac had saved him. For a moment everything faded before Brown's eyes, and he saw himself in a dingy room, with the gaunt figure of the author of "The Yellow Dragon," and the maker of his fortune, before him.

"Shall I open it, sir?" Simmonds' voice reached him as from a far distance, and Brown roused himself with an effort.

"No," he said, "give it to me, and go for the present."

When the bent figure of the clerk had passed out of the room, Brown looked at the envelope carefully. It bore a penny stamp and the impress of the postmark was not legible. The superscription was in white ink, and it was addressed to Mr. John Brown. The "Mr." on the letter irritated Brown, for he was now The Right Hon'ble John Brown, and was punctilious on that score. He was so annoyed that at first he thought of casting the letter unopened into the waste-paper basket beside him, but changed his mind, and tore open the cover. A note-card discovered itself. The contents were brief and to the point:

"Get ready to start. I will call for you at the close of the day. L. De B."

For a moment Brown was puzzled, then the remembrance of his old compact with De Bac came to him. He fairly laughed. To think that he, The Right Hon'ble John Brown, the richest man in England, and one of the most powerful, should be written to like that! Ordered to go somewhere he did not even know! Addressed like a servant! The cool insolence of the note amused Brown first, and then he became enraged. He tore the note into fragments and cast it from him. "Curse the madman," he said aloud, "I'll give him in charge if he annoys me." A sudden twinge in his right wrist made him hurriedly look at the spot. There was a broad pink circle, as large as a florin, around the mark of the trident, and it smarted and burned as the sting of a wasp. He ran to a basin of water and dipped his arm in to the elbow; but the pain became intolerable, and, finally, ordering his carriage, he drove home. That evening there was a great civic banquet in the city, and amongst the guests was The Right Hon'ble John Brown.

All through the afternoon he had been in agony with his wrist, but towards evening the pain ceased as suddenly as it had come on, and Brown attended the banquet, a little pale and shaken, but still himself. On Brown's right hand sat the Bishop of Browboro', on his left a most distinguished scientist, and amongst the crowd of waiters was Simmonds, who had hired himself out for the evening to earn an extra shilling or so to eke out his miserable subsistence. The man of science had just returned from Mount Atlas, whither he had gone to observe the transit of Mercury, and had come back full of stories of witchcraft. He led the conversation in that direction, and very soon the Bishop, Brown, and himself were engaged in the discussion of *diablerie*. The Bishop was a learned and a saintly man, and was a "believer"; the scientist was puzzled by what he had seen, and Brown openly scoffed.

"Look here!" and pulling back his cuff, he showed the red mark on his wrist to his companions, "if I were to tell you how that came here, you would say the devil himself marked me."

"I confess I am curious," said the scientist; and the Bishop fixed an inquiring gaze upon Brown. Simmonds was standing behind, and unconsciously drew near. Then the man, omitting many things, told the history of the mark on his wrist. He left out much, but he told enough to make the scientist edge his chair a little further from him, and a look of grave compassion, not untinged with scorn, to come into the eyes of the Bishop. As Brown came to the end of his story he became unnaturally excited, he raised his voice, and, with a sudden gesture, held his wrist close to the Bishop's face. "There!" he said, "I suppose you would say the devil did that?"

And as the Bishop looked, a voice seemed to breathe in his ear: "*And he caused all... to receive a mark in their right hand, or in their foreheads.*" It was as if his soul was speaking to him and urging him to say the words aloud. He did not; but with a pale face gently put aside Brown's hand. "I do not know, Mr. Brown—but I think you are called upon for a speech."

It was so; and, after a moment's hesitation, Brown rose. He was a fluent speaker, and the occasion was one with which he was peculiarly qualified to deal. He began well; but as he went on those who looked upon him saw that he was ghastly pale, and that the veins stood out on his high forehead in blue cords. As he spoke he made some allusion to those men who have risen to eminence from an obscure position. He spoke of himself as one of these, and then began to tell the story of "The Devil's Manuscript," as he called it, with a mocking look at the Bishop. As he went on he completely lost command over himself, and the story of the manuscript became the story of his life. He concealed nothing, he passed over nothing. He laid all his sordid past before his hearers with a vivid force. His listeners were astonished into silence; perhaps curiosity kept them still. But, as the long tale of infamy went on, some, in pity for the man, and believing him struck mad, tried to stop him, but in vain. He came at last to the incident of the letter, and told how De Bac was to call for him tonight. "The Bishop of Browboro'," he said with a jarring laugh, "thought De Bac was the fiend himself," but he (Brown) knew better; he—he stopped, and, with a half-inarticulate cry, began to back slowly from the table, his eyes fixed on the entrance to the room. And now a strange thing happened. There was not a man in the room who had the power to move or to speak; they were as if frozen to their seats; as if struck into stone. Some were able to follow Brown's glance, but could see nothing. All were able to see that in Brown's face was an awful fear, and that he was trying to escape from a horrible presence which was moving slowly towards him, and which was visible to himself alone. Inch by inch Brown gave way, until he at last reached the wall, and stood with his back to it, with his arms spread out, in the position of one crucified. His face was marble white, and a dreadful terror and a pitiful appeal shone in his eyes. His blue lips were parted as of one in the dolours of death.

The silence was profound.

There were strong men there; men who had faced and overcome dangers, who had held their lives in their hands, who had struggled against desperate odds and won; but there was not a man who did not now feel weak, powerless, helpless as a child before that invisible, advancing terror that Brown alone could see. They could move no hand to aid, lift no voice to pray. All they could do was to wait in that dreadful silence and to watch. Time itself seemed to stop. It was as if the stillness had lasted for hours.

Suddenly Brown's face, so white before, flushed a crimson purple, and with a terrible cry he fell forwards on the polished woodwork of the floor.

As he fell it seemed as if the weight which held all still was on the moment removed, and they were free. With scared faces they gathered around the fallen man and raised him. He was quite dead; but on his forehead, where there was no mark before, was the impress of a red trident.

A man, evidently one of the waiters, who had forced his way into the group, laid his finger on the mark and looked up at the Bishop. There was an unholy exultation in his face as he met the priest's eyes, and said:

"He's marked twice—*curse him!*"

THE TRACTATE MIDDOTH

M. R. James

Montague Rhodes James (1862–1936) was one of the greatest and most influential writers of ghost stories in the twentieth century. An academic and a manuscripts expert at Cambridge University for much of his life, in the 1890s James started a tradition of writing ghost stories to read to friends and colleagues at Christmas. His narratives are infused with his own interest in antiquarianism and often feature the motif of a found manuscript or other artefact which unleashes a ghost or demon onto the unsuspecting academic who studies it. His stories can act as a sort of dramatisation of a power struggle between the historian and the past, in which research which can seem pedantic and outdated awakens forces of the occult, imposing its horrors onto the modern world.

"The Tractate Middoth" is set partially in Cambridge University Library, in its original location within the "Old Schools" (the present building was not constructed until the early 1930s). The titular work is a part of the Talmud which describes in detail the rebuilt Temple in Jerusalem, including architectural measurements, although the particular annotated edition James describes is fictitious. Part of the story hinges on the fact that it was purposefully difficult for people who were not members of the University to access the Library. Female students were not granted access to the Library on the same basis as men until 1923, and were not allowed to graduate from the University until 1948—despite the fact that the first two colleges for women (Girton and Newnham) had been established in 1869 and 1871. It seems odd that James, who disapproved of women's education and would certainly have voted against allowing women access to the Library, demonstrates the unfair advantage this gives the villainous male character Eldred over the sympathetic female character Mrs. Simpson.

"The Tractate Middoth" was first published in *More Ghost Stories of an Antiquary* (1911), and is the most overtly library-themed of all James's stories, including evocative descriptions of the old book-stacks and an investigation into the structure of a shelfmark which will please the nerdiest of readers. It also has the distinction of being one of several stories in which James's lifelong fear of spiders makes an appearance.

Towards the end of an autumn afternoon an elderly man with a thin face and grey Piccadilly weepers pushed open the swing door leading into the vestibule of a certain famous library, and addressing himself to an attendant, stated that he believed he was entitled to use the library, and inquired if he might take a book out. Yes, if he were on the list of those to whom that privilege was given. He produced his card—Mr. John Eldred—and, the register being consulted, a favourable answer was given. "Now, another point," said he. "It is a long time since I was here, and I do not know my way about your building; besides, it is near closing-time, and it is bad for me to hurry up and down stairs. I have here the title of the book I want: is there any one at liberty who could go and find it for me?" After a moment's thought the doorkeeper beckoned to a young man who was passing. "Mr. Garrett," he said, "have you a minute to assist this gentleman?" "With pleasure," was Mr. Garrett's answer. The slip with the title was handed to him. "I think I can put my hand on this; it happens to be in the class I inspected last quarter, but I'll just look it up in the catalogue to make sure. I suppose it is that particular edition that you require, sir?" "Yes, if you please; that, and no other," said Mr. Eldred; "I am exceedingly obliged to you." "Don't mention it, I beg, sir," said Mr. Garrett, and hurried off.

"I thought so," he said to himself, when his finger, travelling down the pages of the catalogue, stopped at a particular entry. "Talmud:

Tractate Middoth, with the commentary of Nachmanides, Amsterdam, 1707. 11.3.34. Hebrew class, of course. Not a very difficult job this."

Mr. Eldred, accommodated with a chair in the vestibule, awaited anxiously the return of his messenger—and his disappointment at seeing an empty-handed Mr. Garrett running down the staircase was very evident. "I'm sorry to disappoint you, sir," said the young man, "but the book is out." "Oh dear!" said Mr. Eldred, "is that so? You are sure there can be no mistake?" "I don't think there is much chance of it, sir; but it's possible, if you like to wait a minute, that you might meet the very gentleman that's got it. He must be leaving the library soon, and I *think* I saw him take that particular book out of the shelf." "Indeed! You didn't recognise him, I suppose? Would it be one of the professors or one of the students?" "I don't think so: certainly not a professor. I should have known him; but the light isn't very good in that part of the library at this time of day, and I didn't see his face. I should have said he was a shortish old gentleman, perhaps a clergyman, in a cloak. If you could wait, I can easily find out whether he wants the book very particularly."

"No, no," said Mr. Eldred, "I won't—I can't wait now, thank you—no. I must be off. But I'll call again tomorrow if I may, and perhaps you could find out who has it."

"Certainly, sir, and I'll have the book ready for you if we—" but Mr. Eldred was already off, and hurrying more than one would have thought wholesome for him.

Garrett had a few moments to spare; and, thought he, "I'll go back to that case and see if I can find the old man. Most likely he could put off using the book for a few days. I dare say the other one doesn't want to keep it for long." So off with him to the Hebrew class. But when he got there it was unoccupied, and the volume marked 11.3.34 was in its place on the shelf. It was vexatious to Garrett's self-respect to have disappointed an inquirer with so little reason: and he would have liked, had it not been against library rules, to take the book down to the vestibule then and there, so that it might be ready for Mr. Eldred when he called. However, next morning he would be on the look-out for him, and he begged the doorkeeper to send and let him know when the moment came. As a matter of fact he was himself in the vestibule when Mr. Eldred arrived, very soon after the library opened, and when hardly anyone besides the staff were in the building.

"I'm very sorry," he said; "it's not often that I make such a stupid mistake, but I did feel sure that the old gentleman I saw took out that very book and kept it in his hand without opening it, just as people do, you know, sir, when they mean to take a book out of the library and not merely refer to it. But, however, I'll run up now at once and get it for you this time."

And here intervened a pause. Mr. Eldred paced the entry, read all the notices, consulted his watch, sat and gazed up the staircase, did all that a very impatient man could, until some twenty minutes had run out. At last he addressed himself to the doorkeeper and inquired if it was a very long way to that part of the library to which Mr. Garrett had gone.

"Well, I was thinking it was funny, sir: he's a quick man as a rule, but to be sure he might have been sent for by the libarian, but even so I think he'd have mentioned to him that you was waiting. I'll just speak him up on the toob and see." And to the tube he addressed himself. As he absorbed the reply to his question his face changed, and he made one or two supplementary inquiries which were shortly answered. Then he came forward to his counter and spoke in a lower tone. "I'm sorry to hear, sir, that something seems to have 'appened a little awkward. Mr. Garrett has been took poorly, it appears, and the libarian sent him 'ome in a cab the other way. Something of an attack, by what I can hear." "What, really? Do you mean that some one has injured him?" "No, sir, not violence 'ere, but, as I should judge, attacted with an attack, what you might term it, of illness. Not a strong constitootion, Mr. Garrett. But as to your book, sir, perhaps you might be able to find it for yourself. It's too bad you should be disappointed this way twice over—" "Er—well, but I'm so sorry that Mr. Garrett should have been taken ill in this way while he was obliging me. I think I must leave the book, and call and inquire after him. You can give me his address, I suppose." That was easily done: Mr. Garrett, it appeared, lodged in rooms not far from the station. "And, one other question. Did you happen to notice if an old gentleman, perhaps a clergyman, in a—yes—in a black cloak, left the library after I did yesterday. I think he may have been a—I think, that is, that he may be staying—or rather that I may have known him."

"Not in a black cloak, sir; no. There were only two gentlemen left later than what you done, sir, both of them youngish men. There was Mr. Carter took out a music-book and one of the prefessors with a couple o' novels. That's the lot, sir; and then I went off to me tea, and glad to get it. Thank you, sir, much obliged."

Mr. Eldred, still a prey to anxiety, betook himself in a cab to Mr. Garrett's address, but the young man was not yet in a condition to receive visitors. He was better, but his landlady considered that he must have had a severe shock. She thought most likely from what the doctor said that he would be able to see Mr. Eldred tomorrow. Mr. Eldred returned to his hotel at dusk and spent, I fear, but a dull evening.

On the next day he was able to see Mr. Garrett. When in health Mr. Garrett was a cheerful and pleasant-looking young man. Now he was a very white and shaky being, propped up in an armchair by the fire, and inclined to shiver and keep an eye on the door. If however there were visitors whom he was not prepared to welcome, Mr. Eldred was not among them. "It really is I who owe you an apology, and I was despairing of being able to pay it, for I didn't know your address. But I am very glad you have called. I do dislike and regret giving all this trouble, but you know I could not have foreseen this—this attack which I had."

"Of course not; but now, I am something of a doctor. You'll excuse my asking; you have had, I am sure, good advice. Was it a fall you had?"

"No. I did fall on the floor—but not from any height. It was, really, a shock."

"You mean something startled you. Was it anything you thought you saw?"

"Not much *thinking* in the case, I'm afraid. Yes, it was something I saw. You remember when you called the first time at the library?"

"Yes, of course. Well, now, let me beg you not to try to describe it—it will not be good for you to recall it, I'm sure."

"But indeed it would be a relief to me to tell any one like yourself: you might be able to explain it away. It was just when I was going into the class where your book is—"

"Indeed, Mr. Garrett, I insist; besides, my watch tells me I have but very little time left in which to get my things together and take the train. No—not another word—it would be more distressing to you than you imagine, perhaps. Now there is just one thing I want to say. I feel that I am really indirectly responsible for this illness of yours, and I think I ought to defray the expense which it has—eh?"

But this offer was quite distinctly declined. Mr. Eldred, not pressing it, left almost at once: not however, before Mr. Garrett had insisted upon his taking a note of the class mark of the Tractate Middoth, which, as he said, Mr. Eldred could at leisure get for himself. But Mr. Eldred did not reappear at the library.

William Garrett had another visitor that day in the person of a contemporary and colleague from the library, one George Earle. Earle had been one of those who found Garrett lying insensible on the floor just inside the "class" or cubicle (opening upon the central alley of a spacious gallery) in which the Hebrew books were placed, and Earle had naturally been very anxious about his friend's condition. So as soon as library hours were over he appeared at the lodgings. "Well," he said (after other conversation), "I've no notion what it was that put you wrong, but I've got the idea that there's something wrong in the atmosphere of the library. I know this, that just before we found you I was coming along the gallery with Davis, and I said to him, 'Did ever you know such a musty smell anywhere as there is about here? It can't be wholesome.' Well now, if one goes on living a long time with a smell of that kind (I tell you it was worse than I ever knew it) it must get into the system and break out some time, don't you think?"

Garrett shook his head. "That's all very well about the smell—but it isn't always there, though I've noticed it the last day or two—a sort of unnaturally strong smell of dust. But no—that's not what did for me. It was something I *saw*. And I want to tell you about it. I went into that Hebrew class to get a book for a man that was inquiring for it down below. Now that same book I'd made a mistake about the day before. I'd been for it, for the same man, and made sure that I saw an old parson in a cloak taking it out. I told my man it was out: off he went, to call again next day. I went back to see if I could get it out of the parson: no parson there, and the book on the shelf. Well, yesterday, as I say, I went again. This time, if you please—ten o'clock in the morning, remember, and as much light as ever you get in those classes, and there was my parson again, back to me, looking at the books on the shelf I wanted. His hat was on the table, and he had a bald head. I waited a second or two looking at him rather particularly. I tell you, he had a very nasty bald head. It looked to me dry, and it looked dusty, and the streaks of hair across it were much less like hair than like cobwebs. Well, I made a bit of a noise on purpose, coughed and moved my feet. He turned round and let me see his face—which I hadn't seen before. I tell you again, I'm not mistaken. Though, for one reason or another I didn't take in the lower part of his face, I did see the upper part; and it was perfectly dry, and the eyes were very deep-sunk; and over them, from the eyebrows to the cheek-bone there were *cobwebs*—thick. Now that closed me up, as they say, and I can't tell you anything more."

What explanations were furnished by Earle of this phenomenon it does not very much concern us to inquire; at all events they did not convince Garrett that he had not seen what he had seen.

Before William Garrett returned to work at the library, the librarian insisted upon his taking a week's rest and change of air. Within a few days' time, therefore, he was at the station with his bag, looking for a desirable smoking compartment in which to travel to Burnstow-on-Sea, which he had not previously visited. One compartment and one only seemed to be suitable. But, just as he approached it, he saw, standing in front of the door, a figure so like one bound up with recent unpleasant associations that, with a sickening qualm, and hardly knowing what he did, he tore open the door of the next compartment and pulled himself into it as quickly as if Death were at his heels. The train moved off, and he must have turned quite faint, for he was next conscious of a smelling-bottle being put to his nose. His physician was a nice-looking old lady, who, with her daughter, was the only passenger in the carriage.

But for this incident it is not very likely that he would have made any overtures to his fellow-travellers. As it was, thanks and inquiries and general conversation supervened inevitably: and Garrett found himself provided before the journey's end not only with a physician, but with a landlady: for Mrs. Simpson had apartments to let at Burnstow, which seemed in all ways suitable. The place was empty at that season, so that Garrett was thrown a good deal into the society of the mother and daughter. He found them very acceptable company. On the third evening of his stay he was on such terms with them as to be asked to spend the evening in their private sitting-room.

During their talk it transpired that Garrett's work lay in a library. "Ah, libraries are fine places," said Mrs. Simpson, putting down her work with a sigh; "but for all that, books have played me a sad turn, or rather *a* book has."

"Well, books give me my living, Mrs. Simpson, and I should be sorry to say a word against them: I don't like to hear that they have been bad for you."

"Perhaps Mr. Garrett could help us to solve our puzzle, Mother," said Miss Simpson.

"I don't want to set Mr. Garrett off on a hunt that might waste a lifetime, my dear, nor yet to trouble him with our private affairs."

"But if you think it in the least likely that I could be of use, I do beg you to tell me what the puzzle is, Mrs. Simpson. If it is finding out anything about a book, you see, I am in rather a good position to do it."

"Yes, I do see that, but the worst of it is that we don't know the name of the book."

"Nor what it is about?"

"No, nor that either."

"Except that we don't think it's in English, Mother—and that is not much of a clue."

"Well, Mr. Garrett," said Mrs. Simpson, who had not yet resumed her work, and was looking at the fire thoughtfully, "I shall tell you the story. You will please keep it to yourself, if you don't mind? Thank you. Now it is just this. I had an old uncle, a Dr. Rant. Perhaps you may have heard of him. Not that he was a distinguished man, but from the odd way he chose to be buried."

"I rather think I have seen the name in some guide-book."

"That would be it," said Miss Simpson. "He left directions—horrid old man!—that he was to be put, sitting at a table in his ordinary clothes, in a brick room that he'd had made underground in a field near his house. Of course the country people say he's been seen about there in his old black cloak."

"Well, dear, I don't know much about such things," Mrs. Simpson went on, "but anyhow he is dead, these twenty years and more. He was a clergyman, though I'm sure I can't imagine how he got to be one: but he did no duty for the last part of his life, which I think was a good thing; and he lived on his own property: a very nice estate not a great way from here. He had no wife or family; only one niece, who was myself, and one nephew, and he had no particular liking for either of us—nor for any one else, as far as that goes. If anything, he liked my cousin better than he did me—for John was much more like him in his temper, and, I'm afraid I must say, his very mean sharp ways. It might have been different if I had not married; but I did, and that he very much resented. Very well: here he was with this estate and a good deal of money, as it turned out, of which he had the absolute disposal, and it was understood that we—my cousin and I—would share it equally at his death. In a certain winter, over twenty years back, as I said, he was taken ill, and I was sent for to nurse him. My husband was alive then, but the old man would not hear of *his* coming. As I drove up to the house I saw my cousin John driving away from it in an open fly and looking, I noticed, in very good spirits. I went up and did what I could for my uncle, but I was very soon sure that this would be his last illness; and he was convinced of it too. During the day before he died he got me to sit by him all the time, and I could see there was something, and probably something unpleasant, that he was saving up to tell me, and putting it off as long as he felt he could afford the strength—I'm afraid purposely in order to keep me on the stretch. But, at last, out it came. 'Mary,' he said,—'Mary, I've made my will in John's favour; he has everything, Mary.' Well, of course that came as a bitter shock to me, for we—my husband and I—were not rich people, and if he could have managed to live a little easier than he was obliged to do, I felt it might be the prolonging of his life. But I said little or nothing to my uncle, except that he had a right to do what he pleased: partly because I could not think of anything to say, and partly because I was sure there was more to come: and so there was. 'But Mary,' he said, 'I'm not very fond of John, and I've made another will in *your* favour. *You* can have everything. Only you've got to find the will, you see: and I don't mean to tell you where it is.' Then he chuckled to himself, and I waited, for again I was sure he hadn't finished. 'That's a good girl,' he said after a time,—'you wait, and I'll tell you as much as I told John. But just let me remind you, you can't go into court with what I'm saying to you, for *you* won't be able to produce any collateral evidence beyond your own word, and John's a man that can do a little hard swearing if necessary. Very well then, that's understood. Now, I had the fancy that I wouldn't write this will quite in the common way, so I wrote it in a book, Mary, a printed book. And there's several thousand books in this house. But there! you needn't trouble yourself with them, for it isn't one of them. It's in safe keeping elsewhere: in a place where John can go and find it any day, if he only knew, and you can't. A good will it is: properly signed and witnessed, but I don't think you'll find the witnesses in a hurry.'

"Still I said nothing: if I had moved at all I must have taken hold of the old wretch and shaken him. He lay there laughing to himself, and at last he said—

"'Well, well, you've taken it very quietly, and as I want to start you both on equal terms, and John has a bit of a purchase in being able to go where the book is, I'll tell you just two other things which I didn't tell him. The will's in English, but you won't know that if ever you see it. That's one thing, and another is that when I'm gone you'll find an envelope in my desk directed to you, and inside it something that would help you to find it, if only you have the wits to use it.'

"In a few hours from that he was gone, and though I made an appeal to John Eldred about it—"

"John Eldred? I beg your pardon, Mrs. Simpson—I think I've seen a Mr. John Eldred. What is he like to look at?"

"It must be ten years since I saw him: he would be a thin elderly man now, and unless he has shaved them off, he has that sort of whiskers which people used to call Dundreary or Piccadilly something."

"—weepers. Yes, that *is* the man."

"Where did you come across him, Mr. Garrett?"

"I don't know if I could tell you," said Garrett mendaciously, "in some public place. But you hadn't finished."

"Really I had nothing much to add, only that John Eldred, of course, paid no attention whatever to my letters, and has enjoyed the estate ever since, while my daughter and I have had to take to the lodging-house business here, which I must say has not turned out by any means so unpleasant as I feared it might."

"But about the envelope."

"To be sure! Why the puzzle turns on that. Give Mr. Garrett the paper out of my desk."

It was a small slip, with nothing whatever on it but five numerals, not divided or punctuated in any way: 11334.

Mr. Garrett pondered, but there was a light in his eye. Suddenly he "made a face," and then asked, "Do you suppose that Mr. Eldred can have any more clue than you have to the title of the book?"

"I have sometimes thought he must," said Mrs. Simpson, "and in this way: that my uncle must have made the will not very long before he died (that, I think, he said himself), and got rid of the book immediately afterwards. But all his books were very carefully catalogued: and John has the catalogue: and John was most particular that no books whatever should be sold out of the house. And I'm told that he is always journeying about to booksellers and libraries; so I fancy that he must have found out just which books are missing from my uncle's library of those which are entered in the catalogue, and must be hunting for them."

"Just so, just so," said Mr. Garrett, and relapsed into thought.

No later than next day he received a letter which, as he told Mrs. Simpson with great regret, made it absolutely necessary for him to cut short his stay at Burnstow.

Sorry as he was to leave them (and they were at least as sorry to part with him), he had begun to feel that a crisis, all-important to Mrs. (and shall we add, Miss?) Simpson, was very possibly supervening.

In the train Garrett was uneasy and excited. He racked his brains to think whether the press mark of the book which Mr. Eldred had been inquiring after was one in any way corresponding to the numbers on Mrs. Simpson's little bit of paper. But he found to his dismay that the shock of the previous week had really so upset him that he could neither remember any vestige of the title or nature of the book, or even of the locality to which he had gone to seek it. And yet all other parts of library topography and work were clear as ever in his mind.

And another thing—he stamped with annoyance as he thought of it—he had at first hesitated, and then had forgotten, to ask Mrs. Simpson for the name of the place where Eldred lived. That, however, he could write about.

At least he had his due in the figures on the paper. If they referred to a press mark in his library, they were only susceptible of a limited number of interpretations. They might be divided into 1.13.34, 11.33.4, or 11.3.34. He could try all these in the space of a few minutes, and if any one were missing he had every means of tracing it. He got very quickly to work, though a few minutes had to be spent in explaining his early return to his landlady and his colleagues. 1.13.34 was in place and contained no extraneous writing. As he drew near to Class 11 in the same gallery, its association struck him like a chill. But he *must* go on. After a cursory glance at 11.33.4 (which first confronted him, and was a perfectly new book) he ran his eye along the line of quartos which fills 11.3. The gap he feared was there: 34 was out. A moment was spent in making sure that it had not been misplaced, and then he was off to the vestibule.

"Has 11.3.34 gone out? Do you recollect noticing that number?"

"Notice the number? What do you take me for, Mr. Garrett? There, take and look over the tickets for yourself, if you've got a free day before you."

"Well then, has a Mr. Eldred called again—the old gentleman who came the day I was taken ill. Come! you'd remember him."

"What do you suppose? Of course I recollect of him: no, he haven't been in again, not since you went off for your 'oliday. And yet I seem to—there now. Roberts 'll know. Roberts, do you recollect of the name of Heldred?"

"Not arf," said Roberts. "You mean the man that sent a bob over the price for the parcel, and I wish they all did."

"Do you mean to say you've been sending books to Mr. Eldred? Come, do speak up! Have you?"

"Well now, Mr. Garrett, if a gentleman sends the ticket all wrote correct and the secketry says this book may go and the box ready addressed sent with the note, and a sum of money sufficient to deefray the railway charges, what would be *your* action in the matter, Mr. Garrett, if I may take the liberty to ask such a question? Would you or would you not have taken the trouble to oblige, or would you have chucked the 'ole thing under the counter and—"

"You were perfectly right, of course, Hodgson—perfectly right: only, would you kindly oblige me by showing me the ticket Mr. Eldred sent, and letting me know his address?"

"To be sure, Mr. Garrett, so long as I'm not 'ectored about and informed that I don't know my duty, I'm willing to oblige in every way feasible to my power. There is the ticket on the file. J. Eldred, 11.3.34. Title of work: T—a—i—m—well, there, you can make what you like of it—not a novel, I should 'azard the guess. And here is Mr. Heldred's note applying for the book in question, which I see he terms it a track."

"Thanks, thanks: but the address? There's none on the note."

"Ah, indeed; well, now... stay now, Mr. Garrett, I 'ave it. Why, that note come inside of the parcel, which was directed very thoughtful to save all trouble, ready to be sent back with the book inside; and if I *have* made any mistake in this 'ole transaction, it lays just in the one point that I neglected to enter the address in my little book here what I keep. Not but what I daresay there was good reasons for me not entering of it: but there, I haven't the time, neither have you, I dare say, to go into 'em just now. And—no, Mr. Garrett, I do *not* carry it in my 'ed, else what would be the use of me keeping this little book here—just a ordinary common notebook, you see, which I make a practice of entering all such names and addresses in it as I see fit to do?"

"Admirable arrangement, to be sure—but—all right, thank you. When did the parcel go off?"

"Half-past ten, this morning."

"Oh, good; and it's just one now."

Garrett went upstairs in deep thought. How was he to get the address? A telegram to Mrs. Simpson: he might miss a train by waiting for the answer. Yes, there was one other way. She had said that Eldred lived on his uncle's estate. If this were so, he might find that place entered in the donation-book. That he could run through quickly, now that he knew the title of the book. The register was soon before him, and, knowing that the old man had died more than twenty years ago, he gave him a good margin, and turned back to 1870. There was but one entry possible. "1875, August 14th. *Talmud: Tractatus Middoth cum comm. R. Nachmanidoe.* Amstelod. 1707. Given by J. Rant, D. D., of Bretfield Manor."

A gazetteer showed Bretfield to be three miles from a small station on the main line. Now to ask the doorkeeper whether he recollected if the name on the parcel had been anything like Bretfield.

"No, nothing like. It was, now you mention it, Mr. Garrett, either Bredfield or Britfield, but nothing like that other name what you coated."

So far well. Next, a time-table. A train could be got in twenty minutes—taking two hours over the journey. The only chance, but one not to be missed; and the train was taken.

If he had been fidgety on the journey up, he was almost distracted on the journey down. If he found Eldred, what could he say? That it had been discovered that the book was a rarity and must be recalled? An obvious untruth. Or that it was believed to contain important manuscript notes? Eldred would of course show him the book, from which the leaf would already have been removed. He might, perhaps, find traces of the removal—a torn edge of a flyleaf probably—and who could disprove, what Eldred was certain to say, that he too had noticed and regretted the mutilation? Altogether the chase seemed very hopeless. The one chance was this. The book had left the library at 10.30: it might not have been put into the first possible train, at 11.20. Granted that, then he might be lucky enough to arrive simultaneously with it and patch up some story which would induce Eldred to give it up.

It was drawing towards evening when he got out upon the platform of his station, and, like most country stations, this one seemed unnaturally quiet. He waited about till the one or two passengers who got out with him had drifted off, and then inquired of the stationmaster whether Mr. Eldred was in the neighbourhood.

"Yes, and pretty near too, I believe. I fancy he means calling here for a parcel he expects. Called for it once today already, didn't he, Bob?" (to the porter).

"Yes sir, he did; and appeared to think it was all along of me that it didn't come by the two o'clock. Anyhow, I've got it for him now," and the porter flourished a square parcel, which a glance assured Garrett contained all that was of any importance to him at that particular moment.

"Bretfield, sir? Yes—three miles just about. Short cut across these three fields brings it down by half a mile. There: there's Mr. Eldred's trap."

A dog-cart drove up with two men in it, of whom Garrett, gazing back as he crossed the little station yard, easily recognised one. The fact that Eldred was driving was slightly in his favour—for most likely he would not open the parcel in the presence of his servant. On the other hand, he would get home quickly, and unless Garrett were there within a very few minutes of his arrival, all would be over. He must hurry; and that he did. His short cut took him along one side of a triangle, while the cart had two sides to traverse; and it was delayed a little at the station, so that Garrett was in the third of the three fields when he heard the wheels fairly near. He had made the best progress possible, but the pace at which the cart was coming made him despair. At this rate it *must* reach home ten minutes before him, and ten minutes would more than suffice for the fulfilment of Mr. Eldred's project.

It was just at this time that the luck fairly turned. The evening was still, and sounds came clearly. Seldom has any sound given greater relief than that which he now heard: that of the cart pulling up. A few words were exchanged, and it drove on. Garrett, halting in the utmost anxiety, was able to see as it drove past the stile (near which he now stood), that it contained only the servant and not Eldred; further, he made out that Eldred was following on foot. From behind the tall hedge by the stile leading into the road he watched the thin wiry figure pass quickly by with the parcel beneath its arm, and feeling in its pockets. Just as he passed the stile something fell out of a pocket upon the grass, but with so little sound that Eldred was not conscious of it. In a moment more it was safe for Garrett to cross the stile into the road and pick up—a box of matches. Eldred went on, and, as he went, his arms made hasty movements, difficult to interpret in the shadow of the trees that overhung the road. But, as Garrett followed cautiously, he found at various points the key to them—a piece of string, and then the wrapper of the parcel—meant to be thrown *over* the hedge, but sticking in it.

Now Eldred was walking slower, and it could just be made out that he had opened the book and was turning over the leaves. He stopped, evidently troubled by the failing light. Garrett slipped into a gate-opening, but still watched. Eldred, hastily looking around, sat down on a felled tree-trunk by the roadside and held the open book up close to his eyes. Suddenly he laid it, still open, on his knee, and felt in all his pockets: clearly in vain, and clearly to his annoyance. "You would be glad of your matches now," thought Garrett. Then he took hold of a leaf, and was carefully tearing it out, when two things happened. First, something black seemed to drop upon the white leaf and run down it, and then as Eldred started and was turning to look behind him, a little dark form appeared to rise out of the shadow behind the tree-trunk and from it two arms enclosing a mass of blackness came before Eldred's face and covered his head and neck. His legs and arms were wildly flourished, but no sound came. Then, there was no more movement. Eldred was alone. He had fallen back into the grass behind the tree-trunk. The book was cast into the roadway. Garrett, his anger and suspicion gone for the moment at the sight of this horrid struggle, rushed up with loud cries of "Help!" and so too, to his enormous relief, did a labourer who had just emerged from a field opposite. Together they bent over and supported Eldred, but to no purpose. The conclusion that he was dead was inevitable. "Poor gentleman!" said Garrett to the labourer, when they had laid him down, "what happened to him, do you think?" "I wasn't two hundred yards away," said the man, "when I see Squire

Eldred setting reading in his book, and to my thinking he was took with one of these fits—face seemed to go all over black." "Just so," said Garrett. "You didn't see any one near him. It couldn't have been an assault?" "Not possible—no one couldn't have got away without you or me seeing them." "So I thought. Well, we must get some help, and the doctor and the policeman; and perhaps I had better give them this book."

It was obviously a case for an inquest, and obvious also that Garrett must stay at Bretfield and give his evidence. The medical inspection showed that, though some black dust was found on the face and in the mouth of the deceased, the cause of death was a shock to a weak heart, and not asphyxiation. The fateful book was produced, a respectable quarto printed wholly in Hebrew, and not of an aspect likely to excite even the most sensitive.

"You say, Mr. Garrett, that the deceased gentleman appeared at the moment before his attack to be tearing a leaf out of this book?"

"Yes; I think one of the fly-leaves."

"There is here a flyleaf partially torn through. It has Hebrew writing on it. Will you kindly inspect it?"

"There are three names in English, sir, also, and a date. But I am sorry to say I cannot read Hebrew writing."

"Thank you. The names have the appearance of being signatures. They are John Rant, Walter Gibson, and James Frost, and the date is 20 July, 1875. Does any one here know any of these names?"

The Rector, who was present, volunteered a statement that the uncle of the deceased, from whom he inherited, had been named Rant.

The book being handed to him, he shook a puzzled head. "This is not like any Hebrew I ever learnt."

"You are sure that it is Hebrew?"

"What? Yes—I suppose No—my dear sir, you are perfectly right—that is, your suggestion is exactly to the point. Of course—it is not Hebrew at all. It is English, and it is a will."

It did not take many minutes to show that here was indeed a will of Dr. John Rant, bequeathing the whole of the property lately held by John Eldred to Mrs. Mary Simpson. Clearly the discovery of such a document would amply justify Mr. Eldred's agitation. As to the partial tearing of the leaf, the coroner pointed out that no useful purpose could be attained by speculations whose correctness it would never be possible to establish.

The Tractate Middoth was naturally taken in charge by the coroner for further investigation, and Mr. Garrett explained privately to him the history of it, and the position of events so far as he knew or guessed them.

He returned to his work next day, and on his walk to the station passed the scene of Mr. Eldred's catastrophe. He could hardly leave it without another look, though the recollection of what he had seen there made him shiver, even on that bright morning. He walked round, with some misgivings, behind the felled tree. Something dark that still lay there made him start back for a moment: but it hardly stirred. Looking closer, he saw that it was a thick black mass of cobwebs; and, as he stirred it gingerly with his stick, several large spiders ran out of it into the grass.

There is no great difficulty in imagining the steps by which William Garrett, from being an assistant in a great library, attained to his present position of prospective owner of Bretfield Manor, now in the occupation of his mother-in-law, Mrs. Mary Simpson.

THE WHISPERERS

Algernon Blackwood

Algernon Henry Blackwood (1869–1951) established a new kind of weird fiction, describing supernatural encounters in which the natural world possesses sinister powers. He was born into a wealthy family, the son of a man who had been a playboy known as "Beauty Blackwood" but who had been converted into a deeply conservative and evangelical Christian during the Crimean War. Blackwood rebelled against his upbringing, becoming interested in mysticism and involved in the Hermetic Order of the Golden Dawn, an occult group that also included Bram Stoker, Arthur Machen and Aleister Crowley.

In addition to fiction exploring the natural world as the source of a dark, mystical force, Blackwood was famed for ghost stories. He featured on the BBC's first ever television programme, *Picture Page*, relating a ghost story at the broadcast from Alexandra Palace on 2 November 1936. He later made regular appearances on both television and radio, and became known as "the Ghost Man".

This is one of his less famous stories, which was first published on 23 May 1912 in *The Eye-Witness*, and reprinted in Blackwood's collection *Ten-Minute Stories* (1914). It is less overtly spooky than most of the others in this collection, but is worthy of inclusion because of its interesting and evocative concept.

To be too impressionable is as much a source of weakness as to be hyper-sensitive: so many messages come flooding in upon one another that confusion is the result; the mind chokes, imagination grows congested.

Jones, as an imaginative writing man, was well aware of this, yet could not always prevent it; for if he dulled his mind to one impression, he ran the risk of blunting it to all. To guard his main idea, and picket its safe conduct through the seethe of additions that instantly flocked to join it, was a psychological puzzle that sometimes overtaxed his powers of critical selection. He prepared for it, however. An editor would ask him for a story—"about five thousand words, you know"; and Jones would answer, "I'll send it you with pleasure—when it comes." He knew his difficulty too well to promise more. Ideas were never lacking, but their length of treatment belonged to machinery he could not coerce. They were alive; they refused to come to heel to suit mere editors. Midway in a tale that started crystal clear and definite in its original germ, would pour a flood of new impressions that either smothered the first conception, or developed it beyond recognition. Often a short story exfoliated in this bursting way beyond his power to stop it. He began one, never knowing where it would lead him. It was ever an adventure. Like Jack the Giant Killer's beanstalk it grew secretly in the night, fed by everything he read, saw, felt, or heard. Jones was too impressionable; he received too many impressions, and too easily.

For this reason, when working at a definite, short idea, he preferred an empty room, without pictures, furniture, books, or anything suggestive, and with a skylight that shut out scenery—just ink, blank paper, and the clear picture in his mind. His own interior, unstimulated by the geysers of external life, he made some pretence of regulating; though even under these favourable conditions the matter was not too easy, so prolifically does a sensitive mind engender.

His experience in the empty room of the carpenter's house was a curious case in point—in the little Jura village where his cousin lived to educate his children. "We're all in a pension above the Post Office here," the cousin wrote, "but just now the house is full, and besides is rather noisy. I've taken an attic room for you at the carpenter's near the forest. Some things of mine have been stored there all the winter, but I moved the cases out this morning. There's a bed, writing-table, wash-handstand, sofa, and a skylight window—otherwise empty, as I know you prefer it. You can have your meals with us," etc. And this just suited Jones, who had six weeks' work on hand for which he needed empty solitude. His "idea" was slight and very tender; accretions would easily smother clear presentment; its treatment must be delicate, simple, unconfused.

The room really was an attic, but large, wide, high. He heard the wind rush past the skylight when he went to bed. When the cupboard was open he heard the wind there too, washing the outer walls and tiles. From his pillow he saw a patch of stars peep down upon him. Jones knew the mountains and the woods were close, but he could not see them. Better still, he could not smell them. And he went to bed dead tired, full of his theme for work next morning. He saw it to the end. He could almost have promised five thousand words. With the dawn he would be up and "at it," for he usually woke very early, his mind surcharged, as though subconsciousness had matured the material in sleep. Cold bath, a cup of tea, and then—his writing-table; and the quicker he could reach the writing-table the richer was the content of imaginative thought. What had puzzled him the night before was invariably cleared up in the morning. Only illness could interfere with the process and routine of it.

But this time it was otherwise. He woke, and instantly realised, with a shock of surprise and disappointment, that his mind was— groping. It was groping for his little lost idea. There was nothing physically wrong with him; he felt rested, fresh, clear-headed; but his brain was searching, searching, moreover, in a crowd. Trying to seize hold of the train it had relinquished several hours ago, it caught at an evasive, empty shell. The idea had utterly changed; or rather it seemed smothered by a host of new impressions that came pouring in upon it—new modes of treatment, points of view, in fact development. In the light of these extensions and novel aspects, his original idea had altered beyond recognition. The germ had marvellously exfoliated, so that a whole volume could alone express it. An army of fresh suggestions clamoured for expression. His subconsciousness had grown thick with life; it surged—active, crowded, tumultuous.

And the darkness puzzled him. He remembered the absence of accustomed windows, but it was only when the candlelight brought close the face of his watch, with two o'clock upon it, that he heard the sound of confused whispering in the corners of the room, and realised with a little twinge of fear that those who whispered had just been standing beside his very bed. The room was full.

Though the candlelight proclaimed it empty—bare walls, bare floor, five pieces of unimaginative furniture, and fifty stars peeping through the skylight—it was undeniably thronged with living people whose minds had called him out of heavy sleep. The whispers, of course, died off into the wind that swept the roof and skylight; but the Whisperers remained. They had been trying to get at him; waking suddenly, he had caught them in the very act... And all had brought new interpretations with them; his thought had fundamentally altered; the original idea was snowed under; new images brimmed his mind, and his brain was working as it worked under the high pressure of creative moments.

Jones sat up, trembling a little, and stared about him into the empty room that yet was densely packed with these invisible Whisperers. And he realised this astonishing thing—that he was the object of their deliberate assault, and that scores of other minds, deep, powerful, very active minds, were thundering and beating upon the doors of his imagination. The onset of them was terrific and bewildering, the attack of aggressive ideas obliterating his original story beneath a flood of new suggestions. Inspiration had become suddenly torrential, yet so vast as to be unwieldy, incoherent, useless. It was like the tempest of images that fever brings. His first conception seemed no longer "delicate", but petty. It had turned unreal and tiny, compared with this enormous choice of treatment, extension, development, that now overwhelmed his throbbing brain.

Fear caught vividly at him, as he searched the empty attic-room in vain for explanation. There was absolutely nothing to produce this tempest of new impressions. People seemed talking to him all together, jumbled somewhat, but insistently. It was obsession, rather than inspiration; and so bitingly, dreadfully real.

"Who are you all?" his mind whispered to blank walls and vacant corners.

Back from the shouting floor and ceiling came the chorus of images that stormed and clamoured for expression. Jones lay still and listened; he let them come. There was nothing else to do. He lay fearful, negative, receptive. It was all too big for him to manage, set to some scale of high achievement that submerged his own small powers. It came, too, in a series of impressions, all separate, yet all somehow interwoven.

In vain he tried to sort them out and sift them. As well sort out waves upon an agitated sea. They were too self-assertive for direction or control. Like wild animals, hungry, thirsty, ravening, they rushed from every side and fastened on his mind.

Yet he perceived them in a certain sequence.

For, first, the unfurnished attic-chamber was full of human passion, of love and hate, revenge and wicked cunning, of jealousy, courage, cowardice, of every vital human emotion ever longed for, enjoyed, or frustrated, all clamouring for—expression.

Flaming across and through these, incongruously threaded in and out, ran next a yearning softness of incredible beauty that sighed in the empty spaces of his heart, pleading for impossible fulfilment...

And, after these, carrying both one and other upon their surface, huge questions flashed and dived and thundered in a patterned, wild entanglement, calling to be unravelled and made straight. Moreover, with every set came a new suggested treatment of the little clear idea he had taken to bed with him five hours before.

Jones adopted each in turn. Imagination writhed and twisted beneath the stress of all these potential modes of expression he must choose between. His small idea exfoliated into many volumes, work enough to fill a dozen lives. It was most gorgeously exhilarating, though so hopelessly unmanageable. He felt like many minds in one...

Then came another chain of impressions, violent, yet steady owing to their depth; the voices, questions, pleadings turned to pictures; and he saw, struggling through the deeps of him, enormous quantities of people, passing along like rivers, massed, herded, swayed here and there by some outstanding figure of command who directed them like flowing water. They shrieked, and fought, and battled, then sank out of sight, huddled and destroyed in—blood...

And their places were taken instantly by white crowds with shining eyes, and yearning in their faces, who climbed precipitous heights towards some Radiance that kept ever out of sight, like sunrise behind mountains that clouds then swallow... The pelt and thunder of images was destructive in its torrent; his little, first idea was drowned and wrecked... Jones sank back exhausted, utterly dismayed. He gave up all attempt to make selection.

The driving storm swept through him, on and on, now waxing, now waning, but never growing less, and apparently endless as the sky. It rushed in circles, like the turning of a giant wheel. All the activities that human minds have ever battled with since thought began came booming, crashing, straining for expression against the imaginative stuff whereof his mind was built. The walls began to yield and settle. It was like the chaos that madness brings. He did not struggle against it; he let it come, lying open and receptive, pliant and plastic to every detail of the vast invasion. And the only time he attempted a complete obedience, reaching out for the pencil and notebook that lay beside his bed, he desisted instantly again, sinking back upon his pillows with a kind of frightened laughter. For the tempest seemed then to knock him down and bruise his very brain. Inextricable confusion caught him. He might as well have tried to make notes of the entire Alexandrian Library in half an hour...

Then, most singular of all, as he felt the sleep of exhaustion fall upon his tired nerves, he heard that deep, prodigious sound. All that had preceded, it gathered marvellously in, mothering it with a sweetness that seemed to his imagination like some harmonious, geometrical skein including all the activities men's minds have ever known. Faintly he realised it only, discerned from infinitely far away. Into the streams of apparent contradiction that warred so strenuously about him, it seemed to bring some hint of unifying, harmonious explanation... And, here and there, as sleep buried him, he imagined that chords lay threaded along strings of cadences, breaking sometimes even into melody—music that rose everywhere from life and wove Thought into a homogeneous Whole...

"Sleep well?" his cousin inquired, when he appeared very late next day for *déjeuner*. "Think you'll be able to work in that room all right?"

"I slept, yes, thanks," said Jones. "No doubt I shall work there right enough—when I'm rested. By the bye," he asked presently, "what has the attic been used for lately? What's been in it, I mean?"

"Books, only books," was the reply. "I've stored my 'library' there for months, without a chance of using it. I move about so much, you see. Five hundred books were taken out just before you came. I often think," he added lightly, "that when books are unopened like that for long, the minds that wrote them must get restless and—"

"What sort of books were they?" Jones interrupted.

"Fiction, poetry, philosophy, history, religion, music. I've got two hundred books on music alone."

FINGERS OF A HAND

H. D. Everett

Henrietta Dorothy Everett (1851–1923), née Huskisson, was born in Gillingham, Kent, into a naval family. Her father was a first lieutenant and quartermaster in the Royal Marines, rising to the senior rank of Major Paymaster by the 1870s. Henrietta married a solicitor in 1869 and settled in the West Midlands. From the mid-1890s onwards she became a reasonably prolific and very popular novelist, publishing historical romances and fantastical stories under the pen name Theo Douglas. After 1910 she wrote under her own name. This story was published in her final book, *The Death-Mask and Other Ghosts*, in 1920. M. R. James praised the volume in his essay "Some Remarks on Ghost Stories" (1929), describing it as "of a rather quieter tone on the whole, but with some excellently conceived stories".

The epigraph at the start of this story is a quotation from the King James Bible, referring to the story of Belshazzar's Feast, where the king receives a warning through mysterious writing that appears on the wall.

"In the same hour came forth
the fingers of a man's hand and wrote...
and the king saw the part of the hand that wrote."

The children were supposed to need a seaside change, and I daresay they did, poor wee things, as they had had whooping-cough in the spring, and measles to follow. As you know, we are taking care of them for Bernard, who is in India with his wife, and so we are even more anxious about them than if they were our own. That is one great use of unmarried aunts—to shoulder other people's responsibilities; and I, for one, think the world would be a poorer place if the "million of unwanted women" were, by some convulsion of nature, to be swept away. I only mention the children's measles as the reason why we took those lodgings at Cove at the beginning of July, for, now one has to economise, we should not have gone in for a seaside change as a luxury for ourselves.

The lodgings were clean and fairly comfortable, and we took them for two months certain, letting our own pretty cottage in the Midlands for a similar term. And that was why we had no home of our own to retreat to when—But I am telling my story upside down, as Sara says I always do. You would not be likely to understand, if I did not begin in the right place, with what went before.

The house was Number Seven, Cliff Terrace, a row of detached villas above the road, on the other side of which was the esplanade and the sea. There were no other lodgers, as we took both Mrs. Mills's "sets"; nobody in the house but ourselves and the bairns, and that important person Nurse, except Mrs. Mills herself, and her daughter who waited on us. So you see there was no one who could have played tricks—But again I am getting on too fast.

We had never been to Cove before, or to St. Eanswyth either, the larger watering-place which lies to the east of Cove; but we thought our choice of place for a summer holiday was amply justified by the pretty inland neighbourhood and the sweet air, and a safe beach close at hand, where the children could be out playing early and late under the guardian wing of Nurse. For the first fortnight we were all satisfied and happy, and, both in metaphor and actually, there was not a cloud in the sky.

Then the rain began, not brief summer showers and sunshine in between, but the worst weather of a wet July—a continuous downpour with hardly ten minutes intermission, and going on for days: such rain as Noah must have witnessed before the beginning of the Flood.

Of course the poor children had to keep to the house, and, though they and Nurse had the dining-room set to themselves, there was but little space for them to play about. Sara and I occupied the drawing-room, and she had been sketching from the window—not that there was much visible to make into a picture: a leaden sea and slanting lines of rain, and boats drawn up on the beach. At last she pushed away colour-box and pencils.

"I can't stand this any longer," she said. "Rain or no rain, I am going out. It will be a good opportunity to test the resisting powers of my new cloak. You must stay in today, as I believe you have caught cold."

I did not dispute her fiat. Sara always decides what is, or what is not to be done, and I, who am a biddable person, submit to be ruled. And, to say the truth, I was not particularly anxious to get wet. I went on with my sewing till it was nearly time for Miss Mills to appear with the luncheon-tray, and then I began to clear the table of Sara's scattered possessions.

Some blank sheets of paper were lying about, besides the one pinned to her board with the half-finished sketch; and on one of these I noticed some large scrawled writing. Not Sara's writing, which is particularly small and neat; not the writing of any one I knew. The words were quite legible, but they were very odd. GO—by itself at the top of the sheet; and the same word repeated twice below, followed by GET OUT AT ONCE.

Of course I showed Sara this when she came in to luncheon, and she could not account for it any more than I. The sheets were unmarked when she took them out of her portfolio; of that she seemed to be certain.

"Some one has been playing a trick on us," she said. "If it is Mrs. Mills, it is an odd sort of notice"; and at this very mild witticism both of us laughed.

But the idea of a trick being played was absurd: I had been in the room the whole time, as I said.

"Unless you think I dozed off while you were out, and did it in my sleep!"

Sara laughed again, and began to sort the loose papers back into place.

"Why, here is more of it," she exclaimed; and I saw on the sheet she held out, in the same large scrawl, a repetition of the words— GET OUT—GET OUT AT ONCE.

Now I could have sworn—had swearing been of any use—that

I had looked those papers over on both sides after finding the first writing, and with that sole exception they bore no mark whatever. So these last words must have been written after my discovery and before Sara's return, and while I was beside them in the room. Surely they had been traced by no mortal hand!

You will not wonder that such a curious happening was the subject of discussion between us during the rest of that wet day. "I'd give anything to know who did it," Sara was saying, while I added: "I should like better still to know what it means." I am more credulous than Sara, and it seemed to me there must be some meaning in anything so unaccountable. I had this feeling from the very first, and, as you will see, both the conviction and the reason for it grew.

I pass on to the following Sunday. The weather was still wet, and the children were kept mainly to the house. For the sake of variety for them, Sara had little Dick and Nancy upstairs in our sitting-room for their Sunday lessons, which as a rule devolve on her to give, as she is a cleverer teacher than I. Lessons of the simplest, as they generally consist of showing pictures and giving explanations; and to be allowed to look at Sara's illustrated Bible is a frequent Sabbath treat. The children had gone down again to Nurse, and Sara was about to tidy the book away, when she gave a sharp exclamation.

"Grace, look here. Who can have done this?"

The volume was lying open at the nineteenth chapter of Genesis, and these words in the twenty-second verse were scored under blackly in pencil—*Haste thee: escape.*

Now Sara, who is particular in everything, is especially so about her books. She hates any soil or mark upon them, and nothing irritates her more than to have a lent volume returned with "purple passages" scored beside in the margin, whether in approval or otherwise. "Tut-tut," she was saying, at the usual pitch of exasperation. "It is really unpardonable. *Where* is my india-rubber? I must see if I can take it out. It could not have been the children. And the Millses would never—! But there is nobody else."

"You would have seen, had it been the children. They are good little things, and would not: besides, they had not a pencil"—(thus I weakened an argument based on their righteousness). "And what odd words to have chosen to mark, when you think of the other scrawls. I wonder if this is all. It is possible there may be more."

"I shall look the book right through and see, and then I shall lock it in my box."

Sara sat down to her task armed with the piece of rubber, and by no means in a Sabbath spirit of peace and good-will. She did find two other texts scored under, and these were the marked words:

2 Kings, ninth chapter and third verse. *Open the door and flee and tarry not.*

St. Matthew, seventh chapter and twenty-seventh verse. *The... house... fell, and great was the fall thereof.*

I was superstitious, because disturbed by these happenings. So I was told, yet who would not have been affected in my place? I believe Sara too was disquieted in her secret mind, though she would not allow it. But then she was used to pride herself on being an *esprit fort*.

I kept saying to myself, What next?—and the next came quickly. I did not tell Sara what I purposed doing, but I left a couple of sheets of paper and a freshly cut pencil displayed on the table when we were going out. More writing might be done with the opportunity given, and "it" might vouchsafe to make clear "its" meaning. I could not then have analysed what I meant by the convenient impersonal pronoun, nor am I clear of the exact meaning now.

We were about to do some shopping in the town, and I had stupidly left my purse on the mantel-shelf in the sitting-room, so I was obliged to turn back to get it. As I opened the door, my eyes fell at once upon the papers, and I saw some dark object moving across the white surface, and then quickly disappearing over the table edge. It was too big for a mouse; could it have been a rat? The thought of a rat gave me a nervous shiver; I think I would have a greater terror of rats than of ghosts. I looked at the papers though I did not touch them; yes, a vague scrawl was begun upon the upper one, not developed into legible words. I had disturbed the writer too soon. But what could the writer be, coming in the form of a rat, or the shadow of a rat, and yet able to write words which appeared to convey a message? I left the papers as they were, but the scrawl was not continued; no doubt that unexpected first return had scared away the writer.

I said nothing to Sara of my failed experiment; but next day about the same time I laid my trap again, this time staying in the room, but retired into a distant corner, where I set myself to watch.

For a long while there was nothing. Then an object ill-defined and shadowy crept across the paper, stealing towards the pencil as it lay. I hardly dared breathe, the excitement was so tense. Over the pencil this shadow paused, and now became denser, taking solid form. It was not the whole of a hand, but a thumb and two fingers, forming something like a claw. But, if you consider, a thumb and two fingers are all a hand needs to manipulate a pencil, and "it" may not have cared to materialise anything superfluous. The pencil now slanted upwards between these fingers and the thumb, and—yes, no doubt remained—the claw was writing. Now we would know all, such was my sanguine thought, not forecasting how deep the mystery would remain.

It was Sara this time who interrupted, coming in. The pencil dropped, the claw from a solid form became a shadow, and slipped away over the edge of the table, as I had seen it vanish before. Sara noticed nothing; she was too full of her news, and of the letter open in her hand.

"Look at this. We ought to have had it two days ago, but there was a mistake in the address. It is from Mrs. Bernard's mother" (Mrs. Bernard is our brother's wife). "She is at Diplake for ten days before they go to Scotland, and she wants one of us to bring the children there just for the time they stay. She says she is sorry she cannot have us both, but it is a case of a single room, as the house is full. She is expecting us tomorrow, so I shall have to wire, and tell Nurse to get ready. Will you go, Grace, or shall I?"

"Of course you must be the one. I should never get on at Diplake, and with a large, gay party. You must go, Sara, and put your best foot foremost, for Bernard's sake. And—I'm glad you have to take the children. For look what is written here!"

I showed her the paper on which the claw had scrawled. Over and over again the word DANGER, as if it could not be too often insisted on. Then, also repeated: GO. GET OUT. Then an attempt at *children*, afterwards clearly written: DANGER. CHILDREN MUST GO.

I think Sara was impressed at last, though she hardly believed in the claw I had seen writing. As to that, I must—she said—have been hallucinated, or else slept and dreamed. But little time remained for argument, as all was in a hurry of preparation—boxes to be packed, and the children to be consoled, for their enjoyment of the seaside pleasures was very keen, and the attraction small of going to stay with an almost unknown grandmother. "But we are coming back?" said little Nancy. "We are coming back again here?" I believe I told her yes, but as to what will happen in the future, who can say?

They set out early next morning, Sara and the three children and Nurse, and I saw them off at the station. Sara said almost at the last:

"I don't half like leaving you alone here, Grace. If you find the lodgings too solitary, why not take a room at the hotel for the days I am away?"

I said I would think of it, but in truth I felt no special nervousness or concern, only an intense curiosity to see what would happen now we had (by pure accident) obeyed the dictation of the writing, and sent the children away.

The lonely evening passed for me without disturbance; Miss Mills came at the usual time to carry down my supper tray, and wished me goodnight, and shortly after this I went to bed.

I slept, and do not remember any warning dreams. But in the very early daylight I was suddenly startled broad awake—not I think by any noise, but by an alteration in the level of my bed. My head was low, almost on the floor, and my feet were high in air. Everything in the room was sliding and altering; basin and ewer slipped from the washstand, crashed and broke, and pictures flapped from the wall. Then came a greater crash like the jolting of a thunder-clap, and it was close at hand; chimney-pots falling, walls and roofs collapsing: was it an earthquake that had happened? I heard screams and shouts, but the sliding movement had stopped.

I struggled up and to my feet, for I had been half buried by the bedclothes falling back upon me; and there opposite was a great crack or rent in the outer wall, wide enough to admit my arm, with the new morning looking through, and a waft of air blowing in keenly from the sea. It was as if the house had broken in two. What but an earthquake could have caused such a disaster?—and again I heard people screaming. The often repeated warning, the scored words in the Bible ran in my head. I could be thankful indeed that Sara and the children were safe at Diplake out of the way: what an agony had they been still here, and those screams possibly theirs!

I do not know how long it took me to scramble up the slanting floor, to find my clothes, my shoes, where all was confusion, so that if it were possible to get out of the house I might go forth clad. Then I tried the door.

It was in some way jammed, and it seemed as if ages passed before I could wrench it open. When at last it gave way, the wreck revealed without was worse than the wreck within. The staircase was a heap of broken wood, and the back wall had fallen inwards; there was no getting down that way. What had become, I wondered, of Mrs. Mills and her daughter, and was it their screams that I heard? I called to them by name, but there was no answer.

Baffled so, I looked from the window, which had hardly a whole pane left. It was as if the terrace had disappeared: the road was broken up, and the house had been carried down with the sliding earth, many yards nearer the sea. A crowd had assembled, staring at this phenomenon, but at a safe distance. I shouted to them, and a man called up to me instructions to stay where I was, as a ladder would presently be brought.

I knew later that they feared at first to touch the house, lest it should collapse in total ruin like the one next on the terrace, where, alas! two people had been killed, overwhelmed and buried in their sleep.

This was a danger indeed, about which that warning came. The part of our house which fell, was where the children would have been sleeping. I was told that tons and tons of masonry had crushed in their little beds; even now it makes me sick to think of what we so narrowly escaped. The Millses, mother and daughter, were dug out of the basement quite unharmed, but I am afraid, poor people, they are heavy losers. I myself had not a scratch.

The great landslip at Cove, with all its damage and disaster, will surely pass into history: the slide of the undercliff down into the sea, the gaping fissure torn above, hundreds of feet in length—the alteration of the ground below, heaped into mounds and billows like the waves of the sea, while the buildings in the course of the slide are broken up and displaced like a set of children's toys, playthings in the hands of a giant. People who are wise about the geological formation, talk of a bed of slippery clay underlying the upper strata, and say water had percolated down to it owing to the wet spring, and, following upon that, the heavy rains of that dismal week in July. But they are wise after the event and did not forecast it: indeed it was anticipated by no one other than the writer of those mysterious words.

MR. TALLENT'S GHOST

Mary Webb

Mary Gladys Webb (1881–1927), née Meredith, is best known today for her novels of the Shropshire countryside, such as *Gone to Earth* (1917) and *Precious Bane* (1924). She spent most of her life as an invalid suffering from Graves' disease, and felt keenly the pain of others too. As well as tremendous generosity towards the poor (even when semi-impoverished herself), she vehemently opposed blood sports and was a vegetarian. Her novels are passionate and tragic, and although she never achieved real fame in her lifetime, a year after her premature death the prime minister Stanley Baldwin gave a speech in praise of her at the Royal Literary Fund dinner, and her popularity grew.

In total contrast to Webb's novels, "Mr. Tallent's Ghost" is a light-hearted pastiche of a ghost story. It was published in Lady Cynthia Asquith's hugely influential edited collection *The Ghost Book* in 1926.

The first time I ever met Mr. Tallent was in the late summer of 1906, in a small, lonely inn on the top of a mountain. For natives, rainy days in these places are not very different from other days, since work fills them all, wet or fine. But for the tourist, rainy days are boring. I had been bored for nearly a week, and was thinking of returning to London, when Mr. Tallent came. And because I could not "place" Mr. Tallent, nor elucidate him to my satisfaction, he intrigued me. For a barrister should be able to sum up men in a few minutes.

I did not see Mr. Tallent arrive, nor did I observe him entering the room. I looked up, and he was there, in the small firelit parlour with its Bible, wool mats and copper preserving pan. He was reading a manuscript, slightly moving his lips as he read. He was a gentle, moth-like man, very lean and about six foot three or more. He had neutral-coloured hair and eyes, a nondescript suit, limp-looking hands and slightly turned-up toes. The most noticeable thing about him was an expression of passive and enduring obstinacy.

I wished him good evening, and asked if he had a paper, as he seemed to have come from civilisation.

"No," he said softly, "no. Only a little manuscript of my own."

Now, as a rule I am as wary of manuscripts as a hare is of greyhounds. Having once been a critic, I am always liable to receive parcels of these for advice. So I might have saved myself and a dozen or so of other people from what turned out to be a terrible, an appalling, incubus. But the day had been so dull, and having exhausted Old Moore and sampled the Imprecatory Psalms, I had nothing else to read. So I said, "Your own?"

"Even so," replied Mr. Tallent modestly.

"May I have the privilege?" I queried, knowing he intended me to have it.

"How kind!" he exclaimed. "A stranger, knowing nothing of my hopes and aims, yet willing to undertake so onerous a task."

"Not at all!" I replied, with a nervous chuckle.

"I think," he murmured, drawing near and, as it were, taking possession of me, looming above me with his great height, "it might be best for me to read it to you. I am considered to have rather a fine reading voice."

I said I should be delighted, reflecting that supper could not very well be later than nine. I knew I should not like the reading.

He stood before the cloth-draped mantelpiece.

"This," he said, "shall be my rostrum." Then he read.

I wish I could describe to you that slow, expressionless, unstoppable voice. It was a voice for which at the time I could find no comparison. Now I know that it was like the voice of the loud speaker in a dull subject. At first one listened, taking in even the sense of the words. I took in all the first six chapters, which were unbelievably dull. I got all the scenery, characters, undramatic events clearly marshalled. I imagined that something would, in time, happen. I thought the characters were going to develop, do fearful things or great and holy deeds. But they did nothing. Nothing happened. The book was flat, formless, yet not vital enough to be inchoate. It was just a meandering expression of a negative personality, with a plethora of muted, borrowed, stale ideas. He always said what one expected him to say. One knew what all his people would do. One waited for the culminating platitude as for an expected twinge of toothache. I thought he would pause after a time, for even the most arrogant usually do that, apologising and at the same time obviously waiting for one to say, "Do go on, please."

This was not necessary in his case. In fact, it was impossible. The slow, monotonous voice went on without a pause, with the terrible tirelessness of a gramophone. I longed for him to whisper or shout—anything to relieve the tedium. I tried to think of other things, but he read too distinctly for that. I could neither listen to him nor ignore him. I have never spent such an evening. As luck would have it the little maidservant did not achieve our meal till nearly ten o'clock. The hours dragged on.

At last I said: "Could we have a pause, just for a few minutes?"

"Why?" he enquired.

"For... for discussion," I weakly murmured.

"Not," he replied, "at the most exciting moment. Don't you realise that now, at last, I have worked up my plot to the most dramatic moment? All the characters are waiting, attent, for the culminating tragedy."

He went on reading. I went on awaiting the culminating tragedy. But there was no tragedy. My head ached abominably. The voice flowed on, over my senses, the room, the world. I felt as if it would wash me away into eternity. I found myself thinking, quite solemnly:

"If she doesn't bring supper soon, I shall kill him."

I thought it in the instinctive way in which one thinks it of an earwig or a midge. I took refuge in the consideration how to do it? This was absorbing. It enabled me to detach myself completely from the sense of what he read. I considered all the ways open to me. Strangling. The bread knife on the sideboard. Hanging. I gloated over them, I was beginning to be almost happy, when suddenly the reading stopped.

"She is bringing supper," he said. "Now we can have a little discussion. Afterwards I will finish the manuscript."

He did. And after that, he told me all about his will. He said he was leaving all his money for the posthumous publication of his manuscripts. He also said that he would like me to draw up this for him, and to be trustee of the manuscripts.

I said I was too busy. He replied that I could draw up the will tomorrow.

"I'm going tomorrow," I interpolated passionately.

"You cannot go until the carrier goes in the afternoon," he triumphed. "Meanwhile, you can draw up the will. After that you need do no more. You can pay a critic to read the manuscripts. You can pay a publisher to publish them. And I in them shall be remembered."

He added that if I still had doubts as to their literary worth, he would read me another.

I gave in. Would anyone else have done differently? I drew up the will, left an address where he could send his stuff, and left the inn.

"Thank God!" I breathed devoutly, as the turn of the lane hid him from view. He was standing on the doorstep, beginning to read what he called a pastoral to a big cattle-dealer who had called for a pint of bitter. I smiled to think how much more he would get than he had bargained for.

After that, I forgot Mr. Tallent. I heard nothing more of him for some years. Occasionally I glanced down the lists of books to see if anybody else had relieved me of my task by publishing Mr. Tallent. But nobody had.

It was about ten years later, when I was in hospital with a "Blighty" wound, that I met Mr. Tallent again. I was convalescent, sitting in the sun with some other chaps, when the door opened softly, and Mr. Tallent stole in. He read to us for two hours. He remembered me, and had a good deal to say about coincidence. When he had gone, I said to the nurse, "If you let that fellow in again while I'm here, I'll kill him."

She laughed a good deal, but the other chaps all agreed with me, and as a matter of fact, he never did come again.

Not long after this I saw the notice of his death in the paper.

"Poor chap!" I thought, "he's been reading too much. Somebody's patience has given out. Well, he won't ever be able to read to me again."

Then I remembered the manuscripts, realising that, if he had been as good as his word, my troubles had only just begun.

And it was so.

First came the usual kind of letter from a solicitor in the town where he had lived. Next I had a call from the said solicitor's clerk, who brought a large tin box.

"The relations," he said, "of the deceased are extremely angry. Nothing has been left to them. They say that the manuscripts are worthless, and that the living have rights."

I asked how they knew that the manuscripts were worthless.

"It appears, sir, that Mr. Tallent has, from time to time, read these aloud—"

I managed to conceal a grin.

"And they claim, sir, to share equally with the—er—manuscripts. They threaten to take proceedings, and have been getting legal opinions as to the advisability of demanding an investigation of the material you have."

I looked at the box. There was an air of Joanna Southcott about it. I asked if it were full.

"Quite, sir. Typed MSS. Very neatly done."

He produced the key, a copy of the will, and a sealed letter.

I took the box home with me that evening. Fortified by dinner, a cigar and a glass of port, I considered it. There is an extraordinary air of fatality about a box. For bane or for blessing, it has a perpetual fascination for mankind. A wizard's coffer, a casket of jewels, the alabaster box of precious nard, a chest of bridal linen, a stone sarcophagus—what a strange mystery is about them all! So when I opened Mr. Tallent's box, I felt like somebody letting loose a genie. And indeed I was. I had already perused the will and the letter, and discovered that the fortune was moderately large. The letter merely repeated what Mr. Tallent had told me. I glanced at some of the manuscripts. Immediately the room seemed full of Mr. Tallent's presence and his voice. I looked towards the now dusky corners of the room as if he might be looming there. As I ran through more of the papers, I realised that what Mr. Tallent had chosen to read to me had been the best of them. I looked up Johnson's telephone number and asked him to come round. He is the kind of chap who never makes any money. He is a freelance journalist with a conscience. I knew he would be glad of the job.

He came round at once. He eyed the manuscripts with rapture. For at heart he is a critic, and has the eternal hope of unearthing a masterpiece.

"You had better take a dozen at a time, and keep a record," I said. "Verdict at the end."

"Will it depend on me whether they are published?"

"*Which* are published," I said. "Some will have to be. The will says so."

"But if I found them all worthless, the poor beggars would get more of the cash? Damnable to be without cash."

"I shall have to look into that. I am not sure if it is legally possible. What, for instance, is the standard?"

"I shall create the standard," said Johnson rather haughtily. "Of course, if I find a masterpiece—"

"If you find a masterpiece, my dear chap," I said, "I'll give you a hundred pounds."

He asked if I had thought of a publisher. I said I had decided on Jukes, since no book, however bad, could make his reputation worse than it was, and the money might save his credit.

"Is that quite fair to poor Tallent?" he asked. Mr. Tallent had already got hold of him.

"If," I said as a parting benediction, "you wish you had never gone into it (as, when you have put your hand to the plough, you will), remember that at least they were never read aloud to you, and be thankful."

Nothing occurred for a week. Then letters began to come from Mr. Tallent's relations. They were a prolific family. They were all very poor, very angry and intensely uninterested in literature. They wrote from all kinds of view-points, in all kinds of styles. They were, however, all alike in two things—the complete absence of literary excellence and legal exactitude.

It took an increasing time daily to read and answer these. If I gave them any hope, I at once felt Mr. Tallent's hovering presence, mute, anxious, hurt. If I gave no hope, I got a solicitor's letter by return of post. Nobody but myself seemed to feel the pathos of Mr. Tallent's ambitions and dreams. I was notified that proceedings were going to be taken by firms all over England. Money was being recklessly spent to rob Mr. Tallent of his immortality, but it appeared, later, that Mr. Tallent could take care of himself.

When Johnson came for more of the contents of the box, he said that there was no sign of a masterpiece yet, and that they were as bad as they well could be.

"A pathetic chap, Tallent," he said.

"Don't, for God's sake, my dear chap, let him get at you," I implored him. "Don't give way. He'll haunt you, as he's haunting me, with that abominable pathos of his. I think of him and his box continually just as one does of a life and death plea. If I sit by my own fireside, I can hear him reading. When I am just going to sleep, I dream that he is looming over me like an immense, wan moth. If I forget him for a little while, a letter comes from one of his unutterable relations and recalls me. Be wary of Tallent."

Needless to tell you that he did not take my advice. By the time he had finished the box, he was as much under Tallent's thumb as I was. Bitterly disappointed that there was no masterpiece, he was still loyal to the writer, yet he was emotionally harrowed by the pitiful letters that the relations were now sending to all the papers.

"I dreamed," he said to me one day (Johnson always says "dreamed", because he is a critic and considers it the elegant form of expression), "I dreamed that poor Tallent appeared to me in the watches of the night and told me exactly how each of his things came to him. He said they came like 'Kubla Khan'."

I said it must have taken all night.

"It did," he replied. "And it has made me dislike a masterpiece."

I asked him if he intended to be present at the general meeting.

"Meeting?"

"Yes. Things have got to such a pitch that we have had to call one. There will be about a hundred people. I shall have to entertain them to a meal afterwards. I can't very well charge it up to the account of the deceased."

"Gosh! It'll cost a pretty penny."

"It will. But perhaps we shall settle something. I shall be thankful."

"You're not looking well, old chap," he said, "Worn, you seem."

"I am," I said. "Tallent is ever with me. Will you come?"

"Rather. But I don't know what to say."

"The truth, the whole truth—"

"But it's so awful to think of that poor soul spending his whole life on those damned... and then that they should never see the light of day."

"Worse that they should. Much worse."

"My dear chap, what a confounded position!"

"If I had foreseen *how* confounded," I said, "I'd have strangled the fellow on the top of that mountain. I have had to get two clerks to deal with the correspondence. I get no rest. All night I dream of Tallent. And now I hear that a consumptive relation of his has died of disappointment at not getting any of the money, and his wife has written me a wild letter threatening to accuse me of manslaughter. Of course that's all stuff, but it shows what a hysterical state everybody's in. I feel pretty well done for."

"You'd feel worse if you'd read the boxful."

I agreed.

We had a stormy meeting. It was obvious that the people did need the money. They were the sort of struggling, under-vitalised folk who always do need it. Children were waiting for a chance in life, old people were waiting to be saved from death a little longer, middle-aged people were waiting to set themselves up in business or buy snug little houses. And there was Tallent, out of it all, in a spiritual existence, not needing beef and bread any more, deliberately keeping it from them.

As I thought this, I distinctly saw Tallent pass the window of the room I had hired for the occasion. I stood up; I pointed; I cried out to them to follow him. The very man himself.

Johnson came to me.

"Steady, old man," he said. "You're overstrained."

"But I did see him," I said. "The very man. The cause of all the mischief. If I could only get my hands on him!"

A medical man who had married one of Tallent's sisters said that these hallucinations were very common, and that I was evidently not a fit person to have charge of the money. This brought me a ray of hope, till that ass Johnson contradicted him, saying foolish things about my career. And a diversion was caused by a tremulous old lady calling out, "The Church! The Church! Consult the Church! There's something in the Bible about it, only I can't call it to mind at the moment. Has anybody got a Bible?"

A clerical nephew produced a pocket New Testament, and it transpired that what she had meant was, "Take ten talents."

"If I could take one, madam," I said, "it would be enough."

"It speaks of that too," she replied triumphantly. "Listen! 'If any man have one talent...' Oh, there's everything in the Bible!"

"Let us," remarked one of the thirteen solicitors, "get to business. Whether it's in the Bible or not, whether Mr. Tallent went past the window or not, the legality or illegality of what we propose is not affected. Facts are facts. The deceased is dead. *You've* got the money. *We* want it."

"I devoutly wish you'd got it," I said, "and that Tallent was haunting you instead of me."

The meeting lasted four hours. The wildest ideas were put forward. One or two sporting cousins of the deceased suggested a decision by games—representatives of the would-be beneficiaries and representatives of the manuscript. They were unable to see that this could not affect the legal aspect. Johnson was asked for his opinion. He said that from a critic's point of view the MSS. were balderdash. Everybody looked kindly upon him. But just as he was sunning himself in this atmosphere, and trying to forget Tallent, an immense lady, like Boadicea, advanced upon him, towering over him in a hostile manner.

"I haven't read the books, and I'm not going to," she said, "but I take exception to that word balderdash, sir, and I consider it libellous. Let me tell you, I brought Mr. Tallent into the world!" I looked at her with awesome wonder. She had brought that portent into the world! But how... whom had she persuaded?... I pulled myself up. And as I turned away from the contemplation of Boadicea, I saw Tallent pass the window again.

I rushed forward and tried to push up the sash. But the place was built for meetings, not for humanity, and it would not open. I seized the poker, intending to smash the glass. I suppose I must have looked rather mad, and as everybody else had been too intent on business to look out of the window, nobody believed that I had seen anything.

"You might just go round to the nearest chemist's and get some bromide," said the doctor to Johnson. "He's overwrought."

Johnson, who was thankful to escape Boadicea, went with alacrity.

The meeting was, however, over at last. A resolution was passed that we should try to arrange things out of court. We were to take the opinions of six eminent lawyers—judges preferably. We were also to submit what Johnson thought the best story to a distinguished critic. According to what they said we were to divide the money up or leave things as they were.

I felt very much discouraged as I walked home. All these opinions would entail much work and expense. There seemed no end to it.

"Damn the man!" I muttered, as I turned the corner into the square in which I live. And there, just the width of the square away from me, was the man himself. I could almost have wept. What had I done that the gods should play with me thus?

I hurried forward, but he was walking fast, and in a moment he turned down a side-street. When I got to the corner, the street was empty. After this, hardly a day passed without my seeing Tallent. It made me horribly jumpy and nervous, and the fear of madness began to prey on my mind. Meanwhile, the business went on. It was finally decided that half the money should be divided among the relations. Now I thought there would be peace, and for a time there was—comparatively.

But it was only about a month from this date that I heard from one of the solicitors to say that a strange and disquieting thing had happened—two of the beneficiaries were haunted by Mr. Tallent to such an extent that their reason was in danger. I wrote to ask what form the haunting took. He said they continually heard Mr. Tallent reading aloud from his works. Wherever they were in the house, they still heard him. I wondered if he would begin reading to me soon. So far it had only been visions. If he began to read...

In a few months I heard that both the relations who were haunted had been taken to an asylum. While they were in the asylum they heard nothing. But, some time after, on being certified as cured and released, they heard the reading again, and had to go back. Gradually the same thing happened to others, but only to one or two at a time.

During the long winter, two years after his death, it began to happen to me.

I immediately went to a specialist, who said there was acute nervous prostration, and recommended a "home". But I refused. I would fight Tallent to the last. Six of the beneficiaries were now in "homes", and every penny of the money they had had was used up.

I considered things. "Bell, book and candle" seemed to be what was required. But how, when, where to find him? I consulted a spiritualist, a priest and a woman who has more intuitive perception than anyone I know. From their advice I made my plans. But it was Lesbia who saved me.

"Get a man who can run to go about with you," she said. "The moment *He* appears, let your companion rush round by a side-street and cut him off."

"But how will that—?"

"Never mind. I know what I think."

She gave me a wise little smile.

I did what she advised, but it was not till my patience was nearly exhausted that I saw Tallent again. The reading went on, but only in the evenings when I was alone, and at night. I asked people in evening after evening. But when I got into bed, it began.

Johnson suggested that I should get married.

"What?" I said, "offer a woman a ruined nervous system, a threatened home, and a possible end in an asylum?"

"There's one woman who would jump at it. I love my love with an L."

"Don't be an ass," I said. I felt in no mood for jokes. All I wanted was to get things cleared up.

About three years after Tallent's death, my companion and I, going out rather earlier than usual, saw him hastening down a long road which had no side-streets leading out of it. As luck would have it, an empty taxi passed us. I shouted. We got in. Just in front of Tallent's ghost we stopped, leapt out, and flung ourselves upon him.

"My God!" I cried. "He's *solid*!"

He was perfectly solid, and not a little alarmed.

We put him into the taxi and took him to my house.

"*Now*, Tallent!" I said, "you will answer for what you have done."

He looked scared, but dreamy.

"Why aren't you dead?" was my next question.

He seemed hurt.

"I never died," he replied softly.

"It was in the papers."

"I put it in. I was in America. It was quite easy."

"And that continual haunting of me, and the wicked driving of your unfortunate relations into asylums?" I was working myself into a rage. "Do you know how many of them are there now?"

"Yes. I know. Very interesting."

"Interesting?"

"It was in a great cause," he said. "Possibly you didn't grasp that I was a progressive psycho-analyst, and that I did not take those novels of mine seriously. In fact, they were just part of the experiment."

"In heaven's name, *what* experiment?"

"The plural would be better, really," he said, "for there were many experiments."

"But what for, you damned old blackguard?" I shouted.

"For my *magnum opus*," he said modestly.

"And what is your abominable *magnum opus*, you wicked old man?"

"It will be famous all over the world," he said complacently. "All this has given me exceptional opportunities. It was so easy to get into my relations' houses and experiment with them. It was regrettable, though, that I could not follow them to the asylum."

This evidently worried him far more than the trouble he had caused.

"So it was *you* reading, every time?"

"Every time."

"And it was you who went past the window of that horrible room when we discussed your will?"

"Yes. A most gratifying spectacle!"

"And now, you old scoundrel, before I decide what to do with you," I said, "what is the *magnum opus?*"

"It is a treatise," he said, with the pleased expression that made me so wild. "A treatise that will eclipse all former work in that field, and its title is—'An Exhaustive Enquiry, with numerous Experiments, into the Power of Human Endurance'."

THE BOOK

Margaret Irwin

Margaret Emma Faith Irwin (1889–1967) was once best known as an historical novelist focusing mainly on the Elizabethan and Stuart periods, but she also wrote fantasy novels and a large number of short stories (the latter mostly for publication in *The London Mercury*). She grew up in Bristol where she lived with her uncle, a classics master at Clifton College—where A. N. L. Munby would later be a pupil.

This story on a Faustian theme appeared in the September 1930 edition of *The London Mercury*, and was republished in Irwin's collection of supernatural tales, *Madame Fears the Dark* (1935). Here Irwin appears to have been inspired by M. R. James; although Mr. Corbett in the story cannot be said to be an antiquarian, the act of reading allows a demonic force to infiltrate an ordinary contemporary setting and endanger the vulnerable.

On a foggy night in November, Mr. Corbett, having guessed the murderer by the third chapter of his detective story, arose in disappointment from his bed and went downstairs in search of something more satisfactory to send him to sleep.

The fog had crept through the closed and curtained windows of the dining-room and hung thick on the air in a silence that seemed as heavy and breathless as the fog. The atmosphere was more choking than in his room, and very chill, although the remains of a large fire still burned in the grate.

The dining-room bookcase was the only considerable one in the house and held a careless unselected collection to suit all the tastes of the household, together with a few dull and obscure old theological books that had been left over from the sale of a learned uncle's library. Cheap red novels, bought on railway stalls by Mrs. Corbett, who thought a journey the only time to read, were thrust in like pert, undersized intruders among the respectable nineteenth-century works of culture, chastely bound in dark blue or green, which Mr. Corbett had considered the right thing to buy during his Oxford days; beside these there swaggered the children's large gaily bound story-books and collections of Fairy Tales in every colour.

From among this neat new cloth-bound crowd there towered here and there a musty sepulchre of learning, brown with the colour of dust rather than leather, with no trace of gilded letters, however faded, on its crumbling back to tell what lay inside. A few of these moribund survivors from the Dean's library were inhospitably fastened with rusty clasps; all remained closed, and appeared impenetrable, their blank, forbidding backs uplifted above their frivolous surroundings with the air of scorn that belongs to a private and concealed knowledge. For only the worm of corruption now bored his way through their evil-smelling pages.

It was an unusual flight of fancy for Mr. Corbett to imagine that the vaporous and fog-ridden air that seemed to hang more thickly about the bookcase was like a dank and poisonous breath exhaled by one or other of these slowly rotting volumes. Discomfort in this pervasive and impalpable presence came on him more acutely than at any time that day; in an attempt to clear his throat of it he choked most unpleasantly.

He hurriedly chose a Dickens from the second shelf as appropriate to a London fog, and had returned to the foot of the stairs when he decided that his reading tonight should by contrast be of blue Italian skies and white statues, in beautiful rhythmic sentences. He went back for a Walter Pater.

He found *Marius the Epicurean* tipped sideways across the gap left by his withdrawal of *The Old Curiosity Shop*. It was a very wide gap to have been left by a single volume, for the books on that shelf had been closely wedged together. He put the Dickens back into it and saw that there was still space for a large book. He said to himself in careful and precise words: "This is nonsense. No one can possibly have gone into the dining-room and removed a book while I was crossing the hall. There must have been a gap before in the second shelf." But another part of his mind kept saying in a hurried, tumbled torrent: "There was no gap in the second shelf. There was no gap in the second shelf."

He snatched at both the *Marius* and *The Old Curiosity Shop*, and went to his room in a haste that was unnecessary and absurd, since even if he believed in ghosts, which he did not, no one had the smallest reason for suspecting any in the modern Kensington house wherein he and his family had lived for the last fifteen years. Reading was the best thing to calm the nerves, and Dickens a pleasant, wholesome and robust author.

Tonight, however, Dickens struck him in a different light. Beneath the author's sentimental pity for the weak and helpless, he could discern a revolting pleasure in cruelty and suffering, while the grotesque figures of the people in Cruikshank's illustrations revealed too clearly the hideous distortions of their souls. What had seemed humorous now appeared diabolic, and in disgust at these two favourites he turned to Walter Pater for the repose and dignity of a classic spirit.

But presently he wondered if this spirit were not in itself of a marble quality, frigid and lifeless, contrary to the purpose of nature. "I have often thought," he said to himself, "that there is something evil in the austere worship of beauty for its own sake." He had never thought so before, but he liked to think that this impulse of fancy was the result of mature consideration, and with this satisfaction he composed himself for sleep.

He woke two or three times in the night, an unusual occurrence, but he was glad of it, for each time he had been dreaming horribly of these blameless Victorian works. Sprightly devils in whiskers and peg-top trousers tortured a lovely maiden and leered in delight at her anguish; the gods and heroes of classic fable acted deeds whose naked crime and shame Mr. Corbett had never appreciated in Latin and Greek Unseens. When he had woken in a cold sweat from the spectacle of the ravished Philomel's torn and bleeding tongue, he decided there was nothing for it but to go down and get another book that would turn his thoughts in some more pleasant direction. But his increasing reluctance to do this found a hundred excuses. The recollection of the gap in the shelf now occurred to him with a sense of unnatural importance; in the troubled dozes that followed, this gap between two books seemed the most hideous deformity, like a gap between the front teeth of some grinning monster.

But in the clear daylight of the morning Mr. Corbett came down to the pleasant dining-room, its sunny windows and smell of coffee and toast, and ate an undiminished breakfast with a mind chiefly occupied in self-congratulation that the wind had blown the fog away in time for his Saturday game of golf. Whistling happily, he was pouring out his final cup of coffee when his hand remained arrested in the act as his glance, roving across the bookcase, noticed that there was now no gap at all in the second shelf. He asked who had been at the bookcase already, but neither of the girls had, nor Dicky, and Mrs. Corbett was not yet down. The maid never touched the books. They wanted to know what book he missed in it, which made him look foolish, as he could not say. The things that disturb us at midnight are negligible at 9 a.m.

"I thought there was a gap in the second shelf," he said, "but it doesn't matter."

"There never is a gap in the second shelf," said little Jean brightly. "You can take out lots of books from it and when you go back the gap's always filled up. Haven't you noticed that? I have."

Nora, the middle one in age, said Jean was always being silly; she had been found crying over the funny pictures in *The Rose and the Ring* because she said all the people in them had such wicked faces, and the picture of a black cat had upset her because she thought it was a witch. Mr. Corbett did not like to think of such fancies for his Jeannie. She retaliated briskly by saying Dicky was just as bad, and he was a big boy. He had kicked a book across the room and said, "Filthy stuff," just like that. Jean was a good mimic; her tone expressed a venom of disgust, and she made the gesture of dropping a book as though the very touch of it were loathsome. Dicky, who had been making violent signs at her, now told her she was a beastly little sneak and he would never again take her for rides on the step of his bicycle. Mr. Corbett was disturbed. Unpleasant housemaids and bad schoolfriends passed through his head, as he gravely asked his son how he had got hold of this book.

"Took it out of that bookcase of course," said Dicky furiously.

It turned out to be the *Boy's Gulliver's Travels* that Granny had given him, and Dicky had at last to explain his rage with the devil who wrote it to show that men were worse than beasts and the human race a wash-out. A boy who never had good school reports had no right to be so morbidly sensitive as to penetrate to the underlying cynicism of Swift's delightful fable, and that moreover in the bright and carefully expurgated edition they bring out nowadays. Mr. Corbett could not say he had ever noticed the cynicism himself, though he knew from the critical books it must be there, and with some annoyance he advised his son to take out a nice bright modern boy's adventure story that could not depress anybody. It appeared, however, that Dicky was "off reading just now", and the girls echoed this.

Mr. Corbett soon found that he too was "off reading". Every new book seemed to him weak, tasteless and insipid; while his old and familiar books were depressing or even, in some obscure way, disgusting. Authors must all be filthy-minded; they probably wrote what they dared not express in their lives. Stevenson had said that literature was a morbid secretion; he read Stevenson again to discover his peculiar morbidity, and detected in his essays a self-pity masquerading as courage, and in *Treasure Island* an invalid's sickly attraction to brutality.

This gave him a zest to find out what he disliked so much, and his taste for reading revived as he explored with relish the hidden infirmities of minds that had been valued by fools as great and noble. He saw Jane Austen and Charlotte Bronte as two unpleasant examples of spinsterhood; the one as a prying, sub-acid busybody in everyone else's flirtations, the other as a raving, craving maenad seeking self-immolation on the altar of her frustrated passions. He compared Wordsworth's love of nature to the monstrous egoism of an ancient bell-wether, isolated from the flock.

These powers of penetration astonished him. With a mind so acute and original he should have achieved greatness, yet he was a mere solicitor and not prosperous at that. If he had but the money, he might do something with those ivory shares, but it would be a pure gamble, and he had no luck. His natural envy of his wealthier acquaintances now mingled with a contempt for their stupidity that approached loathing. The digestion of his lunch in the City was ruined by meeting sentimental yet successful dotards whom he had once regarded as pleasant fellows. The very sight of them spoiled his game of golf, so that he came to prefer reading alone in the dining-room even on sunny afternoons.

He discovered also and with a slight shock that Mrs. Corbett had always bored him. Dicky he began actively to dislike as an impudent blockhead, and the two girls were as insipidly alike as white mice; it was a relief when he abolished their tiresome habit of coming in to say good night.

In the now unbroken silence and seclusion of the dining-room, he read with feverish haste as though he were seeking for some clue to knowledge, some secret key to existence which would quicken and inflame it, transform it from its present dull torpor to a life worthy of him and his powers.

He even explored the few decaying remains of his uncle's theological library. Bored and baffled, he yet persisted, and had the occasional relief of an ugly woodcut of Adam and Eve with figures like bolsters and hair like dahlias, or a map of the Cosmos with Hellmouth in the corner, belching forth demons. One of these books had diagrams and symbols in the margin which he took to be mathematical formulae of a kind he did not know. He presently discovered that they were drawn, not printed, and that the book was in manuscript, in a very neat, crabbed black writing that resembled black-letter printing. It was moreover in Latin, a fact that gave Mr. Corbett a shock of unreasoning disappointment. For while examining the signs in the margin, he had been filled with an extraordinary exultation as though he knew himself to be on the edge of a discovery that should alter his whole life. But he had forgotten his Latin.

With a secret and guilty air which would have looked absurd to anyone who knew his harmless purpose, he stole to the schoolroom for Dicky's Latin dictionary and grammar and hurried back to the dining-room, where he tried to discover what the book was about with an anxious industry that surprised himself. There was no name to it, nor of the author. Several blank pages had been left at the end, and the writing ended at the bottom of a page, with no flourish or superscription, as though the book had been left unfinished. From what sentences he could translate, it seemed to be a work on theology rather than mathematics. There were constant references to the Master, to his wishes and injunctions, which appeared to be of a complicated kind. Mr. Corbett began by skipping these as mere accounts of ceremonial, but a word caught his eye as one unlikely to occur in such an account. He read this passage attentively, looking up each word in the dictionary, and could hardly believe the result of his translation. "Clearly," he decided, "this book must be by some early missionary, and the passage I have just read the account of some horrible rite practised by a savage tribe of devil-worshippers." Though he called it "horrible", he reflected on it, committing each detail to memory. He then amused himself by copying the signs in the margin near it and trying to discover their significance. But a sensation of sickly cold came over him, his head swam, and he could hardly see the figures before his eyes. He suspected a sudden attack of influenza, and went to ask his wife for medicine.

They were all in the drawing-room, Mrs. Corbett helping Nora and Jean with a new game, Dicky playing the pianola, and Mike, the Irish terrier, who had lately deserted his accustomed place on the dining-room hearthrug, stretched by the fire. Mr. Corbett had an instant's impression of this peaceful and cheerful scene, before his family turned towards him and asked in scared tones what was the matter. He thought how like sheep they looked and sounded; nothing in his appearance in the mirror struck him as odd; it was their gaping faces that were unfamiliar. He then noticed the extraordinary behaviour of Mike, who had sprung from the hearthrug and was crouched in the furthest corner, uttering no sound, but with his eyes distended and foam round his bared teeth. Under Mr. Corbett's glance, he slunk towards the door, whimpering in a faint and abject manner, and then as his master called him, he snarled horribly, and the hair bristled on the scruff of his neck. Dicky let him out, and they heard him scuffling at a frantic rate down the stairs to the kitchen, and then, again and again, a long-drawn howl.

"What *can* be the matter with Mike?" asked Mrs. Corbett.

Her question broke a silence that seemed to have lasted a long time. Jean began to cry. Mr. Corbett said irritably that he did not know what was the matter with any of them.

Then Nora asked, "What is that red mark on your face?"

He looked again in the glass and could see nothing.

"It's quite clear from here," said Dicky; "I can see the lines in the finger-print."

"Yes, that's what it is," said Mrs. Corbett in her brisk staccato voice; "the print of a finger on your forehead. Have you been writing in red ink?"

Mr. Corbett precipitately left the room for his own, where he sent down a message that he was suffering from headache and would have his dinner in bed. He wanted no one fussing round him. By next morning he was amazed at his fancies of influenza, for he had never felt so well in his life.

No one commented on his looks at breakfast, so he concluded that the mark had disappeared. The old Latin book he had been translating on the previous night had been moved from the writing bureau, although Dicky's grammar and dictionary were still there. The second shelf was, as always in the daytime, closely packed; the book had, he remembered, been in the second shelf. But this time he did not ask who had put it back.

That day he had an unexpected stroke of luck in a new client of the name of Crab, who entrusted him with large sums of money: nor was he irritated by the sight of his more prosperous acquaintances, but with difficulty refrained from grinning in their faces, so confident was he that his remarkable ability must soon place him higher than any of them. At dinner he chaffed his family with what he felt to be the gaiety of a schoolboy. But on them it had a contrary effect, for they stared, either at him in stupid astonishment, or at their plates, depressed and nervous. Did they think him drunk? he wondered, and a fury came on him at their low and bestial suspicions and heavy dullness of mind. Why, he was younger than any of them!

But in spite of this new alertness he could not attend to the letters he should have written that evening and drifted to the bookcase for a little light distraction, but found that for the first time there was nothing he wished to read. He pulled out a book from above his head at random, and saw that it was the old Latin book in manuscript. As he turned over its stiff and yellow pages, he noticed with pleasure the smell of corruption that had first repelled him in these decaying volumes, a smell, he now thought, of ancient and secret knowledge.

This idea of secrecy seemed to affect him personally, for on hearing a step in the hall he hastily closed the book and put it back in its place. He went to the schoolroom where Dicky was doing his homework, and told him he required his Latin grammar and dictionary again for an old law report. To his annoyance he stammered and put his words awkwardly; he thought that the boy looked oddly at him and he cursed him in his heart for a suspicious young devil, though of what he should be suspicious he could not say. Nevertheless, when back in the dining-room, he listened at the door and then softly turned the lock before he opened the books on the writing-bureau.

The script and Latin seemed much clearer than on the previous evening, and he was able to read at random a passage relating to a trial of a German midwife in 1620 for the murder and dissection of 783 children. Even allowing for the opportunities afforded by her profession, the number appeared excessive, nor could he discover any motive for the slaughter. He decided to translate the book from the beginning.

It appeared to be an account of some secret society whose activities and ritual were of a nature so obscure, and when not, so vile and terrible, that Mr. Corbett would not at first believe that this could be a record of any human mind, although his deep interest in it should have convinced him that from his humanity at least it was not altogether alien.

He read until far later than his usual hour for bed and when at last he rose, it was with the book in his hands. To defer his parting with it, he stood turning over the pages until he reached the end of the writing, and was struck by a new peculiarity.

The ink was much fresher and of a far poorer quality than the thick rusted ink in the bulk of the book; on close inspection he would have said that it was of modern manufacture and written quite recently were it not for the fact that it was in the same crabbed late seventeenth-century handwriting.

This however did not explain the perplexity, even dismay and fear, he now felt as he stared at the last sentence. It ran: "Confine te in perennibus studiis," and he had at once recognised it as a Ciceronian tag that had been dinned into him at school. He could not understand how he had failed to notice it yesterday.

Then he remembered that the book had ended at the bottom of a page. But now, the last two sentences were written at the very top of a page. However long he looked at them, he could come to no other conclusion than that they had been added since the previous evening.

He now read the sentence before the last: "Re imperfecta mortuus sum," and translated the whole as: "I died with my purpose unachieved. Continue, thou, the never-ending studies."

With his eyes still fixed upon it, Mr. Corbett replaced the book on the writing-bureau and stepped back from it to the door, his hand outstretched behind him, groping and then tugging at the door-handle. As the door failed to open, his breath came in a faint, hardly articulate scream. Then he remembered that he had himself locked it, and he fumbled with the key in frantic ineffectual movements until at last he opened it and banged it after him as he plunged backwards into the hall.

For a moment he stood there looking at the door-handle; then with a stealthy, sneaking movement, his hand crept out towards it, touched it, began to turn it, when suddenly he pulled his hand away and went up to his bedroom, three steps at a time.

There he behaved in a manner only comparable with the way he had lost his head after losing his innocence when a schoolboy of sixteen. He hid his face in the pillow, he cried, he raved in meaningless words, repeating: "Never, never, never. I will never do it again. Help me never to do it again." With the words, "Help me," he noticed what he was saying, they reminded him of other words, and he began to pray aloud. But the words sounded jumbled, they persisted in coming into his head in a reverse order so that he found he was saying his prayers backwards, and at this final absurdity he suddenly began to laugh very loud. He sat up on the bed, delighted at this return to sanity, common sense and humour, when the door leading into Mrs. Corbett's room opened, and he saw his wife staring at him with a strange, grey, drawn face that made her seem like the terror-stricken ghost of her usually smug and placid self.

"It's not burglars," he said irritably. "I've come to bed late, that is all, and must have waked you."

"Henry," said Mrs. Corbett, and he noticed that she had not heard him, "Henry, didn't you hear it?"

"What?"

"That laugh."

He was silent, an instinctive caution warning him to wait until she spoke again. And this she did, imploring him with her eyes to reassure her.

"It was not a human laugh. It was like the laugh of a devil."

He checked his violent inclination to laugh again. It was wiser not to let her know that it was only his laughter she had heard. He told her to stop being fanciful, and Mrs. Corbett, gradually recovering her docility, returned to obey an impossible command, since she could not stop being what she had never been.

The next morning, Mr. Corbett rose before any of the servants and crept down to the dining-room. As before, the dictionary and grammar alone remained on the writing-bureau; the book was back in the second shelf. He opened it at the end. Two more lines had been added, carrying the writing down to the middle of the page. They ran:

Ex auro canceris
In dentem elephantis.

which he translated as:

Out of the money of the crab
Into the tooth of the elephant.

From this time on, his acquaintances in the City noticed a change in the mediocre, rather flabby and unenterprising "old Corbett". His recent sour depression dropped from him: he seemed to have grown twenty years younger, strong, brisk and cheerful, and with a self-confidence in business that struck them as lunacy. They waited with a not unpleasant excitement for the inevitable crash, but his every speculation, however wild and hare-brained, turned out successful. He no longer avoided them, but went out of his way to display his consciousness of luck, daring and vigour, and to chaff them in a manner that began to make him actively disliked. This he welcomed with delight as a sign of others' envy and his superiority.

He never stayed in town for dinners or theatres, for he was always now in a hurry to get home, where, as soon as he was sure of being undisturbed, he would take down the manuscript book from the second shelf of the dining-room and turn to the last pages.

Every morning he found that a few words had been added since the evening before, and always they formed, as he considered, injunctions to himself. These were at first only with regard to his money transactions, giving assurance to his boldest fancies, and since the brilliant and unforeseen success that had attended his gamble with Mr. Crab's money in African ivory, he followed all such advice unhesitatingly.

But presently, interspersed with these commands, were others of a meaningless, childish, yet revolting character such as might be invented by a decadent imbecile, or, it must be admitted, by the idle fancies of any ordinary man who permits his imagination to wander unbridled. Mr. Corbett was startled to recognise one or two such fancies of his own, which had occurred to him during his frequent boredom in church, and which he had not thought any other mind could conceive.

He at first paid no attention to these directions, but found that his new speculations declined so rapidly that he became terrified not merely for his fortune but for his reputation and even safety, since the money of various of his clients was involved. It was made clear to him that he must follow the commands in the book altogether or not at all, and he began to carry out their puerile and grotesque blasphemies with a contemptuous amusement, which however gradually changed to a sense of their monstrous significance. They became more capricious and difficult of execution, but he now never hesitated to obey blindly, urged by a fear that he could not understand, but knew only that it was not of mere financial failure.

By now he understood the effect of this book on the others near it, and the reason that had impelled its mysterious agent to move the books into the second shelf so that all in turn should come under the influence of that ancient and secret knowledge.

In respect to it, he encouraged his children, with jeers at their stupidity, to read more, but he could not observe that they ever now took a book from the dining-room bookcase. He himself no longer needed to read, but went to bed early and slept sound. The things that all his life he had longed to do when he should have enough money now seemed to him insipid. His most exciting pleasure was the smell and touch of these mouldering pages as he turned them to find the last message inscribed to him.

One evening it was in two words only: "Canem occide."

He laughed at this simple and pleasant request to kill the dog, for he bore Mike a grudge for his change from devotion to slinking aversion. Moreover, it could not have come more opportunely, since in turning out an old desk he had just discovered some packets of rat poison bought years ago and forgotten. No one therefore knew of its existence and it would be easy to poison Mike without any further suspicion than that of a neighbour's carelessness. He whistled light-heartedly as he ran upstairs to rummage for the packets, and returned to empty one in the dog's dish of water in the hall.

That night the household was awakened by terrified screams proceeding from the stairs. Mr. Corbett was the first to hasten there, prompted by the instinctive caution that was always with him these days. He saw Jean, in her nightdress, scrambling up on to the landing on her hands and knees, clutching at anything that afforded support and screaming in a choking, tearless, unnatural manner. He carried her to the room she shared with Nora, where they were quickly followed by Mrs. Corbett.

Nothing coherent could be got from Jean. Nora said that she must have been having her old dream again; when her father demanded what this was, she said that Jean sometimes woke in the night, crying, because she had dreamed of a hand passing backwards and forwards over the dining-room bookcase, until it found a certain book and took it out of the shelf. At this point she was always so frightened that she woke up.

On hearing this, Jean broke into fresh screams, and Mrs. Corbett would have no more explanations. Mr. Corbett went out on to the stairs to find what had brought the child there from her bed. On looking down into the lighted hall, he saw Mike's dish overturned. He went down to examine it and saw that the water he had poisoned must have been upset and absorbed by the rough doormat which was quite wet.

He went back to the little girls' room, told his wife that she was tired and must go to bed, and he would take his turn at comforting Jean. She was now much quieter. He took her on his knee where at first she shrank from him. Mr. Corbett remembered with an angry sense of injury that she never now sat on his knee, and would have liked to pay her out for it by mocking and frightening her. But he had to coax her into telling him what he wanted, and with this object he soothed her, calling her by pet names that he thought he had forgotten, telling her that nothing could hurt her now he was with her.

At first his cleverness amused him; he chuckled softly when Jean buried her head in his dressing-gown. But presently an uncomfortable sensation came over him, he gripped at Jean as though for her protection, while he was so smoothly assuring her of his. With difficulty, he listened to what he had at last induced her to tell him.

She and Nora had kept Mike with them all the evening and taken him to sleep in their room for a treat. He had lain at the foot of Jean's bed and they had all gone to sleep. Then Jean began her old dream of the hand moving over the books in the dining-room bookcase; but instead of taking out a book, it came across the dining-room and out on to the stairs. It came up over the banisters and to the door of their room, and turned their door-handle very softly and opened it. At this point she jumped up wide awake and turned on the light, calling to Nora. The door, which had been shut when they went to sleep, was wide open, and Mike was gone.

She told Nora that she was sure something dreadful would happen to him if she did not go and bring him back, and ran down into the hall where she saw him just about to drink from his dish. She called to him and he looked up, but did not come, so she ran to him, and began to pull him along with her, when her nightdress was clutched from behind and then she felt a hand seize her arm.

She fell down, and then clambered upstairs as fast as she could, screaming all the way.

It was now clear to Mr. Corbett that Mike's dish must have been upset in the scuffle. She was again crying, but this time he felt himself unable to comfort her. He retired to his room, where he walked up and down in an agitation he could not understand, for he found his thoughts perpetually arguing on a point that had never troubled him before.

"I am not a bad man," he kept saying to himself. "I have never done anything actually wrong. My clients are none the worse for my speculations, only the better. Nor have I spent my new wealth on gross and sensual pleasures; these now have even no attraction for me."

Presently he added: "It is not wrong to try and kill a dog, an ill-tempered brute. It turned against me. It might have bitten Jeannie."

He noticed that he had thought of her as Jeannie, which he had not done for some time; it must have been because he had called her that tonight. He must forbid her ever to leave her room at night, he could not have her meddling. It would be safer for him if she were not there at all.

Again that sick and cold sensation of fear swept over him: he seized the bed-post as though he were falling, and held on to it for some minutes. "I was thinking of a boarding school," he told himself, and then, "I must go down and find out—find out—" He would not think what it was he must find out.

He opened his door and listened. The house was quiet. He crept on to the landing and along to Nora's and Jean's door where again he stood, listening. There was no sound, and at that he was again overcome with unreasonable terror. He imagined Jean lying very still in her bed, too still. He hastened away from the door, shuffling in his bedroom slippers along the passage and down the stairs.

A bright fire still burned in the dining-room grate. A glance at the clock told him it was not yet twelve. He stared at the bookcase. In the second shelf was a gap which had not been there when he had left. On the writing-bureau lay a large open book. He knew that he must cross the room and see what was written in it. Then, as before, words that he did not intend came sobbing and crying to his lips, muttering, "No, no, not that. Never, never, never." But he crossed the room and looked down at the book. As last time, the message was in only two words: "Infantem occide."

He slipped and fell forward against the bureau. His hands clutched at the book, lifted it as he recovered himself and with his finger he traced out the words that had been written. The smell of corruption crept into his nostrils. He told himself that he was not a snivelling dotard, but a man stronger and wiser than his fellows, superior to the common emotions of humanity, who held in his hands the sources of ancient and secret power.

He had known what the message would be. It was after all the only safe and logical thing to do. Jean had acquired dangerous knowledge. She was a spy, an antagonist. That she was so unconsciously, that she was eight years old, his youngest and favourite child, were sentimental appeals that could make no difference to a man of sane reasoning power such as his own. Jean had sided with Mike against him. "All that are not with me are against me," he repeated softly. He would kill both dog and child with the white powder that no one knew to be in his possession. It would be quite safe.

He laid down the book and went to the door. What he had to do, he would do quickly, for again that sensation of deadly cold was sweeping over him. He wished he had not to do it tonight; last night it would have been easier, but tonight she had sat on his knee and made him afraid. He imagined her lying very still in her bed, too still. But it would be she who would lie there, not he, so why should he be afraid? He was protected by ancient and secret powers. He held on to the door-handle, but his fingers seemed to have grown numb, for he could not turn it. He clung to it, crouched and shivering, bending over it until he knelt on the ground, his head beneath the handle which he still clutched with upraised hands. Suddenly the hands were loosened and flung outwards with the frantic gesture of a man falling from a great height, and he stumbled to his feet. He seized the book and threw it on the fire. A violent sensation of choking overcame him, he felt he was being strangled, as in a nightmare he tried again and again to shriek aloud, but his breath would make no sound. His breath would not come at all. He fell backwards heavily, down on the floor, where he lay very still.

In the morning, the maid who came to open the dining-room windows found her master dead. The sensation caused by this was scarcely so great in the City as that given by the simultaneous collapse of all Mr. Corbett's recent speculations. It was instantly assumed that he must have had previous knowledge of this and so committed suicide.

The stumbling-block to this theory was that the medical report defined the cause of Mr. Corbett's death as strangulation of the wind-pipe by the pressure of a hand which had left the marks of its fingers on his throat.

THE LIBRARY

Hester Holland

Hester Gaskell Gorst (1887–1992), née Holland, was born in Liverpool into a wealthy and well-connected family. Her father was a partner in the shipping firm Lamport and Holt, and her grandmother's sister-in-law was the novelist Elizabeth Gaskell. When Hester was a small child, her uncle Edgar was murdered by the actress Catherine Kempshall, after he reneged on a marriage proposal. The family supported Kempshall's death sentence being commuted to life imprisonment in Broadmoor.

Hester Holland attended the Slade School of Art and had some success as a painter (specialising in imaginary and fantastical scenes), and as a sculptor. She married Elliot Gorst, a barrister, in 1914, and the couple lived in London. In her 40s Hester turned her hand to writing, publishing this story in *Keep on the Light* (edited by Christine Campbell Thomson, 1933) and four books, including the thriller *A Man Must Live*, over the next 15 years.

This story revolves around the mysterious library in the fictional Witcombe Court, and the secretary who is employed to assist in the maintenance of the grand house and its contents. It was perhaps inspired by Holland's childhood home. Carnatic Hall in the Mossley Hill area of Liverpool had originally been built in 1779 for the slave trader Peter Baker and named after a French ship he had captured. In 1891 a major fire destroyed the house and Hester's father Walter had it rebuilt to a similar design. When Walter died the house went out of the family, eventually being bought by the University of Liverpool in 1947, and demolished in 1964.

The drive was punctuated at intervals by lodges and gates. These were opened by shadowy figures who emerged from their doors at the sound of the motor horn. Then they drove on through endless woods and pasture land. All very lovely in the daytime, thought Margaret, but on this winter night she only wanted to see a fire and a cup of tea. Margaret was essentially practical. Life had meant very little to her from an early age—finding jobs and trying to keep them in the face of ill health. It had always been a struggle to give people the value for their money and keep fit enough to do it.

After Dick had left her, things had seemed harder than ever. There had been the hope that some day they would get married. He had loved her once, and she still loved him. But that was all over, he would never come back any more. After six months of trying to forget him and typing in an underground office, she had broken down. The doctor whom she saw advised a complete rest. "Go home," he said, "and loaf round." Margaret laughed; she had no relations and nobody cared a button whether she died or not.

"Well," he said, "if you have got to work, get some work in the country. Be out of doors all day."

That was why she answered Lady Farrell's advertisement. Her ladyship wanted a capable young lady to take charge of her country house whilst she was away. Margaret could hardly believe her good luck when she was engaged. Here was a chance to get out of town, so full of memories of Dick, and recuperate. It might even mean a permanent job.

Her ladyship explained that Witcombe Court was lonely. Though there was a full staff always there whether she was away or not. The house must not be neglected. She was very particular about Margaret's family. Had she many relatives? Would they mind her going to a lonely place? When the girl said she had no relatives and was alone in the world, it seemed to please the old lady.

"Poor child!" she exclaimed, jumping up and taking the girl's hand. "I'm sure you'll suit me. I'm sure we shall like each other."

She explained the reason of her visits abroad.

"I have to be away half the year for my health. And I must have a lady to look after things for me. The servants are all excellent, but of course a lady at the head of things makes so much difference. One thing I must insist upon, though it does not apply in your case, my dear. I do object to strangers being asked to the house in my absence."

Lady Farrell was very old, with an ancestry which dated back to Saxon times and earlier. Dressed in a fashion which had been new in the Seventies, she created a sensation in London whenever she appeared. Witcombe Court with its hundreds of acres had been guarded by her with the tenderness of a mother. She was the last of her race and the estate would be sold at her death. There had been reckless gambling by members of the family, who had sold parts of the estate to pay their debts. One of her forebears had despoiled the library of its collection of rare books and sold some historical furniture. There was a legend that the stone wolves mounting guard on the terrace howled when the treasures were taken away. Lady Farrell, incongruous in a West End hotel, spoke of these things as if someone had ill-treated a child.

"My ancestors behaved shamefully. They robbed the house which was defenceless against them. And to think I must die and leave it to be sold to someone who does not understand it. The thought is torture to me. That is why I go for treatment abroad. I must live as long as I can to protect it."

Margaret's duties would evidently be those of a watchdog. Yet Lady Farrell spoke of her large and efficient staff of servants which were kept on during her absence and seemed an adequate body-guard. The house must have constant service and constant attention. Margaret must see that there was no jarring note. The girl promised to be vigilant. She had a strong historical sense, though it had been thwarted in London offices. It would be pleasant to wander through rooms which had no recollections of Dick to haunt her; there were sure to be relics, swords, and flags of warriors who had fought against Norman and Yorkist and Roundhead. From earliest times Witcombe Court had been a regular buffer state for invading forces. And always there had been blood spilt in its name. The house expected sacri-fices. Lives had been given for it. Margaret decided to read up all its history. It would be wonderful to live so near the past. But with the question of reading came the first disappointment. Lady Farrell was strict about certain things.

"Not yet, my dear," she said, patting Margaret's hand affection-ately. "I quite realise how eager you will be to go into the library, but we must be ready."

"Ready for what?" thought the girl. It must be that Lady Farrell did not trust her alone with the rare books. After all, she was a stranger. Great care must be taken to fall in with her employer's ways. She wondered how the other secretaries had fared. There seemed to have been a lot of going and coming as far as they were concerned; perhaps they had got fed up with the country. Well, Witcombe Court might be lonely, but it was better than town, with those imaginary Dicks in every street. On the night of her arrival a silent-footed butler showed her into an immense drawing room. Here she found Lady Farrell sunk on a wide settee in front of a virile fire; the lavish tea and glowing heat of burning wood soon cheered Margaret. She began to feel happy. A tenderness woke in her heart for the fragile old lady who seemed lost in the vastness of her abode. The house was enormous, and was a quaint mixture of early and late architecture. The great hall was hung with flags and battered armour. The wide rooms adjoining were a museum of pathetic relics, telling of the struggle to keep invading foes at bay.

Oddly enough, though it gave the sensation of vastness, there was no atmosphere of peace. The girl noticed this at once. Entering the dark, lofty hall, she had been met by a breath of hostility which conveyed itself forcibly to her sensitive nature. It was as if the house did not want her. Resented the entrance of strangers. The walls which rose darkly around her held no friendliness. As she entered the hall she was conscious of an extraordinary sensation. It was like entering some enormous clock. There was a steady beat coming from a distance, like a pulse, far away certainly, but plain enough to hear. Margaret supposed some engine used for procuring light or water. She got used to this noise as one gets used to the beat of a pendulum, and for a while thought no more of it. But the feeling of hostility remained. This had been enhanced by the first glimpse of the house as the car turned into the drive. There had been no lights in the upper windows. The only illumination came from the porch. It gave the impression of two slit-like eyes. Red eyes gazing out at the night-bound park.

The effect was sinister. The heap of building crouched lumpily against the sky—a dark bulk waiting to spring. Her heart had given a queer, frightened start. It was like entering a living thing to go through that dim doorway. After a few days she put the feeling down to strangeness. She was not accustomed to such vast rooms. Neither was she used to such harmony. It was like a ritual. A competent, perfectly trained staff of servants vied with each other to make the house beautiful. They were obsessed by it. Margaret could see no work for a secretary. She spent the time with her employer making catalogues of portraits which could easily have been done by one of the footmen. It almost seemed as if Lady Farrell made work for her. There were tapestries shaken from obscure boxes, and laces washed and put away again. She had no time to explore alone. Her employer showed her everything herself. The old lady displayed a reverent pride in her possessions; not for her pleasure, but for the house itself, the work went on. Flowers were heaped in the rooms. The servants walked softly so as not to disturb it.

A few days after Margaret's arrival and the day before Lady Farrell was to leave, the girl was in the billiard room. With notebook and pencil she was busy cataloguing the portraits. Sir Walter Raleigh between the windows. Lady Catherine Grey over the fireplace. It was disagreeable being in the room alone. Somehow none of the picture faces seemed friendly. Her footsteps, as she crossed the parquet floor, sounded unnaturally loud. She had the sensation of being the undigested contents of a maw. An alien Thing waiting to be identified with the whole. That was what made her feel remote. The servants and Lady Farrell were in sympathy with the house. A body moving in accord. She alone was strange to it. Was this why she felt herself hated? But how could bricks and mortar hate her? She stood staring at the wall. The room was one of the few unpanelled in the house, and was painted the colour of elephant's hide.

Suddenly, as if a wind had scudded in, a ripple ran along its surface. It was like the clipped skin of a horse trying to get rid of a fly. Again and again it quivered from floor to ceiling. With a scream Margaret stumbled from the room. All she wanted to do was to get away. The house was alive. She knew it now. Waking in the early morning she fancied she heard it stirring, like a great beast, stretching and preparing to rise. Long before the servants were about, Margaret would lie and listen to that pulse which sounded through the rooms. A dull thud, thud, like a heart's beat. She wanted to go, but her wish was greeted with tears.

"What, go and leave me now, just when I have got someone whom I can trust? I could not go away and leave no one in charge of the house. Stay, stay at least till I return."

Margaret promised to do this, and the old lady was pathetically grateful.

"And you shall go to the library," she whined. "You shall go to the library as soon as it is ready for you."

After her departure the girl tried to engross herself in work. There was very little to do, and what she did seemed futile. The daily round of service which the house received was not in her province. Its requirements were carried out by a competent staff of priests and priestesses who ministered at its shrine. There was no cessation of this ministration now that the Pontiff had gone. Everything went like clockwork. The Catechumens and Acolytes, whom Margaret secretly called the between-maids and under-maids, showed the same zeal as their superiors. Day after day rooms were cleaned and polished. Beds aired, linen sorted, and silver burnished. Labour was sucked up as a plant takes in moisture. What was it all for? There was no one but herself to appreciate this neatness of the linen cupboard or the shine on the brasses. But the house rejected her as a worker. There was nothing to do. One day she discovered that Lady Farrell had left the key of the library with her.

"That's the library key, miss," the cook had said, when she had asked where it belonged.

"Oh, of course, Lady Farrell must have left it on the bunch by mistake."

"Her ladyship always leaves the library key with the secretary," said the cook, and watched Margaret out of the kitchen with a smile.

What trust, thought the girl. Had all the other secretaries kept faith as she intended to do, or had they just peeped. She had a longing to go into that library. It was as if someone was calling from there. The heart of the house, Lady Farrell had called it. Surely in its heart she would find the root of this animosity to herself. As the days passed, she found it easier to consider the house in the light of an idol, for directly she did this everything fell into place.

The labour was no longer futile if it kept the god alive. It was an idol that must be worshipped and ministered to. A very old god that had grown silent and vindictive with the years, watching with an increasingly jealous eye its hive of priests lest one of them should slacken in zeal. But it was her duty to propitiate it. She sought about for a position among its ministries that was not yet appropriated. With not much knowledge of an idol's requirements, it was difficult to create the perfect circle of service necessary to its well-being. Exorcists, those were the cleaners, and I don't clean—Acolytes, but I don't wait on the butler. Lady Farrell was the High Priestess. Margaret was in the woods overlooking the house. It stood, a grey shape against the hill, its windows dull with sleep, a thin turret of smoke rising from each of its many chimneys. Today, by some mischance, she had unearthed a tie which she had once bought for Dick. She had not given it to him because people in torment don't give away ties.

It was just at the time of her discovery that he didn't care any more. The woods had seemed the best place to try and forget in. And then she realised it was that loving she still kept in her heart which put her out of harmony with the house. She was not one with it. Had the other secretaries refused to merge themselves, and was that why they had left? Suddenly Margaret held out her arms.

"House," she said aloud, "try not to hate me. Tell me what you would like me to be."

With dropped arms she waited, fixing anxious eyes on the mountain of stone in front. A voice in her brain whispered:

"Sacrifice."

A sacrifice, why had she not thought of that? The life of a normal idol was incomplete without it. All the endless tending of altar fires and the prayers, vain. And the victim must come from without. They did not offer up the priests. Did the house want her? Was it angry because she held away from it, fought against its demand for her? Did it want to crush her and make her its own, as those thirsty gods of the old days? But the surrender must come from her. The house was waiting. Margaret shivered. She felt afraid to go back through those heavy doors, or feel again that animosity, like a shield against her.

There was a step among the leaves. The gardeners had a tiresome way of creeping about with wheelbarrows disturbing the solitude. An old man was standing among the trees behind her. He was dressed in a black cassock-like garment, and his small, wrinkled face had the yellow texture of ivory. He raised a round black hat and showed a completely bald head. Margaret stood staring at him.

"Excuse me," he said, "but could I come to the house and rest a little? I am so very tired."

"Lady Farrell is away."

"I know, but I am a great friend of hers. In fact, I am her chaplain. I am sure she would not mind."

Well, if he was the chaplain, Lady Farrell could not object. It would be nice to have a chat with someone, she was so lonely.

"Come in," she said, "I'll ask them to give you some tea."

"You are very kind, but I just wanted to rest; you see, I have been on my feet all day, on parish rounds. I thought I would look in here on my way home."

"Yes, of course. I'm the secretary."

"Lady Farrell told me you were coming. My name is Father Collard."

They walked up the drive and on to the terrace. Father Collard stopped to admire the stone wolves which crouched each side of the steps.

"You know the legend about them?" He laid a thin yellow paw on one of the moss-grown heads.

"Oh yes, but there are a lot of legends about the house I should like to know."

"You should read about them. Lady Farrell has a wonderful library."

"I thought it was sold."

"It was sold, but her ladyship bought nearly all the books back. She took the greatest trouble to advertise, and had to pay far more than the books were sold for originally."

"She is devoted to the house."

"We must all love what has been in our family for generations. There is no sacrifice we should not make for our own." The old man spoke with the ardour of fanaticism.

Margaret looked at him. She had a sudden doubt as to his sanity. They were in the lofty hall now, and she saw his pale eyes glitter with excitement as he looked round.

"The house has a lot of disciples." She could not resist saying that. After all, it was only she and the other secretaries who had not fallen under its spell. He turned to her with a smile on his wizened little face.

"I can understand you not feeling the same as we do. You have only been here a short time. You have not felt its influence yet."

"Oh, but I have," began Margaret. Then she stopped. What would be the use of telling him about her fears and fancies? "I should like to know more about its history, but Lady Farrell does not wish strangers to go into her library."

"I am sure she would not mind your looking at one or two books. I should so like to show them to you."

"Well, if you really think it will be all right, and you know their names." Margaret subsided on one of the wide chairs in the drawing room; suddenly she felt extraordinarily tired. Her companion sat opposite. Without his hat he looked like a small black bottle with a round ivory stopper. She felt inclined to laugh, and wondered whether James the footman, who had come in to draw the curtains, noticed how odd the old priest was. The drawing room was not used in Lady Farrell's absence, as Margaret preferred the smaller and sunnier breakfast room. However, with unabated service given to the house, the blinds were drawn up every morning, a fire laid and lighted.

She asked James to bring tea. The old man was still talking of the books.

"There is one full of legends I should like to show you."

"What sort of legends?"

But she knew it was not the stories she wanted to hear. They were an excuse to go into the library, and any excuse was enough. The fact that Lady Farrell had forbidden it did not matter any more.

Something stronger than her will was compelling her. She did not know whether it was the old man's voice or her brain which droned on about an oubliette in the upper regions which no one had ever found. A legend of a Royalist hidden in a secret room in Cromwell's time.

"His pursuers murdered those who had the secret. He was not found till long after."

"How horrible," said Margaret.

There came a chuckle from the chair opposite. A pair of little bony hands were spread out in front of her face in a motion of supplication.

"Do go and fetch the books from the library."

She wondered vaguely why he didn't wear a proper clergyman's collar and why he had never called before. Why, no one ever called at the house.

"All right," she said, "I'll get them."

He told her their titles and exactly where they stood on the shelves. He seemed to know the room extraordinarily well. She was not sure whether the little black figure with the bald head had really asked her to go, or whether it was a voice in her brain.

The library was in the left wing of the house. At the end of a long stone passage. There were no other rooms near it. It was evident that the perpetual cleaning which went on all day stopped when this part of the house was reached. There was dust on the floor, and a litter of dead leaves had blown in from the garden. A low stone arch over the library door was festooned with cobwebs. The key moved smoothly and she turned the handle to face darkness. There were no windows. She relocked the door and went in search of a candle. James was carrying the tea tray across the hall, and she asked him to tell Father Collard she would join him in a moment.

"Very well, miss."

He seemed anxious to be gone with his tray, so she took a silver candlestick from the hall table and went slowly back to the library. She stood just inside the door and looked round expectantly. What would she find besides books? As she stood there the door behind her clicked to, as if someone had pulled it from the outside, and Margaret turned quickly. She saw the door was made of shelves and that there was no trace of a handle on the inside wall. There was no way of getting out unless she discovered some spring.

"But I can knock on the door and they will let me out."

Again she turned and faced the room, and the swaying light of the candle showed her something. It was a small room lined with books from floor to ceiling and furnished only with a few musty-looking chairs. In the centre of it was a table on which for some reason had been heaped a quantity of dead flowers. The slightest breath stirs dead leaves, and these moved continually. What was it which moved them? The girl became aware of a vibration, a beating in the room. The pulsing of a heart which she had heard for so long and not understood. Here was the house's heart. She had entered its shrine, its inner life, its holy of holies. Beat, beat, beat. Her shadow, cast by the feeble light of the candle, trembled along the floor. Thin and long, it was sucked away into the room. It was filled with the smell of hay, and the breath of dying flowers and of incense, and another smell. The terrible smell of decaying flesh. She was not alone. Against the wall, huddled in different positions of abandoned agony and death, were several figures. Figures of women in modern clothes, jerseys, hats, boots. Four in all. Sacrifices. The other secretaries left here to die. Imprisoned sacrifices to the house, whose heart-beats shook the dried flowers on the table. With a scream, Margaret flung herself against the lines of books which formed the door. Wildly, with clenched hands, she struck it. "Let me out—let me out!" But no one ever came to let her out.

They wrote to Lady Farrell and she returned at once. Father Collard was in the hall to meet her, and all the servants, even down to the kitchen-maid.

A service was held in the chapel, and Lady Farrell cried a little as she knelt before the altar.

"I never can bear to be here at the time," she said weakly to her chaplain. "I know it has to be, but it upsets me so. The thought of those dear girls—"

"But, Lady Farrell—if the house requires them, you would not stint it—you would not stint it of sacrifice?"

"No!" exclaimed her ladyship, rising from her knees. "I don't stint it. So long as I am alive we will give it life. I shall not fail it so long as I am alive."

"You have given it lives," whispered Father Collard, "and it is alive."

Lady Farrell clasped her hands in worship.

"I will try to procure another secretary," she murmured.

MIDNIGHT EXPRESS

Alfred Noyes

Alfred Noyes (1880–1958) was born in Wolverhampton, the son of a grocer, and attended Exeter College, Oxford—although he did not graduate, instead choosing to meet with the publisher who went on to publish his first collection of poetry, *The Loom of Years*, in 1902. Today Noyes is best known for his poem "The Highwayman" (1906), which appeared in many poetry anthologies and was taught in schools for a great part of the twentieth century. In 1914 he was appointed to a lectureship at Princeton University which he held until 1923 (with the exception of the wartime period when he was exempted from military service because of poor eyesight and instead worked for the Foreign Office). During his war service he began writing patriotic stories tinged with the uncanny, such as "The Lusitania Waits" (1916), a ghostly tale of revenge on Germany for sinking the British liner.

This story, first published in *This Week* magazine, 3 November 1935, is an eerie work of metafiction, short but effective.

It was a battered old book, bound in red buckram. He found it, when he was twelve years old, on an upper shelf in his father's library; and, against all the rules, he took it to his bedroom to read by candlelight, when the rest of the rambling old Elizabethan house was flooded with darkness. That was how young Mortimer always thought of it. His own room was a little isolated cell, in which, with stolen candle ends, he could keep the surrounding darkness at bay, while everyone else had surrendered to sleep and allowed the outer night to come flooding in. By contrast with those unconscious ones, his elders, it made him feel intensely alive in every nerve and fibre of his young brain. The ticking of the grandfather clock in the hall below, the beating of his own heart; the long-drawn rhythmical "ah" of the sea on the distant coast, all filled him with a sense of overwhelming mystery; and, as he read, the soft thud of a blinded moth, striking the wall above the candle, would make him start and listen like a creature of the woods at the sound of a cracking twig.

The battered old book had the strangest fascination for him, though he never quite grasped the thread of the story. It was called *The Midnight Express*, and there was one illustration, on the fiftieth page, at which he could never bear to look. It frightened him.

Young Mortimer never understood the effect of that picture on him. He was an imaginative, but not a neurotic youngster; and he avoided the fiftieth page as he might have hurried past a dark corner on the stairs when he was six years old, or as the grown man on the lonely road, in *The Ancient Mariner*, who, having once looked round, walks on, and turns no more his head. There was nothing in the picture—apparently—to account for this haunting dread. Darkness, indeed, was almost its chief characteristic. It showed an empty railway platform—at night—lit by a single dreary lamp; an empty railway platform that suggested a deserted and lonely junction in some remote part of the country. There was only one figure on the platform: the dark figure of a man, standing almost directly under the lamp with his face turned away towards the black mouth of a tunnel which—for some strange reason—plunged the imagination of the child into a pit of horror. The man seemed to be listening. His attitude was tense, expectant, as though he were awaiting some fearful tragedy. There was nothing in the text, so far the child read, and could understand, to account for this waking nightmare. He could neither resist the fascination of the book, nor face that picture in the stillness and loneliness of the night. He pinned it down to the page facing it with two long pins, so that he should not come upon it by accident. Then he determined to read the whole story through. But, always, before he came to page fifty, he fell asleep; and the outlines of what he had read were blurred; and the next night he had to begin again; and again, before he came to the fiftieth page, he fell asleep.

He grew up, and forgot all about the book and the picture. But half way through his life, at that strange and critical time when Dante entered the dark wood, leaving the direct path behind him, he found himself, a little before midnight, waiting for a train at a lonely junction; and, as the station-clock began to strike twelve he remembered; remembered like a man awakening from a long dream—

There, under the single dreary lamp, on the long, glimmering platform, was the dark and solitary figure that he knew. Its face was turned away from him towards the black mouth of the tunnel. It seemed to be listening, tense, expectant, just as it had been thirty-eight years ago.

But he was not frightened now, as he had been in childhood. He would go up to that solitary figure, confront it, and see the face that had so long been hidden, so long averted from him. He would walk up quietly, and make some excuse for speaking to it: he would ask it, for instance, if the train was going to be late. It should be easy for a grown man to do this; but his hands were clenched, when he took the first step, as if he, too, were tense and expectant. Quietly, but with the old vague instincts awaking, he went towards the dark figure under the lamp, passed it, swung round abruptly to speak to it; and saw—without speaking, without being able to speak—

It was himself—staring back at himself—as in some mocking mirror, his own eyes alive in his own white face, looking into his own eyes, alive—

The nerves of his heart tingled as though their own electric currents would paralyse it. A wave of panic went through him. He turned, gasped, stumbled, broke into a blind run, out through the deserted and echoing ticket-office, on to the long moonlit road behind the station. The whole countryside seemed to be utterly deserted. The moonbeams flooded it with the loneliness of their own deserted satellite.

He paused for a moment, and heard, like the echo of his own footsteps, the stumbling run of something that followed over the wooden floor within the ticket-office. Then he abandoned himself shamelessly to his fear; and ran, sweating like a terrified beast, down the long white road between the two endless lines of ghostly poplars each answering another, into what seemed like a long straight canal, in which one of the lines of poplars was again endlessly reflected.

He heard the footsteps echoing behind him. They seemed to be slowly, but steadily, gaining upon him. A quarter of a mile away, he saw a small white cottage by the roadside, a white cottage with two dark windows and a door that somehow suggested a human face. He thought to himself that, if he could reach it in time, he might find shelter and security—escape.

The thin implacable footsteps, echoing his own, were still some way off when he lurched, gasping, into the little porch; rattled the latch, thrust at the door, and found it locked against him. There was no bell or knocker. He pounded on the wood with his fists until his knuckles bled. The response was horribly slow. At last, he heard heavier footsteps within the cottage. Slowly they descended the creaking stair. Slowly the door was unlocked. A tall shadowy figure stood before him, holding a lighted candle, in such a way that he could see little either of the holder's face or form; but to his dumb horror there seemed to be a cerecloth wrapped round the face.

No words passed between them. The figure beckoned him in; and, as he obeyed, it locked the door behind him. Then, beckoning him again, without a word, the figure went before him up the crooked stair, with the ghostly candle casting huge and grotesque shadows on the whitewashed walls and ceiling.

They entered an upper room, in which there was a bright fire burning, with an armchair on either side of it, and a small oak table, on which there lay a battered old book, bound in dark red buckram. It seemed as though the guest had been long expected and all things were prepared.

The figure pointed to one of the armchairs, placed the candlestick on the table by the book (for there was no other light but that of the fire) and withdrew without a word, locking the door behind him.

Mortimer looked at the candlestick. It seemed familiar. The smell of the guttering wax brought back the little room in the old Elizabethan house. He picked up the book with trembling fingers. He recognised it at once, though he had long forgotten everything about the story. He remembered the ink stain on the title page; and then, with a shock of recollection, he came on the fiftieth page, which he had pinned down in childhood. The pins were still there. He touched them again—the very pins which his trembling childish fingers had used so long ago.

He turned back to the beginning. He was determined to read the end now, and discover what it was all about. He felt that it must all be set down there, in print; and, though in childhood he could not understand it, he would be able to fathom it now.

It was called *The Midnight Express*; and, as he read the first paragraph, it began to dawn upon him slowly, fearfully, inevitably—

It was the story of a man who, in childhood, long ago, had chanced upon a book, in which there was a picture that frightened him. He had grown up and forgotten it and one night, upon a lonely railway platform, he had found himself in the remembered scene of the picture: he had confronted the solitary figure under the lamp: recognised it, and fled in panic. He had taken shelter in a wayside cottage: had been led to an upper room, found the book awaiting him and had begun to read it right through, to the very end, at last—And this book too was called The Midnight Express. *And it was the story of a man who, in childhood—It would go on thus, forever and forever, and forever. There was no escape.*

But when the story came to the wayside cottage, for the third time, a deeper suspicion began to dawn upon him, slowly, fearfully, inevitably—Although there was no escape, he could at least try to grasp more clearly the details of the strange circle, the fearful wheel, in which he was moving.

There was nothing new about the details. They had been there all the time; but he had not grasped their significance. That was all. *The strange and dreadful being that had led him up the crooked stair—who and what was That?*

The story mentioned something that had escaped him. The strange host, who had given him shelter, was about his own height. Could it be that he also—And was this why the face was hidden?

At the very moment when he asked himself that question he heard the click of the key in the locked door.

The strange host was entering—moving toward him from behind—casting a grotesque shadow, larger than human, on the white walls in the guttering candlelight.

It was there, seated on the other side of the fire, facing him. With a horrible nonchalance, as a woman might prepare to remove a veil, it raised its hands to unwind the cerecloth from its face. He knew to whom it would belong. But would it be dead or living?

There was no way out but one. As Mortimer plunged forward and seized the tormentor by the throat, his own throat was gripped with the same brutal force. The echoes of their strangled cry were indistinguishable; and when the last confused sounds died out together, the stillness of the room was so deep that you might have heard—the ticking of the old grandfather clock, and the long-drawn rhythmical "ah" of the sea, on a distant coast, thirty-eight years ago.

But Mortimer had escaped at last. Perhaps, after all, he had caught the midnight express.

It was a battered old book, bound in red buckram...

1949

HERODES REDIVIVUS

A. N. L. Munby

Alan Noel Latimer Munby (1913–1974), known as Tim, was a later
follower of M. R. James in the antiquarian tradition. His interest in
rare books was first aroused by visits to booksellers in Bristol, near
Clifton College where he was a pupil. Between 1935 and 1947 (except
for during the Second World War), he worked in the book trade,
at the antiquarian book dealers Bernard Quaritch, and in the book
department at Sotheby's. After the war, he became Librarian of King's
College, Cambridge, the college which had formerly been home
to M. R. James. He became an important figure in the librarianship
community, and was made a member of the first ever British Library
Board in 1973.

Munby started writing ghost stories whilst a prisoner at Oflag VII
B, a German prisoner-of-war camp near Eichstätt, after his capture
at Calais in 1940. The Roman Catholic Bishop of Eichstätt, Michael
Rackl, gave the prisoners access to his own printing press, and
they produced a camp magazine called *Touchstone*, which contained
three of Munby's tales as well as poems, illustrations and essays
by other prisoners. The stories recycled Munby's own antiquarian interests and knowledge into escapist fantasy for his fellow
soldiers. Later he had these tales, and others written in the same
period including "Herodes Redivivus", published as *The Alabaster
Hand* (1949).

147

Just as in M. R. James's tales, the supernatural forces in Munby's work are not all ghosts as such. This story features a Bristol schoolboy meeting a bookseller who is rather more than he seems, and plays on our fears about child safety in the modern world. The title of the story is Latin and means "Herod reborn"—a reference to the Biblical figure who ordered the death of babies in an attempt to kill the infant Jesus.

I don't suppose that many people have heard of Charles Auckland, the pathologist, as he isn't the type of man who catches the public eye. What slight reputation he has got is of rather a sinister nature; for he has always tended to avoid the broad, beaten tracks of scientific research, and has branched off to bring light into certain dark cul-de-sacs of the human mind, which many people feel should be left unilluminated. Not that one would suspect it from his appearance. Some men who spend their lives studying abnormalities begin to look distinctly queer themselves, but not Auckland. To look at him one would put him down as a country doctor, a big red-faced man of about sixty, obviously still pretty fit, with a shrewd but kindly face. We belonged to the same club and for years had been on nodding terms, but I didn't discover until quite recently that he was a book-collector, and that only accidentally. I went to refer to Davenport's *Armorial Bookbindings* in the club library, and found him reading it. He deplored its inaccuracies, and I offered to lend him a list of corrections and additions that I had been preparing. This led to further discussion on bindings, and finally he invited me to go back with him to his flat and see his books. It was not yet ten o'clock and I agreed readily.

The night was fine, and we strolled together across the park to Artillery Mansions, where he was living at the time. On arriving we went up in the lift, and were soon seated in the dining-room of his flat, the walls of which were lined with books from floor to ceiling. I was glad to see that one alcove was entirely filled with calf and vellum bindings, the sight of which sent a little thrill of expectation down my spine. I crossed the room to examine them, and my host rose too. A glance showed me that they were all of the class that second-hand booksellers classify comprehensively under the word "Occult". This, however, did not surprise me, as I knew of Auckland's interests. He took down several volumes, and began to expatiate on them—some first editions of the astrological works of Robert Fludd, and a very fine copy of the 1575 *Theatrum Diabolorum*. I expressed my admiration, and we began to talk of trials for witchcraft. He had turned aside to fetch a copy of Scot's *Discoverie* to illustrate some point in his argument when suddenly my eye became riveted on the back of a small book on the top shelf, and my heart missed a beat. Of course it couldn't be, but it was fantastically like it! The same limp vellum cover without any lettering, with the same curious diagonal tear in the vellum at the top of the spine. My hand shook a little as I took it down and opened it. Yes, it was the book. I read once more the title villainously printed on indifferent paper: *Herodes Redivivus seu Liber Scelerosae Vitae et Mortis Sanguinolentae Retzii, Monstri Nannetensis,* Parisiis, MDXLV. As I read the words memories came flooding back of that macabre episode which had overshadowed my school days. Some of the terror that had come to me twenty years before returned, and I felt quite faint.

"I say, you must have a nose for a rarity," said Auckland, pointing to the volume in my hand.

"I've seen this book before," I replied.

"Really?" he said. "I'd be very glad to know where. There's no copy in any public collection in England, and the only one I've traced on the Continent is in the Ambrosian Library at Milan. I haven't even *seen* that. It's in the catalogue, but it's one of those books that librarians are very reluctant to produce. Can you remember where you've met it before?"

"I mean that I've seen this copy before," I answered.

He shook his head dubiously. "I think you must be mistaken about that. I've owned this for nearly twenty years, and before that it was the property of a man that you're most unlikely to have met. In fact, he died in Broadmoor fifteen years ago. His name was—"

"Race," I interposed.

He looked at me with interest. "I shouldn't have expected you to remember that," he said. "You must have been at school during the trial—not that it got much publicity. Thank God, there's legislation to prevent the gutter press from splashing that sort of stuff across their headlines." He half smiled. "You must have been a very precocious child—surely you were only a schoolboy at the time?"

"Yes," I replied. "I was a schoolboy—*the* schoolboy, one might say; the one who gave evidence at the trial and whose name was suppressed."

He put down the book he was holding and looked hard at me. "That's most extraordinarily interesting. I suppose you wouldn't be willing to tell me about it? As you know, cases of that sort are rather my subject. Of course, it would be in the strictest confidence."

I smiled. "There's nothing in my story that I'm particularly ashamed of," I replied, "though I must confess that I occasionally feel that if I'd been a little more intelligent the tragedy might have been averted. However, I've no objection at all. It's only of academic interest now. I haven't thought about the matter for years."

He sat me down in an armchair and poured me out a large whisky-and-soda, then settled himself opposite me.

"Take your time about it," he said. "I'm a very late bird, and it's only a quarter to eleven."

I took a long drink and collected my thoughts.

"I was at a large school on the outskirts of Bristol," I began, "and was not quite sixteen at the time of these events. Even in those days I was extremely interested in old books, a hobby in which I was encouraged by my housemaster. I never cut a great figure on the games field, and when it was wet or I was not put down for a game, I used to go book-hunting in Bristol. Of course, my purse was very limited and my ignorance profound, but I got enormous pleasure out of pottering round the shops and stalls of the town, returning every now and then with a copy of Pope's *Homer* or Theobald's *Shakespeare* to grace my study.

"I don't know whether you're acquainted with Bristol, but it's a most fascinating town. As one descends the hills towards the Avon, one passes from the Georgian crescents and squares of Clifton into the older maritime town, with its magnificent churches and extensive docks. Down by the river are many narrow courts and alleys, which are unchanged since the days when Bristol was a thriving mediaeval port. Much of this poorer area was out of bounds to the boys at school, but having exhausted the bookshops of the University area, I found it convenient to ignore this rule and explored every corner of the old town. One Saturday afternoon—it was in a summer term—I was wandering round the area between St. Mary Redcliffe and the old 'Floating Harbour', and I discovered a little court approached through a narrow passage. It was a miserable enough place, dark and damp, but a joy to the antiquarian—so long as he didn't have to live there! The first floors of the half-timbered houses jutted out and very nearly shut out the sky, and the court ended abruptly in a high blank wall. At the end on the right was a shop—at least the ground-floor window was filled with a collection of books. They were of little interest, and from the accumulation of dust upon them it was obvious that they hadn't been disturbed for years. The place had a deserted air, and it was in no great hope of finding it open that I tried the door. But it did open, and I found myself in its dark interior. Books were everywhere—all the shelves were blocked by great stacks of books on the floor with narrow lanes through which one could barely squeeze sideways, and over everything lay the same thick coating of dust that I'd noticed in the window. I felt as though I were the first person to enter it for years. No bell rang as I opened the door, and I looked round for the proprietor. I saw him sitting in an alcove at my right, and I picked my way through the piles of books to his desk. Did you ever see him yourself?"

"Only later, in Broadmoor," replied Auckland. "I'd like you to describe in your own words exactly how he struck you at the time."

"Well," I resumed, "my first impression of him was the extreme whiteness of his face. One felt on looking at him that he never went out into the sun. He had the unhealthy look that a plant gets if you leave a flower-pot over it and keep the light and air from it. His hair was long and straight and a dirty grey. Another thing that impressed me was the smoothness of his skin. You know how sometimes a man looks as though he has never had any need to shave—attractive in a young man but quite repulsive in an old one—well, that's how he looked. He stood up as I approached, and I saw he was a fat man, not grotesquely so but sufficiently to suggest grossness. His lips particularly were full and fleshy.

"I was half afraid of my own temerity in having entered, but he seemed glad to see me and said in rather a high-pitched voice:

"'Come in, my dear boy; this is a most pleasant surprise. What can I do for you?'

"I mumbled something about being interested in old books and wanting to look round, and he readily assented. Shambling round from pile to pile, he set himself deliberately to interest me. And the man was a fascinating talker—in a very little while he had summed up my small stock of bibliographical knowledge and was enlightening me on dates, editions, issues, values and other points of interest. It was with real regret that I glanced at my watch and found that I had to hurry back to school. I had made no purchase, but he insisted on presenting me with a book, a nicely bound copy of Sterne's *Sentimental Journey*, and made me promise to visit him again as soon as I could."

"Have you still got the Sterne?" asked Auckland.

"No," I said, "my father destroyed it at the time of the trial.

"As the shop was in a part of the town that was strictly out of bounds, I didn't mention my visit to my housemaster, but on the following Thursday it was too wet for cricket and I returned to my newly found friend.

"This time he took me up to a room on the first floor, where there were more books and several portfolios of prints. Race, for such I discovered was his name, was a mine of information on the political history of the eighteenth century, and kept me enthralled by his exposition of a great volume of Gillray cartoons. The man had a sort of magnetism, and at that impressionable age I fell completely under his spell. He drew me out about myself and my work at school, and it was impossible for a boy not to feel flattered by the attention of so learned a man. It was easy to forget his rather repellent physical qualities when he talked so brilliantly.

"Suddenly we heard the shop door below opening, and with an exclamation of annoyance he descended the stairs to attend to the customer. A minute or two passed, and he did not return. I listened and could hear the murmur of conversation below. I idly pulled a book or two from the shelves and glanced at them, but there was little in the room that he had not already shown me. I went to the door and peered down over the stairs, but couldn't see what was going on. My ears caught a scrap of dialogue about the county histories of Somerset. I became bored.

"Across the landing at the top of the stairs was another room, the door of which was very slightly ajar. I'm afraid that I'm of a very inquisitive disposition. I pushed it open and peeped in. It was obviously where Race lived. There was a bed in one corner, a wardrobe, and a circular table in the middle of the room, but what caught my eye at once and held me spellbound was a picture over the fireplace. No words of mine can describe it."

Auckland nodded. "I saw it—an unrecorded Goya—in his most bloodcurdling vein—made his 'Witches' Sabbath' look like a school treat! It was burned by our unimaginative police force. They wouldn't even let me photograph it." He sighed.

I resumed. "I went nearer to have a look at it. On the mantelpiece below it was a book—the book you've got now on your top shelf. I opened it and read the title page. Of course it meant nothing to me. Gille de Retz doesn't feature in the average school curriculum. Suddenly I heard a noise behind me and swung round. There was Race standing in the doorway. He had come up the stairs without my hearing him. I shall never forget the blazing fury in his eyes. His face seemed whiter than ever as he stood there, a terrifying figure literally shaking with rage.

"I quickly tried to make my apologies, but he silenced me with a gesture; then he snatched the book from my hands and replaced it on the mantelpiece. Still without speaking, he pointed to the door and I went quickly down the stairs. He followed me down into the shop. I was about to leave without another word when suddenly his whole manner changed. It was as though he had recollected some powerful reason for conciliating me. He laid a hand on my arm.

"'My dear boy,' he said, 'you must forgive my momentary annoyance. I am a methodical man, and I can't bear people touching the things in my room. I'm afraid that living as something of a recluse has made me rather fussy. I quite realise that you meant no harm. There are some very valuable books and pictures in there—not for sale, but my own private collection, and naturally I can't allow customers to wander in and out of it in my absence.'

"I expressed my contrition awkwardly enough, for the whole situation had embarrassed me horribly and I felt ill at ease. He perceived this and added:

"'Now you mustn't worry about this—and least of all must you let it stop you coming here. I want you to promise that you'll visit me as soon as you can again—just to show that you bear no ill-will. I'll hunt out some interesting things for you to look at.'

"I gave him my promise and hurried back to school. In a day or two I had persuaded myself that I'd been imagining things, that some trick of the light had made him appear so distorted with rage. After all, why should a man get so angry about so little? As for the picture, it made comparatively little impression on my schoolboy mind. Much that it depicted was unintelligible to me at that time. I was, in any case, unlikely to be invited into the private room again. And so I resolved to pay a further visit to the shop.

"An opportunity didn't occur for nearly a fortnight, and when I did manage to slip down to Bristol, there was no mistaking how glad he was to see me. He was almost gushing in his manner. He had been as good as his word in finding more books to show me, and I spent a most pleasant afternoon. Race was as voluble as ever, but I got the impression that he was slightly distrait, as though he were labouring under some sort of suppressed excitement. Several times as I looked up from a book I caught him looking at me in a queer reflective way, which made me feel a little uncomfortable. When I finally said that I must go, he made a suggestion that he had never made before.

"'You've got very dusty,' he said. 'You really must wash your hands before you go. There's a basin downstairs—I'll turn on the light for you.'

"As he said this, he stepped across the shop, opened a door and turned a switch, illuminating a long flight of stairs. I descended them. They were of stone and led apparently into a cellar. As I reached the bottom step the light was extinguished. I turned sharply and saw him standing at the head of the stairs—a fantastic, foreshortened figure at the top of the shaft, silhouetted in the doorway. He had his hands stretched out, holding on to the jambs of the door, and with the half-light of the shop behind him he looked like a misshapen travesty of a cross. I called out to him and started to remount the stairs, but as I did so he quickly closed the door without saying a word.

"I was terribly afraid. Of course, it might have been a joke but I knew inside me that it wasn't and that I was in the most deadly peril. I reached the top of the stairs and groped at the door, but there seemed to be no handle inside. I couldn't find the switch either, it must have been in the shop. I shouted, there was no reply. An awful horror gripped me—the dank smell of the stone cellar, the lack of air and the darkness, all conspired to undermine what little courage I possessed. I shouted again; then listened, holding my breath. All at once I heard the outer shop door open and an unfamiliar footstep inside the shop. With all my strength I pounded on the door, shouting and screaming like a madman. The noise reverberating round the confined space nearly deafened me. I listened again for a second; voices were raised in the shop, but I caught no words. I shouted again until I felt my lungs would burst and hammered on the door until my fists were bruised. Suddenly it was flung open and I stumbled out, hysterical with fear and half-blinded by the daylight. Before me stood an old clergyman, behind him Race, who bore on his face the same look of malevolent fury that I had seen before.

"'What is the matter?' asked the clergyman. 'How did you get shut in there?'

"It was then that I made my fatal mistake. All I wanted was to get away and never come back again. If I lodged a complaint I foresaw endless trouble, with the school authorities, even with the police. My terror had evaporated with the daylight, and I was feeling more than a little ashamed of myself.

"'I went down to wash my hands,' I said. 'The lights went out and I got frightened. I'm quite all right now, though.'

"The clergyman looked enquiringly at Race, but the latter had recovered his self-possession.

"'The lights must have fused,' he said; 'they often do—it's the damp. I was just going to let him out when you came in. No wonder he was frightened. It's a most eerie place in the dark.'

"The clergyman looked from him to me, as if inviting some comment from me, but I merely said, 'I ought to be getting back to school now.'

"We left the shop together, and as we walked through the passage out of the court I looked back, and there was Race standing on the step of his shop following us with baleful eyes. My companion seemed to be debating whether he would ask me a question, but he refrained. I hardly liked to ask him to say nothing about the episode; he obviously wished to satisfy his curiosity, but we were complete strangers and, though old enough to be my grandfather, he seemed to be a diffident man. It was a curious relationship.

"He put me on to a bus, and I thanked him gravely. As we shook hands he said abruptly, 'I shouldn't go there again,' and turned away.

"For a few days I was on tenterhooks lest he should make any report of the occurrence to the school, but as the days became weeks and I heard no more, my mind became at rest. I had firmly decided that nothing would induce me to visit Race's shop again, and soon the whole episode assumed an air of unreality in my mind."

I looked at my watch.

"Good Lord!" I said to Auckland, "it's getting pretty late. Do you want to go to bed? We could have another session tomorrow."

"Certainly not," he replied. "I find your story of the most absorbing interest. It fills in all sorts of gaps in my knowledge of the affair. If you don't mind sitting up, I should greatly appreciate it if you'd carry on."

He refilled my glass and I settled myself more comfortably into my chair.

"Well," I continued, "I'm a bit diffident about telling the rest of the story. Up to now it's been pretty strange, but it has been sober fact; now we get into realms where I find myself a bit out of my depth."

Auckland nodded. "Never mind," he said, "let's have it. Just as it comes back to you—don't try to explain it, just tell me what happened."

"A year passed and I was still at school," I continued; "I'd got into the Sixth Form and was working pretty hard for a scholarship. I'd also got into the House Cricket XI by some miracle, and so I couldn't be so free and easy about games as I had been previously. Public opinion forced me to take them fairly seriously. A dropped catch at a critical point in a match can make a schoolboy's life pretty good hell.

"At that age I used to sleep extraordinarily well—I still do for that matter. It was very rare for me to dream and then only of trivial affairs. But on the night of June 26th—I noted the date in my diary—I had the first of a couple of particularly horrible dreams. I dreamed most vividly that I was back in Race's shop. Every detail of that untidy interior passed in an accurate picture through my brain. I was standing in the middle of the shop, and it was dusk. Very little light came through those dusty windows piled high with books. Race himself was nowhere to be seen. The door to the cellar which had such sinister associations for me was closed. Suddenly from the other side of it came a series of appalling screams and shouts, intermingled with muffled bangs and thumps on the door. I ran across and tried to open it, but it was locked. Then I darted out to the shop steps to see if anyone were at hand to assist me, but the court was deserted. I stood irresolute in the shop, and then all at once the cries seemed to get weaker and the banging on the door ceased. I listened and could hear the sounds of a struggle on the stairs gradually getting fainter as it reached the cellar below.

"At this point I awoke shivering with fright, bathed in a cold sweat. Sleep was impossible for me during the rest of the night. I lay and thought about my dream. It seemed so queer that I should dream, not of my own experience on the stairs, but from the point of view of an observer.

"The next night exactly the same thing occurred, and the horror of the scene so impressed me that I must have cried out in my sleep, for I found that I'd awakened several of the other boys in my dormitory. I couldn't bear the anticipation of having such a dream a third time, and I went to the House Matron on the following day and told her that I couldn't sleep. She moved me from the dormitory into the sick-room and gave me a sedative. On that night and thereafter I slept quite normally again.

"Not quite a fortnight later a further link was forged in this extraordinary chain of events. I was passing the local police-station and I stopped to read a notice posted outside about the protection

of wild birds—I've always been a bit of an ornithologist. Along
the railings in front of the building were hung the usual medley of
notices—Lost, Found and Missing. My eye caught one more recent
than the others—and I idly read it.

"I cannot, of course, remember the exact wording at this date,
but it asked for information about a boy named Roger Weyland, aged
fifteen and a half. He was described in detail, and I remember being
struck at once by his similarity to myself. He had left his home at
Clevedon after lunch on June 26th to bicycle into Bristol, where he
intended to visit the docks. He was last seen near St. Mary Redcliffe
at about half-past five the same afternoon, and the police were asking
anyone to come forward who could throw light on his whereabouts.

"I read and reread the notice. Its implication dawned on me at
once. It's no good asking why, but I assure you that at the moment I
knew what had happened. My dream of the night of June 26th was
still fresh in my memory, and even in the broad sunlit street I shuddered and was oppressed by a feeling of nameless horror.

"I debated what I should do. The police, I felt sure, would laugh
at me. I could never bring myself to walk into the station and blurt
out such a fantastic tale to some grinning sergeant. But I must tell
someone; and after dinner that day I sought an interview with my
housemaster. He was a most understanding man, and listened in
patient silence while I told him the whole story. I must have spoken
with conviction, because at the end of it he rang up a friend of his,
a local Inspector of Police. Half an hour later I repeated my tale to
him. He was very polite, asked one or two searching questions, but
I could see that he was sceptical. He did, however, agree with my
housemaster that Race's activities might profitably be looked into.

"If you followed the trial, I suppose you know all the rest—how
they found the boy's body and God-knows-what other devilish things

beside. My name was suppressed in the evidence, and I left school at the end of that term and went abroad for six months.

"One very odd thing about it all was that they never traced the clergyman. The police were most anxious to get him to corroborate my story, and my father was equally keen to find him—after all, he saved my life—and my father wanted to show some tangible appreciation of the fact, subscribe generously to one of his favourite charities or something. It's very queer really that the police, with all their nation-wide organisation, never got on to him. After all, there aren't a limitless number of clergymen, and the number of those in the Bristol area that afternoon must have been comparatively small. Perhaps he didn't like to come forward and be connected with such a business, but I don't think that's very likely—he didn't strike me as the sort of man who would shirk his obligations.

"That's really all that I can tell you, and I expect you knew some of that already."

"A certain amount," replied Auckland, "but by no means all. I occasionally get asked questions by the police in this kind of case, and I did assist them on this occasion, though I wasn't called in evidence. Race had a damned good counsel in Rutherford, and managed to convince the jury that he was insane. If a man is sufficiently wicked, a British jury will often believe that he must be mad. And so he went to Broadmoor. Of course, he was as sane as you and I are."

"How did you come to get hold of one of his books?" I asked.

"Through the good offices of the police," he said. "Perhaps as a sort of consolation prize for my distress at the destruction of the Goya. The book is really the clue to Race.

"It is a contemporary account of the activities of Gille de Retz, Marshal of France, hanged at Nantes in 1440. I expect you know a certain amount about him; he figures in all the standard works on

Diabolism. The contemporary authorities are a bit vague on the exact number of children he murdered—Monstrelet says a hundred and sixty, but Chastellain and some others put it at a hundred and forty. But all this is general knowledge.

"What isn't so widely known is that every now and then he seems to reappear in history—at least the devilish practices, with which his name is associated, crop up again and again. He was quite a cult in seventeenth-century Venice, and there was a case in Bohemia in the middle of the last century. A variant of de Retz's name is de Rais and Race himself claimed to be a descendant; but I've no proof of this. The police failed to trace his parentage or to find any details about him before he appeared in Bristol just before the First World War. His shop has gone now; the whole of that area was pulled down in a recent slum-clearance scheme.

"The trial at Nantes in 1440 has always been an interest of mine, and I had a great find the last time I was in Paris. Some early Nantes archives had recently been acquired by the Bibliothèque Nationale, and I spent a happy week examining all the original documents relating to the examination of the woman, La Meffrie, who procured most of the children for de Retz. I've got transcripts of the most important. Would you care to borrow them? They are quite enthralling."

"Not on your life," I replied as I rose to take my leave. "I came far too near to playing the principal role to read about such things with any pleasure. *You* may be able to take a detached, scientific view of the case, but, believe me, I've had enough of de Retz and all his works to last me a lifetime."

W. S.

L. P. Hartley

Leslie Poles Hartley (1895–1972) started his literary career as a book reviewer, before having a first short story collection published in 1924 and later moving on to novel writing. His most famous book is probably *The Go-Between* (1953), generally regarded as a modern classic. He was a close friend of Lady Cynthia Asquith, the editor of the influential *Ghost Book* series, and she supported him by including his work in several of her edited collections. He wrote the introduction to her *Third Ghost Book* in 1955, and contributed the Christmas-themed story "Someone in the Lift" to the same volume. "W.S.", which first appeared in the journal *World Review* in January 1952, was reprinted twice that year—once in the August issue of *The Magazine of Fantasy and Science Fiction*, and again in Asquith's collection *The Second Ghost Book*.

Hartley's ghost stories are natural successors to the works of M. R. James, relying on scenarios in which comfortable ordinariness becomes a source of terror. "W. S." is a work of psychological horror based around the humble picture postcard. The editors of *The Magazine of Fantasy and Science Fiction* described it as "a new variation on a classic Pirandellian theme". This is a reference to the Italian playwright Luigi Pirandello, who wrote the influential absurdist metatheatrical play *Six Characters in Search of an Author* (1921).

The first postcard came from Forfar. *I thought you might like a picture of Forfar*, it began. *You have always been so interested in Scotland, and that is one reason why I am interested in you. I have enjoyed all your books, but do you really get to grips with people? I doubt it. Try to think of this as a handshake from your devoted admirer.—W. S.*

Like other novelists, Walter Streeter was used to getting communications from strangers. Usually they were friendly but sometimes they were critical. In either case he always answered them, for he was conscientious. But answering them took up the time and energy he needed for his writing, so that he was rather relieved that W. S. had given no address. The photograph of Forfar was uninteresting and he tore it up. His anonymous correspondent's criticism, however, lingered in his mind. Did he really fail to come to grips with his characters? Perhaps he did. He was aware that in most cases they were either projections of his own personality or, in different forms, the antitheses of it. The Me and the Not Me. Perhaps W. S. had spotted this. Not for the first time Walter made a vow to be more objective.

About ten days later arrived another postcard, this time from Berwick-on-Tweed. *What do you think of Berwick-on-Tweed?* it said. *Like you, it's on the Border. I hope this doesn't sound rude. I don't mean that you are a borderline case! You know how much I admire your stories. Some people call them other-worldly. I think you should plump for one world or the other. Another warm handshake from.—W. S.*

Walter Streeter pondered over this and began to wonder about the sender. Was his correspondent a man or a woman? It looked like a man's handwriting—commercial, un-selfconscious, and the criticism was like a man's. On the other hand, it was like a woman to probe—to want to make him feel at the same time flattered and unsure of himself. He felt the faint stirrings of curiosity but soon dismissed them; he was not a man to experiment with acquaintances. Still, it was odd to think of this unknown person speculating about him, sizing him up. Other-worldly, indeed! He reread the last two chapters he had written. Perhaps they didn't have their feet firm on the ground. Perhaps he was too ready to escape, as other novelists were nowadays, into an ambiguous world, a world where the conscious mind did not have things too much its own way. But did that matter? He threw the picture of Berwick-on-Tweed into his November fire and tried to write; but the words came haltingly, as though contending with an extra-strong barrier of self-criticism. And as the days passed, he became uncomfortably aware of self-division, as though someone had taken hold of his personality and was pulling it apart. His work was no longer homogeneous; there were two strains in it, unreconciled and opposing, and it went much slower as he tried to resolve the discord. Never mind, he thought; perhaps I was getting into a groove. These difficulties may be growing pains; I may have tapped a new source of supply. If only I could correlate the two and make their conflict fruitful, as many artists have!

The third postcard showed a picture of York Minster. *I know you are interested in cathedrals*, it said. *I'm sure this isn't a sign of megalomania in your case, but smaller churches are sometimes more rewarding. I'm seeking a good many churches on my way south. Are you busy writing or are you looking round for ideas? Another hearty handshake from your friend.—W. S.*

It was true that Walter Streeter was interested in cathedrals. Lincoln Cathedral had been the subject of one of his youthful fantasies and he had written about it in a travel book. And it was also true that he admired mere size and was inclined to undervalue parish churches. But how could W. S. have known that? And was it really a sign of megalomania? And who was W. S., anyhow?

For the first time it struck him that the initials were his own. No, not for the first time. He had noticed it before, but they were such commonplace initials; they were Gilbert's, they were Maugham's, they were Shakespeare's—a common possession. Anyone might have them. Yet now it seemed to him an odd coincidence; and the idea came into his mind—suppose I have been writing postcards to myself? People did such things, especially people with split personalities. Not that he was one of them, of course. And yet there were these unexplained developments—the dichotomy in his writing, which had now extended from his thought to his style, making one paragraph languorous with semicolons and subordinate clauses, and another sharp and incisive with main verbs and fullstops.

He looked at the handwriting again. It had seemed the perfection of ordinariness—anybody's hand—so ordinary as perhaps to be disguised. Now he fancied he saw in it resemblances to his own. He was just going to pitch the postcard in the fire when suddenly he decided not to. I'll show it to somebody, he thought.

His friend said, "My dear fellow, it's all quite plain. The woman's a lunatic. I'm sure it's a woman. She has probably fallen in love with you and wants to make you interested in her. I should pay no attention whatsoever. People in the public eye are always getting letters from lunatics. If they worry you, destroy them without reading them.

That sort of person is often a little psychic, and if she senses that she's getting a rise out of you, she'll go on."

For a moment Walter Streeter felt reassured. A woman, a little mouse-like creature, who had somehow taken a fancy to him! What was there to feel uneasy about in that? Then his subconscious mind, searching for something to torment him with, and assuming the authority of logic, said: Supposing those postcards are a lunatic's, and you are writing them to yourself; doesn't it follow that you must be a lunatic too?

He tried to put the thought away from him; he tried to destroy the postcard as he had the others. But something in him wanted to preserve it. It had become a piece of him, he felt. Yielding to an irresistible compulsion, which he dreaded, he found himself putting it behind the clock on the chimney piece. He couldn't see it, but he knew that it was there.

He now had to admit to himself that the postcard business had become a leading factor in his life. It had created a new area of thoughts and feelings, and they were most unhelpful. His being was strung up in expectation of the next postcard.

Yet when it came it took him completely by surprise. He could not bring himself to look at the picture. *I am coming nearer*, the postcard said; *I have got as near as Warwick Castle. Perhaps we shall come to grips after all. I advised you to come to grips with your characters, didn't I? Have I given you any new ideas? If I have, you ought to thank me, for they are what novelists want, I understand. I have been re-reading your novels, living in them. I might say. Je vous serre la main. As always.—W. S.*

A wave of panic surged up in Walter Streeter. How was it that he had never noticed, all this time, the most significant fact about the postcards—that each one came from a place geographically closer to him than the last? *I am coming nearer*. Had his mind, unconsciously self-protective, worn blinkers? If it had, he wished he could put them back. He took an atlas and idly traced out W. S.'s itinerary. An interval of eighty miles or so seemed to separate the stopping places. Walter lived in a large West Country town about eighty miles from Warwick.

Should he show the postcards to an alienist? But what could an alienist tell him? He would not know, what Walter wanted to know, whether he had anything to fear from W. S.

Better go to the police. The police were used to dealing with poison pens. If they laughed at him, so much the better.

They did not laugh, however. They said they thought the postcards were a hoax and that W. S. would never show up in the flesh. Then they asked if there was anyone who had a grudge against him. "No one that I know of," Walter said. They, too, took the view that the writer was probably a woman. They told him not to worry, but to let them know if further postcards came.

A little comforted, Walter went home. The talk with the police had done him good. He thought it over. It was quite true what he had told them—that he had no enemies. He was not a man of strong personal feelings; such feelings as he had went into his books. In his books he had drawn some pretty nasty characters. Not of recent years, however. Of recent years he had felt a reluctance to draw a very bad man or woman; he thought it morally irresponsible and artistically unconvincing, too. There was good in everyone: Iagos were a myth. Latterly—but he had to admit that it was several weeks since he laid pen to paper, so much had this ridiculous business of the postcards weighed upon his mind—if he had to draw a really wicked person he represented him as a Communist or a Nazi—someone who had deliberately put off his human characteristics. But in the past, when he was younger and more inclined to see things as black or white, he had let himself go once or twice. He did not remember his old books very well, but there was a character in one, *The Pariah*, into whom he had really got his knife. He had written about him with extreme vindictiveness, just as if he was a real person whom he was trying to show up. He had experienced a curious pleasure in attributing every kind of wickedness to this man. He never gave him the benefit of the doubt. He never felt a twinge of pity for him, even when he paid the penalty for his misdeeds on the gallows. He had so worked himself up that the idea of this dark creature, creeping about brimful of malevolence, had almost frightened him.

Odd that he couldn't remember the man's name. He took the book down from the shelf and turned the pages—even now they affected him uncomfortably. Yes, here it was, William... William... he would have to look back to find the surname. William Stainsforth.

His own initials.

He did not think the coincidence meant anything, but it coloured his mind and weakened its resistance to his obsession. So uneasy was he that when the next postcard came, it came as a relief.

I am quite close now, he read, and involuntarily turned the postcard over. The splendid central tower of Gloucester Cathedral met his eyes. He stared at it as if it could tell him something, then with an effort went on reading. *My movements, as you may have guessed, are not quite under my control, but all being well, I look forward to seeing you some time this weekend. Then we can really come to grips. I wonder if you'll recognise me! It won't be the first time you have given me hospitality. Ti serro lo mano. As always.—W. S.*

Walter took the postcard straight to the police station, and asked if he could have police protection over the weekend. The officer in charge smiled at him and said he was quite sure it was a hoax; but he would send someone to keep an eye on the place.

"You still have no idea who it would be?" he asked.

Walter shook his head.

It was Tuesday; Walter Streeter had plenty of time to think about the weekend. At first he felt he would not be able to live through the interval but, strange to say, his confidence increased instead of waning. He set himself to work as though he could work, and presently he found he could—differently from before and, he thought, better. It was as though the nervous strain he had been living under had, like an acid, dissolved a layer of nonconductive thought that came between him and his subject; he was nearer to it now, and instead of responding only too readily to his stage directions, his characters responded wholeheartedly and with all their beings to the tests he put them to. So passed the days, and the dawn of Friday seemed like any other day until something jerked him out of his self-induced trance and suddenly he asked himself, "When does a weekend begin?"

A long weekend begins on Friday. At that his panic returned. He went to the street door and looked out. It was a suburban, unfrequented street of detached Regency houses like his own. They had tall square gateposts, some crowned with semicircular iron brackets holding lanterns. Most of these were out of repair: only two or three were ever lit. A car went slowly down the street; some people crossed it; everything was normal.

Several times that day he went to look and saw nothing suspicious, and when Saturday came, bringing no postcard, his panic had almost subsided. He nearly rang up the police to tell them not to bother to send anyone after all.

They were as good as their word: they did send someone. Between tea and dinner, the time when weekend guests most commonly arrive,

Walter went to the door and there, between two unlit gateposts, he saw a policeman standing—the first policeman he had ever seen in Charlotte Street. At the sight and the relief it brought him, he realised how anxious he had been. Now he felt safer than he had ever felt in his life, and also a little ashamed at having given extra trouble to a hard-worked body of men. Should he go and speak to his unknown guardian, offer him a cup of tea and a drink? It would be nice to hear him laugh at Walter's fancies. But no—somehow he felt his security the greater when its source was impersonal and anonymous. "PC Smith" was somehow less impressive than "police protection".

Several times from an upper window (he didn't like to open the door and stare) he made sure that his guardian was still there; and once, for added proof, he asked his housekeeper to verify the strange phenomenon. Disappointingly, she came back saying she had seen no policeman; but she was not very good at seeing things, and when Walter went a few minutes later, he saw him plain enough. The man must walk about, of course; perhaps he had been taking a stroll when Mrs. Kendal looked.

It was contrary to his routine to work after dinner but tonight he did—he felt so much in the vein. Indeed, a son of exaltation possessed him; the words ran off his pen; it would be foolish to check the creative impulse for the sake of a little extra sleep. On, on. They were right who said the small hours were the time to work. When his housekeeper came in to say goodnight, he scarcely raised his eyes.

In the warm, snug little room the silence purred around him like a kettle. He did not even hear the doorbell till it had been ringing for some time.

A visitor at this hour?

His knees trembling, he went to the door, scarcely knowing what he expected to find: so what was his relief, on opening it, to see the doorway filled by the tall figure of a policeman. Without waiting for the man to speak.

"Come in, come in, my dear fellow," he exclaimed. He held his hand out, but the policeman did not take it. "You must have been very cold standing out there. I didn't know that it was snowing, though," he added, seeing the snowflakes on the policeman's cape and helmet. "Come in and warm yourself."

"Thanks," said the policeman. "I don't mind if I do."

Walter knew enough of the phrases used by men of the policeman's stamp not to mistake this for a grudging acceptance. "This way," he prattled on. "I was writing in my study. By Jove, it is cold, I'll turn the gas on more. Now, won't you take your traps off and make yourself at home?"

"I can't stay long," the policeman said, "I've got a job to do, as *you* know."

"Oh yes," said Walter, "such a silly job, a sinecure." He stopped, wondering if the policeman would know what a sinecure was. "I suppose you know what it's about—the postcards?"

The policeman nodded.

"But nothing can happen to me as long as you are here," said Walter. "I shall be as safe... as safe as houses. Stay as long as you can, and have a drink."

"I never drink on duty," said the policeman. Still in his cape and helmet, he looked round. "So this is where you work?" he said.

"Yes, I was writing when you rang."

"Some poor chap's for it, I expect," the policeman said.

"Oh, why?" Walter was hurt by his unfriendly tone, and noticed how hard his eyes were.

"I'll tell you in a minute," said the policeman, and then the telephone bell rang. Walter excused himself and hurried from the room.

"This is the police station," said a voice. "Is that Mr. Streeter?"

Walter said it was.

"Well, Mr. Streeter, how is everything at your place? All right, I hope? I'll tell you why I ask. I'm sorry to say we quite forgot about that little job we were going to do for you. Bad co-ordination, I'm afraid."

"But," said Walter, "you did send someone."

"No, Mr. Streeter, I'm afraid we didn't."

"But there's a policeman here, here in this very house."

There was a pause, then his interlocutor said, in a less casual voice,

"He can't be one of our chaps. Did you see his number by any chance?"

"No."

Another pause and the voice said,

"Would you like us to send somebody now?"

"Yes p—please."

"All right, then; we'll be with you in a jiffy."

Walter put back the receiver. "What now?" he asked himself. Should he barricade the door? Should he run out into the street? While he was debating, the door opened and his guest came in.

"No room's private when the street door's once passed," he said. "Had you forgotten I was a policeman?"

"Was?" said Walter, edging away from him. "You *are* a policeman."

"I have been other things as well," the policeman said. "Thief, pimp, blackmailer, not to mention murderer. *You* should know."

The policeman, if such he was, seemed to be moving towards him, and Walter suddenly became alive to the importance of small distances—from the sideboard to the table, from one chair to another.

"I don't know what you mean," he said. "Why do you speak like that? I've never done you any harm. I've never set eyes on you before."

"Oh, haven't you?" the man said. "But you've thought about me, and"—his voice rose—"and you've written about me. You got some fun out of me, didn't you? Now I'm going to get some fun out of you. You made me just as nasty as you could. Wasn't that doing me harm? You didn't think what it would be like to be me, did you? You didn't put yourself in my place, did you? You hadn't any pity for me, had you? Well, I'm not going to have any pity for you."

"But I tell you," cried Walter, fingering the table's edge, "I don't know you!"

"And now you say you don't know me! You did all that to me and then forget me!" His voice became a whine, charged with self-pity. "You forgot William Stainsforth."

"William Stainsforth!"

"Yes. I was your scapegoat, wasn't I? You unloaded all your self-dislike on me. You felt pretty good while you were writing about me. Now, as one W. S. to another, what shall I do, if I behave in character?"

"I—I don't know," muttered Walter.

"You don't know?" Stainsforth sneered. "You ought to know, you fathered me. What would William Stainsforth do if he met his old dad in a quiet place, his kind old dad who made him swing?"

Walter could only stare at him.

"You know what he'd do as well as I," said Stainsforth. Then his face changed and he said abruptly, "No you don't, because you never really understood me. I'm not so black as you painted me." He paused and a flame of hope flickered in Walter's breast. "You never gave me a chance, did you? Well, I'm going to give you one. That shows you never understood me, doesn't it?"

Walter nodded.

"And there's another thing you have forgotten."

"What is that?"

"I was a kid once," the ex-policeman said.

Walter said nothing.

"You admit that?" said William Stainsforth grimly. "Well, if you can tell me of one virtue you ever credited me with—just one kind thought—just one redeeming feature—"

"Yes," said Walter, trembling.

"Well, then I'll let you off."

"And if I can't?" whispered Walter.

"Well, then, that's just too bad. We'll have to come to grips, and you know what that means. You took off one of my arms but I've still got the other. 'Stainsforth of the iron arm', you called me."

Walter began to pant.

"I'll give you two minutes to remember," Stainsforth said.

They both looked at the clock. At first the stealthy movement of the hand paralysed Walter's thoughts. He stared at William Stainsforth's face, his cruel and crafty face, which seemed to be always in shadow, as if it was something the light could not touch. Desperately he searched his memory for the one fact that would save him; but his memory, clenched like a fist, would give up nothing.

"I must invent something," he thought, and suddenly his mind relaxed and he saw, printed on it like a photograph, the last page of the book. Then, with the speed and magic of a dream, each page appeared before him in perfect clarity until the first was reached, and he realised with overwhelming force that what he looked for was not there. In all that evil there was not one hint of good. And he felt, compulsively and with a kind of exaltation, that unless he testified to this, the cause of goodness everywhere would be betrayed.

"There's nothing to be said for you!" he shouted. "Of all your dirty tricks this is the dirtiest! The very snowflakes on you are turning black! How dare you ask me for a character? I've given you one already! God forbid that I should ever say a good word for you! I'd rather die!"

Stainsforth's one arm shot out. "Then die!" he said.

The police found Walter Streeter slumped across the dining-table. In view of what had happened previously, they did not exclude the possibility of foul play. But the pathologist could not state with certainty the cause of death. There was a clue, but it led nowhere. On the table and on the victim's clothes were flakes of melting snow. It had run down his neck, soaking his underclothes. It had even, in some way, got into his stomach and might have killed him for, on analysis, it was found to be poisonous. Perhaps he had taken his own life. But what the substance was, and where it came from, remained a mystery, for no snow was reported from any district on the day he died.

WHAT SHADOWS WE PURSUE

Russell Kirk

Russell Amos Kirk (1918–1994) was born in Plymouth, Michigan, USA. After graduating in history from Michigan State College and then from Duke University, he travelled to the UK to study for a PhD at the University of St. Andrews. His doctoral thesis traced a philosophical history and pedigree for traditionalist conservative thought in the USA, and when it was published as *The Conservative Mind* in 1953 he was established as an important political theorist of the American right. He became a prolific author, and interspersed his writings on political history with thrillers and collections of ghost stories. "What Shadows We Pursue" is one of his earlier tales, first published in *The Magazine of Fantasy and Science Fiction* in January 1953 and reprinted in his collection *The Surly Sullen Bell* in 1962. An afterword in the latter volume makes a case for the revival of the "Gothick" story in an age that Kirk felt had turned from faith and spirituality to hard science, psychology and the depiction of graphic violence.

"Eleven thousand books," said Mrs. Corr, mildly and factually. In her clear old voice lingered no tone of affection for the vast dusty library, no hint of apprehension of its dignity. "Or nearly eleven thousand. Dr. Corr had Sarah make a card for every one. Why, that's less than thirty cents a volume you're offering, isn't it, Mr. Stoneburner?" With a species of gentle calculation, she let her dim glance slide along the interminable Georgian spines of *A Universal History*. "My... but I suppose that's the best we can hope for?"

From thick, faded carpet to moulded-plaster ceiling fifteen feet above, Dr. Corr's books staunchly filled the walls of the long room. Beyond the archway was another room nearly as large, and there books not only jammed the shelves but lay in heaps upon tables and were monumentally stacked upon the floor. The grand, chill corridor upon which this second room opened also was choked with books, while the shorter hall at right angles, leading from the corridor to what had been Dr. Corr's bedroom, held bound volumes of *The Edinburgh Review* and *Harper's Monthly*. Nor did these comprehend the whole of the collection, for the great skylighted attic, up beyond the graceful curve of the mahogany stair rail, was a storehouse for countless periodicals never bound but neatly tied together in volumes; for obscure governmental reports; for a welter of cheap and damaged editions that Dr. Corr should have sold as waste. But, of course, Dr. Corr never had parted with a book, however wretchedly printed or wretchedly written. He would as soon have sold his daughter—sooner, old Mr. Hanchett said. Hanchett, who had been Stoneburner's cataloguer for five years and cataloguer to other booksellers decades before that, was given to uncharitable judgments. And for all these books, William Stoneburner, bookdealer, now was writing a check.

"Not much more than a quarter each," Stoneburner replied, with his apologetic nod, blowing upon the check. "If you could find a man who wanted the collection for himself, Mrs. Corr, he could give you more than any of us dealers. But who'd have the space for them, in these days? Or the money? Or the leisure to read?" Stoneburner was a little vain of the mien with which he could deliver his genteel and recurrent sigh of *in hoc tempori*. It sat well upon a man who inhabited the valley of the shadow of books, even though he dwelt there as a bourgeois.

"A friend told me," murmured Mrs. Corr, rocking her little chair softly and inspecting the buttons of her shiny shoes of a fashion forty years obsolete, "that the old Bibles might be worth a great deal, just by themselves. There's a man somewhere who collects old Bibles, this friend said." Despite her having tucked the check into her work basket only this minute, already she was displaying the recriminations so frequently encountered among sellers of books. Stoneburner, knowing the mood, was tolerant.

"I'm sure some people must collect Bibles," he assured the venerable Mrs. Corr in a voice nearly as artless as her own. "Here's what you and I'll do: you can have all the old Bibles. Put them aside and keep them, and sell them to somebody else, if you like. I own too many old Bibles. The price for the library will stand. But I do want to take just one Bible—the Cranmer. I think I know where I can sell that. The rest are yours."

A harsh tone, neither masculine nor feminine, broke in upon this colloquy: the voice of Miss Sarah Corr, who had entered by the door at Stoneburner's back. "What Bible is that, Mr. Stoneburner?" She moved ponderously toward the window seat where a half dozen folio and quarto Bibles clustered, a black dust thick upon their exposed top edges. "You'll get a lot of money for it, I imagine?" She poked unfeelingly the thick book in vellum that Stoneburner indicated.

And Miss Sarah Corr turned her set smile upon Mr. Stoneburner. Larger far than Stoneburner, larger than most men, she was a massive spinster. Fifty? Sixty? Had she ever been young? Not to judge by her dress, which was as timeless as her frail mother's. To be beamed upon by Miss Sarah Corr was not altogether pleasant. When Stoneburner first had seen that broad smile, he had been standing upon the steps of the austere stone house of Dr. Corr, a house somber even on an Indian-summer evening; and Miss Corr had opened to his ring with some caution, and then had said, with that peculiar smile, "You're the gentlemen who buys books? The one with the advertisement in the telephone directory?"

A month gone, that evening. The month had been a time of delicate negotiation with Mrs. Corr and Miss Corr, two recluses mightily ignorant of the contents of these eleven thousand volumes, mightily afraid of losing a fortune. It was a good library, but there was no fortune in it: the library of a man who read, not of a man who collected.

"It's going to bring me sixty or seventy dollars, Miss Corr," Stoneburner told her, unruffled. "Only that for a Cranmer Bible. On all these shelves, perhaps there are six or eight books people will pay that much for. The rest—why, they're good books, the kind of books Dr. Corr read. I think I'd have liked to know Dr. Corr."

"Yes, yes?" sighed Mrs. Corr, civilly, still rocking. She accepted Stoneburner's remark as a conventional compliment, apparently, and volunteered no comment upon her husband. Her *late* husband, Stoneburner had thought when initially he browsed through this house; but while the Corr women spoke of the doctor as one forever gone, they never seemed quite to use the past tense. So Stoneburner had inquired of old Hanchett, who knew something of every man within this century that had bought very many books in the city.

"Dr. Corr is one of those chaps that wither up and the wind blows away," old Hanchett had said, being himself invincibly portly and rubicund. "Haven't seen him in several years. He let his friends go because he liked the books better, and he came out into the light less and less... Well, you've seen his wife and daughter. Books cost; the Corr women had to manage with one new dress a year, or every other year. And then they gave up their card-parties. As time went on, Corr decided that his women's mission in life was to make catalogue cards for his books and to do a bit of dusting. He used to take his wife for an hour's walk after supper; then back to his library, and she to her parlor to sew, until it was time for sleep—Corr to his bedroom (books helter-skelter on the floor), she to hers.

"The daughter? Oh, the girl was queer to begin with. You'll see it, Mr. Stoneburner: she has her little ways. Maybe she was one of the things that drove Corr away from people, into books. Corr was allergic—allergic to people. Ah, but books, though... I'll hand it to him there. No, it's been years since I had a word with him. As he dried up, even the evening walk got to be too long a vacation from his books. I wonder if he has books where he is now? I don't know exactly when they took him away, but Mrs. Corr told my cousin that they sent him out West for his health. They don't seem to expect him back. His *health*, eh?" Here Hanchett had tapped a plump finger against his forehead, uncharitably. "One-way ticket, Mr. Stoneburner. And is the money nearly gone now, too? I suppose it costs to keep the doctor in the West for his *health*. Why, the doctor would be a screaming devil if he knew the library was being sold. He was a tall, white husk of a man, decent-spoken, a gold mine for the dealers."

Still Mrs. Corr rocked, soothing away this reference of Stoneburner's to her husband as she and her daughter were wont to pass over such comments—nothing of pride in their manner, nothing of resentment. "Yes, yes? Well, now—the house will seem almost empty with the books gone, won't it? All sorts of people are looking for places to live these days, I hear. I suppose we could rent part of this great big house of ours. But who would want to live here? It's too dirty." And Mrs. Corr laughed her delicate little laugh, and Miss Corr added her deep chuckle.

Candid, this. The Corrs were not deficient in a certain withered wit. Undoubtedly the Corr house was too dirty for anyone but the Corrs. From the parlor ceiling, the paper hung down in festoons that obscured the gilt-framed paintings on the walls. Plaster was falling in the attic, for the roof has begun to leak in Dr. Corr's time. One suspected that Dr. Corr's allergy toward humanity extended even to roofers and plumbers and paperers. Certain utilitarian improvements had been installed in his house only with extreme tardiness: the lighting, for instance. Apparently possessed of a reactionary confidence that the days of high old Roman virtue would return, Dr. Corr had cherished three systems of illumination, each ready to function in a pinch. Candelabra and kerosene lamps were to be seen, tarnished and topsy-turvy, in this corner or that; gas jets still protruded from plaster or panelling, and could be lit; but the actual artificial light came from naked bulbs dangling like hanged felons from the ceilings—many of them the early bamboo filament sort that terminate in a glassy spike, since the Corrs lived in three or four rooms and turned on these other switches scarcely more than twice in a month.

Not a practical man, Dr. Corr; nor was Mrs. Corr a practical woman; yet she seemed to have a canny eye for a dollar, possibly out of necessity. Her rocking uninterrupted, she continued, "Now, Mr. Stoneburner, I don't suppose you mean the books in the attic are included, do you? Those still belong to us?"

Stoneburner certainly had thought they were his. All the same, they were trash, except for the periodicals, which needed binding. And it was unpleasant to deny a crumb of victory to an impractical lady in her eighties. He was about to say, "You're quite welcome to them," when Mr. Markashian entered. Mr. Markashian had over-heard something of the conversation. Mr. Markashian had a habit of overhearing, Stoneburner reflected.

"Of course they belong to us, Mother," pronounced Markashian, with emphasis.

Mrs. Corr obviously was not Markashian's mother, for he was a Levantine; despite the Armenian name, he had more the look of an Anatolian Greek. He was her son-in-law, nevertheless, a public accountant from Newark, firm in a decided opinion that he knew the world, and deserved well of it. "Markashian never dared turn up while the doctor was in the house," Hanchett had told Stoneburner. "He married Lilly Corr on the sly. Both of them got cheated."

But the vanishing of the doctor from the scene and the scent of a sale of family assets had drawn the worldly Mr. Markashian from his accustomed pursuits in New Jersey. He left his wife behind to tend the children, informing her that family honor and prosperity now were his responsibility. As a man of business, Mrs. Corr and Miss Sarah Corr appeared to reverence him unwillingly; but it was clear to Stoneburner that Markashian did not want the books to be sold at all, preferring the chance of inheriting the library to the chance of inheriting a remnant of the cash. As a man of business and as a simple man, Stoneburner loathed Markashian, who rejoiced in the best suits and the worst manners Stoneburner had observed for some years.

"You understand that, don't you?" went on Markashian, turning to Stoneburner. "The books in the attic don't go with the others. There's highly valuable property upstairs."

"What money you can extract from the books in the attic," Stoneburner told him sourly, "I make you a present of."

"That's settled, then," grinned Markashian, on a note of triumph. "What's the book you're holding, Sarah?"

Miss Sarah Corr gave Markashian one of her long stares, and then a long smile, and suddenly came out with, "An old Bible worth thirty dollars. Mr. Stoneburner wants this one." A single bond of sympathy joined Stoneburner and Miss Corr: distrust of Markashian.

"What, this lovely old ancestral Bible?" groaned Markashian. "An heirloom! Gutenburg Bible, isn't it? It mustn't leave the family."

"It's not a Gutenburg, I'm sorry to inform you, Mr. Markashian; and it's my property. I can't have more books extracted from my purchase. Would you prefer to return the check to me, Mrs. Corr?" He extended his hand toward her. Though a cheery little man, Stoneburner was capable of firmness.

Patting her work basket in alarm, Mrs. Corr declared she had no intention of breaking the bargain. "Everything but the other Bibles, and the books in the attic, and the few things Mr. Markashian took for himself yesterday after you left—everything else is yours, Mr. Stoneburner. My, what a strange house this will be with the books gone! You'll take them all out yourself, Mr. Stoneburner? You won't bring anyone to help? We'd rather carry them for you ourselves than have strangers running upstairs."

This was a matter of consequence with her and with Sarah Corr, who turned her stagnant look on him. The intensity of the appeal somewhat embarrassed Stoneburner and seemed to surprise even Markashian. But Stoneburner already had agreed to the stipulation. It was natural enough: dirty though they confessed their house to be, still they hardly would want it inspected by chance comers.

"All eleven thousand, Mrs. Corr—I'll lug them to the truck myself. I'll need a whole week, off and on. We'll have to take care with some of the folios: they're shaky. Heavy things, books—I'll be stiff when it's done. Will it suit you if I start at nine tomorrow morning?"

Sarah Corr went with him to the double-bolted front door, through the vaulted corridor where two walnut clocks ticked alternately amid the ashes of magnificence, and she let him out into the night. He swung away from that ponderous, ever-beaming face, with the close-cropped grey hair that turned it almost masculine. "You've seen the attic," she said. "You won't need to go there again, after tonight?"

"Since those books aren't mine, no."

"That's nice of you," Miss Corr concluded, closing the door in his face. He listened to her bolt it, hesitating for a moment on the steps. As he loitered, it occurred to him that he had not heard Sarah Corr's slow stride back through the corridor. She must be standing just inside the door, to make sure he was gone. Shrugging, Stoneburner went.

A light covered truck especially equipped with wooden racks was the property of Stoneburner's Bookshop. And this Stoneburner parked close by the porch of the Corr house next morning, ready to commence moving one tier of the books in the library proper. Greeting him with her invariable hesitant commendation of the weather, Mrs. Corr admitted him. She wore that black dress which hid her ankles—a dowdy figure, but not vulgar. Back into her parlor she tottered, and Stoneburner went his quiet way up the circling stairs to the library. As he trod the stair carpet, he heard feet hastily descending from a higher level—the attic, of course; and he took them for Mr. Markashian's feet. But when he reached the library floor, nothing was to be seen of Markashian. Perhaps he had ducked into one of the chilly bedrooms off the corridor. Markashian was given to judicious ducking.

Methodically dusting the top of each volume with a piece of flannel, Stoneburner took the books from a tier of shelves close to the window and stacked them in tidy heaps convenient for carrying downstairs. A gap appeared upon one of the shelves. The morning before, a set of Bacon had reposed there, and Stoneburner assumed it was part of his purchase. But finding it gone in the afternoon, he had inquired of Mrs. Corr, to be told that "Mr. Markashian thought it ought to be his—useful in his work." Stoneburner had waived the matter.

A decrepit little ladder enabled Stoneburner to reach the higher shelves; he balanced upon it, dusting. In this volume or that, Dr. Corr had inserted neat slips of paper to mark favorite passages; small checks in the margins pointed to some mighty line or kernel of wit. Himself a leisurely man, Stoneburner now and then opened a book to glance at these passages, and generally was much taken with the doctor's choice. He began to form an image of Dr. Corr other than the "sneer of cold command" that Hanchett's description had left in his mind. A solitary man, this Dr. Corr; but then, how could he be other than alien to his mousy wife and queer daughter and infuriating son-in-law? Indeed, Stoneburner experienced the beginnings of awe for a noble mind in provincial obscurity. Corr's family may have paid back his disdain in that ferocious envy the vulgar feel toward the proud. Bound to them he may have been; but until now they had been his slaves.

Stoneburner took down Fuller's *The Holy State and the Profane State*—a fine glossy seventeenth-century binding. "Cesare Borgia, His Life," Corr had underlined in the index, and had marked the page by inserting a note-card. The bookseller ran his eye along the passages checked: "The throne and the bed cannot severally abide partners..." "For he could neither lengthen the land nor lessen the sea in Italie..." "He preferred the state of his body to the body of his state." Why, even a touch of fun in this Dr. Corr. Stoneburner put the quarto upon his dusted stack; and, having done with this shelf, glanced at the books on the window seat There was a gap among them.

What sort of fool did they think him? For the Cranmer Bible was gone. He was inured to pilferage and aware that the average person with whom he dealt thought a single volume could hardly be missed among so many. But in the present instance, Stoneburner had specifically claimed the Cranmer for his own the previous day, and it was too bulky and too valuable for them to suppose he would forget it wholly. This was more than Stoneburner was disposed to endure. Though angry, he was self-possessed, and he turned to face the room, wondering if they could have tucked the book into some drawer. They would not dare hide it absolutely, since that was theft; more probably they would endeavor to lose it in some pile of trash, trusting he might pass it by. And so he recalled the steps he had heard briskly descending from the attic when, an hour before, he had entered the house.

Mrs. Corr was downstairs, and Sarah Corr with her, no doubt; Markashian—for surely it was he who had scuttled from the attic— would not be inclined to face him at this moment, even supposing him only across the corridor. A quiet survey of the attic could do no harm.

Stoneburner walked into the corridor and turned up the spiralling stair. At the top the door stood ajar. Standing on the last step and resting his arm upon the balustrade, Stoneburner sent an exploratory glance within. One enormous room, this attic, into which the sun penetrated dully through a cupola skylight. Sundry boxes and articles of old furniture were scattered about the center of the floor, but Dr. Corr had kept the place fairly clear of rubbish so that he could get to his shelves of magazines along the walls. Right opposite the door, in line with Stoneburner's eyes, was a broad tier of worthless novels, no doubt bought by Dr. Corr with other books at some auction.

These novels had been disturbed. Six or seven had fallen to the floor, and another gap indicated that more had tumbled from the shelves. Had Markashian been sliding the Cranmer among this trash and been interrupted at his game? Stoneburner raised one foot to the final step of the staircase.

But he was prevented. Sharp and resistless, a grip pinned his arm against the balustrade. Half a second he paused to quiet his leaping nerves, and then looked round to see Miss Sarah Corr at his back, her great hand clamped upon his wrist, her face set in that inimitable smile. The smile grew broader. As it spread, her fingers dug into his wrist as if to find a passage through. She must have tiptoed painstakingly after him, weasel behind goose. And in her face there was no more of mercy than of sanity.

"Sarah!" whispered Mrs. Corr from the foot of the staircase, and commenced laboriously to climb toward them. At that soft cry, Miss Sarah Corr relaxed her clutch, and the smile sank into something nearer humanity, but still she did not speak.

Mrs. Corr ascended the infinite way to their side, and said to him, most politely and casually, "Did you need something in the attic,

Mr. Stoneburner?" Her old eyes cried out some awful disturbance. But what?

"Someone seems to have been looking over the Cranmer Bible," Stoneburner answered, something of a quaver in his voice. "Do you suppose it might have been left up here by mistake?"

Embarrassment he had expected, perhaps shamed denial; but not this assuagement that came into the faces of the Corr women. "Oh, I'm sorry you have the trouble of looking for it," said Mrs. Corr with a tiny sigh. "Sarah and I will see if we can help." And together they entered the attic.

To the left of the cupola skylight stood an imposing oak desk, a pile of old ledgers sprawled upon it. Stoneburner had noticed it before. But now the capacious drawers were pulled open, and bundles of letters and papers and photographs tossed out of them and spread in confusion beside the ledgers. Sarah Corr drew a heavy breath, and Mrs. Corr glanced round the big room, and then they went at the desk with a sort of horror-struck frenzy. Markashian's curiosity and covetousness extended beyond the library purchase to the property of his mother-in-law and sister-in-law, Stoneburner surmised; and doubtless his coming had interrupted Mr. Markashian's prowling. As mother and daughter packed papers into drawers and cubby-holes with a gingerly haste, Stoneburner examined a photograph of a white-haired, hollow-cheeked man in a high collar that lay face upward. "Oh, Dr. Corr?" he inquired. "And these are his papers? A fine face."

They stopped sorting the papers, and, wordless, looked at him. Sarah Corr raised a massive hand, and for a foolish moment he thought she meant to strike him; but instead she laid a finger upon her lips. Then she took the picture from his hand, turning it downward in the act, and laid it at the bottom of a drawer. This silence was contagious. Quite dumb, he stood by while they cleared away the confusion and shut the violated drawers and padded back toward the stairs. Then—"Ah, there's the Bible," said Stoneburner, seeing the quarto among a heap of the fallen novels and bending to retrieve it.

"My... Mr. Markashian must have been reading it," murmured Mrs. Corr, touching his coat sleeve—almost tugging at him. As he rose with the Bible, he noticed a deep, an incalculably deep, space behind the gap from which the novels had tumbled.

"Why, what's happened here, Mrs. Corr? Have you lost some books down a hole?" He glanced into it. A hole, yes; a very great hole. A stair well, with steps descending into a black abyss. This tier of shelves veiled, and sealed away, was some disused back way into the attic. When he leaned forward for a closer look, his shoulder brushed against a tottering novel, and that book, too, fell backward from its place, bounding four or five steps into the filthy gloom and then flopping to its rest upon the last visible tread.

"You! Don't you dare!" The stifled scream had come from Sarah Corr—the most nearly feminine expression he had heard from her. Her teeth were gritted, but she seemed beyond smiling. Mrs. Corr ran a hand along her daughter's arm.

"Those are the old stairs for the maids, Mr. Stoneburner," Mrs. Corr explained, looking not at him but at the gap in the shelves. "They've been boarded since I don't know when. That's one reason we hoped you wouldn't need the books up here: the stairs would seem so odd without books to hide them.

"I'm glad the Bible wasn't lost. Do you need us to help you dust downstairs?" She took his arm; he helped her down the staircase, Sarah closing the door tightly behind them. There was no key in it, and Stoneburner suspected that nearly every key in the house had been mislaid years before.

In the library, with the Corr women gone down to the parlor, Stoneburner placed his resurrected Bible among the dusted books and went on with his stacking. A pox upon the book-ignorant folk who think every dog-eared Victorian New Testament a collector's treasure beyond the dreams of avarice! How often had he heard over his telephone some hesitant voice inquiring, "Do you buy old books? Really old books? What do you pay? I've got a *really* old Bible here. Authorized Version. London, *1884*…"

All too strong was this spirit in that nervous pair, the Corr women. Possibly, though, they were endowed with redeeming virtues. They had seemed genuinely shocked at Markashian's profanation of the doctor's papers, presumably left undisturbed, out of sentiment, ever since that gaunt shell of learning was sent somewhere into the West to linger out the little time still vouchsafed his wreck.

Now Stoneburner began taking down the volumes of a good set of Burke, their pages much marked and checked in the doctor's hand. Such pencillings impair the value of second-hand books; but since Stoneburner read books as well as sold them, he did not complain overmuch. What sort of thing had Corr favored in Burke? Opening at random, he found a sentence doubly underlined: "What shadows we are, and what shadows we pursue."

Just so, old doctor. And true for bookworms like you and me, most especially—thus Stoneburner to himself. You even more than I, thank God. He put the volume with the others and stretched his tired arms. As he rested, a noise of voices full of anger drifted faintly to him from the parlor below. Well, had the Corr women had enough of that reluctantly-revered Setebos of a son-in-law, that dandy with the vulturine profile and the flaccid hand? The temptation to eavesdrop was overwhelming. Stoneburner bent over the stair well, where the words could be made out sufficiently.

"... Only to look for the receipts, Mother." Yes, it was Markashian, half the cocksureness gone out of his tones, a Markashian taken aback at such vehemence over a bout of snooping.

Sarah Corr was answering him, or rather drowning him out. "Meddling, meddling, stirring things up! What do you want to poke into? What do you want to bring on us? Take your pictures, take your books, but don't poke. Take your money, but don't pry! No more sense..."

Markashian's reply was not wholly audible, but Stoneburner made out something about "no harm" and "a thousand miles away." Miss Corr roared down the oily voice again, her mother's low entreaty interrupting her. Then a door was shut and Stoneburner was prevented from hearing the rest; but this he caught before the colloquy was suppressed: "He always slept light, and he knew what you were after, and he could get into your dreams, and now he'll stir, the devil! That old, white, sneering, creepy devil! That's what!"

Was it the absent Dr. Corr thus described by his daughter? A nice family, a cordial household. Well, time for lunch, Stoneburner realized. He skipped down the stairs and tapped at the parlor door and glanced within. The three were standing in the middle of the faded room, all taut at his knock. "Back at two, if that's all right," Stoneburner told them, and went his way. Yes, a jolly family.

The grimmest of all aspects of the book trade is the carrying of big volumes upstairs or down; and just this was to be Stoneburner's afternoon task. Commencing at two, he kept at it faithfully for more than an hour. The Corrs and Markashian stayed out of his way, withdrawn in their parlor with its dingy plush chairs. As Stoneburner lugged perhaps the fortieth stack of volumes toward the front door, there came a crash above. Had the books piled in the library fallen? Hardly.

He had arranged them neatly, and the noise seemed more distant. From the parlor peered Markashian and Mrs. Corr.

"Perhaps some magazines in the attic toppled," Stoneburner offered.

"My, no," said Mrs. Corr, almost inaudibly, holding tight to the door-jamb. Markashian went up the stairs; Mrs. Corr opened her mouth as if to call after him, but no words followed. So remarkable was the look she sent up the stair well that Stoneburner waited for Markashian's report.

He came down with his accustomed strut. "Three shelves in the attic tipped over somehow," Markashian informed them. "Sarah ought to pick them up before long—some of the shelves in front of the closed-off stairs."

Without a word, Mrs. Corr vanished back into the parlor, and Stoneburner went on with his load. But as he closed the house door, he heard from the parlor what sounded like an hysterical gurgle; and also it sounded like Sarah Corr.

When five o'clock was chimed by the two clocks in the hall, Stoneburner still was lugging books to his truck. For a moment's rest, he seated himself in a rickety chair amid his dusted stacks and leafed through the first collected edition of Harrington, *Oceana* Harrington. "Dr. Randolph Corr," with a flourish, was written upon the flyleaf. "Purchased in Bristol, April 23, 1912." Ah, how everything passes! The doctor had spent his life amassing these dead men's fancies, and here strove the undoer of the great library, dispersing in some days what Corr had built in as many decades. Perhaps it was as well that he had not known the doctor, Stoneburner reflected: had he ever seen Corr, this work of destruction might have weighed upon his conscience. One man's pleasure, another's agony... He lifted another stack, cradled it in his arms, and proceeded carefully downstairs.

Halfway down, an odor drifted round him. Undeniable—yes, gas. Stoneburner took the books to the stair foot and then tapped at the parlor.

"Who?" It was Mrs. Corr's voice, with a quaver. He entered. Mrs. Corr and Sarah Corr sat near to each other in two armchairs that faced the door. Markashian was not there. They looked at him with disturbing intensity.

"Could you have forgotten to turn off the kitchen range, Miss Corr? I smell gas somewhere."

"Gas, gas, gas," repeated Sarah Corr, with a heave of her heavy body; but she did not rise, nor did her mother. Truly, Miss Corr had her ways.

A pregnant pause; then, from Mrs. Corr, "Mr. Markashian is out. Might I ask you, Mr. Stoneburner, to see if the gas is turned on?"

Still they did not rise nor offer to assist, nor even to come so far as the door with him. And they watched him as he went into the corridor.

No, it was not the kitchen range. Now that he was on the ground floor, it seemed to Stoneburner that the faint gas-odor drifted to him from above. And when he was on the library floor, it came stronger still; and he thought it must emanate from the attic. Up the stair. As evening approached, the attic grew unpleasantly dark. Those books still lay tumbled from the shelves before the sealed staircase. Yes, the odor was most strong in this dim room. Three gas brackets in the attic: the first two securely turned off—indeed, screwed tight so firmly that he could not budge them with his bare hands. But the third was open, the gas pouring from it. Closing the jet, Stoneburner reflected upon his good fortune not to have been smoking. Had Markashian turned on a light while up here, blown it out, and forgotten to twist the little knob below the mantle? A man unfamiliar with gas mantles might well blunder. But why hadn't Markashian switched on the single electric bulb dangling near the skylight? A most eccentric ménage.

"Ah!" cried Stoneburner. And then, "Who is it?" For two or three books had fallen suddenly, an earthquake in this attic silence. He jerked about; but there was no one, and surely there could have been no whisper. Yes, more books had dropped inward from those shelves before the dead-end staircase. He reached into that hole back of the novels to retrieve whatever volumes had escaped downward. But they had tumbled beyond his reach—he could make them out, vaguely, a half-dozen steps down, one flopped open on its spine, its pages slowly slipping from left to right as if turned by fingers indiscernible.

"By God, no!" muttered Stoneburner, low.

For no one could have whispered to him, whispered ever so slyly and incoherently, out of the abyss. Stoneburner shrugged uneasily, dusted off his trouser-knees, and fixed his mind resolutely upon book-prices current.

He trotted down to the library then, picked up his Cranmer Bible to ensure it against another misadventure, and proceeded to the ground-floor corridor. The Corr women still sat immobile in those lumpy chairs.

"Someone didn't close the jet in the attic, but it's all right now. I think I'll go to dinner. Will it inconvenience you people if I finish moving the section I'm on about seven o'clock or so?"

Sarah Corr had worn that smile so literally mordant, but without warning she said fiercely, "Old devil! Old, white, creepy devil!"

Was it extreme old age or a genuine power of dissimulation that enabled Mrs. Corr so placidly to gloss over her daughter's out-bursts? At any rate, she nodded politely to Stoneburner. "We'll be glad to have you back this evening." But ah, her eyes. And she did not accompany him to the porch. So Stoneburner left them in the moldy, tattered parlor.

Nearer eight o'clock than seven, Stoneburner pulled the tarnished bell-knob at Dr. Corr's house. No clang responded within, so far as he could tell; but he always had suspected that the bell did not work, and that Miss Corr had known of his presence only because she had been peering from some window. He knocked, and knocked again. No one came. And now he observed that the whole house was a darker mass of blackness against the night—not one window lit. Had the Corrs gone out? Too early for bed, surely. He tried the door: not locked, fortunately. Closing it behind him, Stoneburner felt for a light switch, and could find none; everything in the Corr house was tucked out of sight.

Ah, well, he knew the stairs and could find the light in the library. Inside the library doorway his fingers encountered the switch, and the old-fashioned bulb sent its radiance into the corridor. And then, as he was about to cross the threshold into the sea of books, out of the corner of his eye he perceived something unfamiliar, something inappropriate, protruding between two posts of the stair rail to the attic. A chill went through him. For the unfamiliar thing was a flabby hand. Behind it? Whoever was behind it must be lying prone on the dark stairs. A quick-witted little man, Stoneburner thought of the miniature flashlight attached to his key-ring. Pulling it from his coat, he stepped to the stairs and sent the beam upward.

Markashian: nothing worse. Mr. Markashian lay with his unconscious face slanting downward, as if he had tripped and fallen—and the blood on one olive cheek seemed to confirm this. A closer look suggested that he was breathing, though thoroughly stunned. Kneeling in the dark by the accountant, Stoneburner listened for any step or rustle. But surely nothing moved within the house, and its stone walls barred the noise of the street. Mrs. Corr and Sarah Corr? Somehow Stoneburner dared not call out. He left Markashian, and slipped with infinite care down the carpeted treads to the ground floor, every hint of a creak from the old boards an agony to his nerves, his own faint shadow on the papered wall a hunched menace.

Hesitating at the parlor door, he still could detect no sound. None? Why, perhaps the gentlest of sounds, not a hiss, not a swish, but the suggestion of a breath of air. Stoneburner did not desire to turn that knob.

All the same, he turned it, and pushed open the door, and was met by a wave of gas, long pent within. Holding his breath, he fumbled for the light-switch. This time, luck being with him, the light came on. Mrs. Corr still sat in her chair, but Sarah Corr had slumped out of hers upon the rug. Their faces were toward him, unmistakably dead, faces with such a look as drifts through dreams.

Several curious and unpleasant matters concerning Mr. Markashian's past were known to the police captain who arrived at Dr. Corr's house ten minutes after Stoneburner's call. No one could doubt that Markashian had been quite as odd, on occasion, as had been his connections by marriage, nor that his mind was seriously impaired at present, nor that his case required not a trial, but committal to an asylum. At least, none could doubt these conclusions but Stoneburner, and he only confusedly. Why Mrs. Corr and Miss Corr had not risen from their chairs to shut off the jets remained unexplained, unless it was from terror of Markashian.

After two hours in the echoing house, the police discovered at the foot of the disused maids' stairs what remained of the doctor—Dr. Corr, who had gone West only figuratively, his body having been crammed into a closet, or large cupboard, in that sealed passage. Within the cupboard was a gas mantle, and the police captain speculated that the old man, still living, had been bound, pushed into the closet, and left for some hours with the gas turned on. He must have been a vigorous old man, Dr. Corr: great strength would have been required to subdue him. Passed from this life for many months, and that by what must have been an act of explosive violence, Corr bore the expression of a domestic hatred that had smouldered many a year. Markashian, rallying, disclaimed any knowledge of the doctor's death. And so far, but no further, the police believed him.

The police put the livid Markashian on a sofa in what had been the doctor's office. After a time—he watching the closed door intently all the while—Markashian defiantly informed them (his slippery vanity somewhat reviving) that he had gone to the attic to rummage the doctor's desk for a will. "My wife has her rights, after all"—and Dr. Corr, presumably never to return from the West, might have left behind a testament of sorts. Stoneburner watched that vulturine bravado pale and sag then; but Markashian went on, stumblingly, to say that he had run downstairs and had fallen, and knew nothing of what followed in the Corr house.

"Why did you hurry on the stairs?" the police captain demanded.

"Because it was coming up, up from behind the books," Markashian cried out, gripping the sofa arm.

"What do you mean?" The captain was infected with this man's dread.

"Oh, it woke. The books falling, the mouth, the long hair, the dusty hands!" That said, Markashian sank sobbing to the floor. From the rim of one high shelf, past the leather spines of fine bindings which gleamed from their cases, a streamer of soot floated downward to settle upon his cheek.

1963

THE WORK OF EVIL

William Croft Dickinson

William Croft Dickinson (1897–1963) was the son of a non-conformist minister. He studied history at the University of St. Andrews with a hiatus for military service during the First World War. After ten years of teaching and running the library at the London School of Economics, in 1943 he became the first ever English-born person to be appointed to the Sir William Fraser Professorship of Scottish History and Palaeography, a prestigious Chair at the University of Edinburgh. It was whilst working there that he began writing ghost stories, the first of which ("The Sweet Singers") appeared in *Blackwood's Magazine* in February 1947.

"The Work of Evil" was published in Dickinson's short-story collection *Dark Encounters* (1963). In it, librarians discover an uncatalogued *incunabulum*—a Latin word meaning "cradle" and "swaddling clothes" and referring to a book printed in the fifteenth century, at the very beginning of European printing. It is a potent story and a warning to librarians who try to make their collections more accessible.

Ever since his return to duty from his long illness, Maitland Allan, our Keeper of Printed Books, had been singularly reluctant to grant any access to the Special Collections which were in his charge; so much so that the Rare Book Room in the library had become well-nigh as sacred and as difficult to enter as the secret courts of an Eastern harem. Thus, when he suddenly said to me: "Come, and I'll show you the whole collection," I was taken completely by surprise.

I had asked for an early Italian work by Aeneas Sylvius. The assistant at the library counter had disappeared with my form. Allan had come back with him. And now, strangely, I was to be shown "the whole collection". Was this simply a piece of unexpected good fortune? Or had the old man some ulterior purpose? I had noticed during the last two or three weeks that he had made a point of stopping to talk to me whenever we met in a room or corridor. Had he singled me out in some way from the rest of my colleagues? And if so, why? Everyone knew that his recent illness had made him a little "queer".

Opening a door marked "Staff Only", Allan led the way through a maze of book-lined passages until at last, passing a heavy steel door, we stopped before an inner iron grille. This he unlocked and, stepping aside, he ushered me into the room.

I glanced around with curiosity; but he gave me time for no more than a quick glance.

"There they are," he said, pointing to one of the stacks. "An extraordinary collection. A frightening collection. The *Lucretia and Eurialus* which you want happens to be in it, but it's very much of a stranger there. For the rest, I hate them," and his voice rose nervously as if in emphasis.

I walked over to the stack, but I noticed he did not accompany me. There, as I saw two long rows of beautiful bindings, I murmured something of my appreciation and delight. Reverently taking down one volume after another, I examined the bindings more closely. All were of rich leather elaborately tooled in a variety of intricate patterns in which whorls and strange cabalistic signs predominated. I also turned to the title-pages: every work was either an *incunabulum* or of a date early in the sixteenth century. But every work was on the same theme. I ran my eye along the shelves, picking out the volumes which bore titles on their spines. Still the same theme.

"Why!" I exclaimed, turning towards him; "they are all on black magic and necromancy. What you might call a collection of evil; or at any rate a collection of evil intent. Who on earth gathered together all this devilry? It looks as though someone was striving hard to find something which at last would work."

"An unfortunate young man whose history you know as well as I do," answered Allan, slowly. "John, third Earl of Gowrie. You may remember that after studying here he became a law student at Padua, and was there said to have dabbled in magic and witchcraft. Well, here's his library—or part of it. And I wish it had never survived."

Again I noticed the nervous pitch in his voice.

"Well," I replied, lightly, "if he did dabble in the forbidden art he must have found it pretty ineffective. The very number of his books shows that. One would have thought that constant experiment followed by constant failure and disappointment would have been bound to bring disillusion."

For a full minute Allan made no reply. Instead, he gazed at me with an odd look in his eyes.

"'Ineffective'!" he said, at last. "I wish to God you were right! Do you see that safe over there? It contains one further book belonging to Gowrie's collection. No one knows it is there but myself—and now you. That book is the one book which, at last, Gowrie found *would* work. Listen to me—you *must* listen to me—and I'll tell you a tale of devilry that has tormented me ever since this collection came in. Then you'll believe in 'effectiveness'."

He had pointed to a small safe in a corner of the room. I made a step towards it, but he seized me by the arm.

"Often I feel I must take the book in that safe and throw it into the middle of the sea," he continued, "but I can't do it. I'm too afraid. Only one small book, yet it is evil itself. That one book seizes a man by the throat and strangles him to death."

I looked at him in astonishment. Could it be Allan who was saying all this, and who was holding my arm so tightly that his fingers were biting into my flesh?

"Whatever do you mean?" I asked, partly disturbed, and partly angry at being held as though I were a child faced with something which might be dangerous.

"I wish I knew," he replied slowly, and in a quieter tone. "All I can tell you is that within the last eighteen months two men have been strangled to death after looking into that book. That's all."

I was dumbstruck. And not without reason. We stood there, tense and silent, like two conspirators surprised by something they couldn't name and fearful of what it might mean.

*

The collection came to us towards the end of the war, said Allan, breaking the silence at last. It came from the local Antiquarian Society, and it came in the wooden boxes in which it had been stored when Gowrie House was pulled down in 1805 and in which it had remained, untouched, until we opened those boxes in this very room nearly one hundred and fifty years later. It is said that the books were discovered in a wall closet which had been panelled in and so lost to sight. It may well be so. Perhaps Gowrie himself entombed them that way. Perhaps he, too, tried to rid himself of an evil incubus. Perhaps Gowrie put one particular book, with all its fellows, into a hidden closet, as I have put that one particular book into a safe. Perhaps he, too, was afraid to do the one thing he ought to have done. Or perhaps he did something else. Perhaps he put his own curse upon the book that no one should again open its pages and live. That, at any rate, has been its history here.

First it was Fraser, who, you will remember, was our professor of chemistry before you came. As soon as the collection arrived he was all agog to see it. Day after day he was here with his notebook. "Working out their formulae," he would say to me. "Damned interesting, some of them."

But one day he read too much. I had been in the Reid Room that afternoon, and I didn't come here until nearly closing time. Fraser, as usual, was in his seat by the window there; but, that afternoon, he didn't look up with his usual cheery nod. Instead, as he looked up at my entrance, I saw that his face was drawn and white. "My God, Allan," he said in a strained voice, "this book is the Devil himself. It should be burned. Burned to ashes." He pushed his chair back and seemed to recover himself. "Look," he continued, glaring at me with fierce earnestness, "I'm putting it here, in this empty case. Lock it in. And let no one, no one, ever read it again."

He strode to that wire-fronted case over there—it was empty then—thrust in the book, and waited for me to lock the door with my master key. Then he pushed past me and went out. It was the last I saw of him.

That same night he was found dead in his own room in the lab. Strangled. And no one could explain how or why.

He had a queer kind of lab-coat of which he was very proud. It was like an old-fashioned smock which was tied by a fancy cord running through the neck. When he was found, his hands were gripping that cord. It had been drawn so tight that it had throttled him. The students working in the lab had seen no one go into his room or come out of it. I know now that they *wouldn't* see anyone. I know, too, that Fraser's hands were at that cord in a vain struggle to loosen it, and live.

No one thought of connecting Fraser's death with the book he had been reading. At first I hardly associated the two events myself. Yet it was not long before I found I was growing frightened of that book, lying by itself in its locked case. I tried to avoid looking at it, but it seemed to force its presence upon me. Perhaps a fortnight passed before I realised the truth. Then, suddenly, I knew. I knew that Fraser's death had been caused by it.

Frightened as I was, I still had courage enough to do one thing. Unknown to the rest of the staff, I removed from the library catalogue all the entries relating to it. Fraser's death should not go unheeded. No one should read that book again. No one should even know of its existence. Had I dared, I would have burned it—as Fraser had said it should be burned. But I couldn't bring myself to touch it. Already it had me in its power. I was afraid of it. And so young Inglis had to die. A second victim.

He had come to us as a part-time student assistant, and had quickly proved his worth. So much so that special tasks were soon assigned to him automatically. And, at a time when I was unluckily absent for a few days with influenza, he was given the task of checking the shelf catalogue of the Special Collections. You can imagine my horror when, on the day of my return to duty, I found him here, holding *the book* in his hands, open, and reading it.

As soon as he saw me he called out: "I've found an *incunabulum* which is not in the catalogue. It's filthy with dust..."

But I rushed up and seized the thing from him. I shoved it back into the case and relocked the door, while he looked at me open-mouthed. But what could I say? I simply dare not tell him the truth. As I saw it, to tell him the truth would be to tell him his own sentence of death. I made some feeble excuse, which I know he didn't believe, and sent him off. Then I sat down, sick and faint. What could I do to save him? Nothing. He was doomed. The evil thing was upon him, and he could never escape. I cursed myself for my own cowardice. Why, at least, had I not warned him? Had the book so laid its spell upon me that I even feared the ridicule which might follow my warning?

Poor beggar. He didn't escape. When the library was closing that night, one of the staff found that the automatic lift wouldn't work. Naturally he assumed that someone, on one of the floors, had failed to shut the door properly; and he went to look. He found the door which wasn't shut. He also found Inglis. He was trapped by the outer door, and, strangely, he was trapped by the neck. Almost as though he had entered the lift and then, as the door was sliding-to, had put out his head to look at something. Stranger still, but only to those who didn't know what I knew, the poor fellow was dead. I tell you, the pressure of the outer doors on that lift is so light that you can hold them back easily with one hand. Yet Inglis was dead. He had been throttled by the light pressure of a lift-door.

Fraser had been strangled on the day he had opened the book. So had Inglis.

Can you wonder that the same night I had what was called a nervous breakdown?

I was away for over a year and, as you probably know, I have only been back for some six weeks or so. Surprisingly, I have kept my reason—though sometimes I'm not sure. Perhaps I am mad; or perhaps I am suffering from some delusion. Yet I was the only person who knew that Inglis had opened the book; I was the only person who knew that Inglis was doomed to die. And he did die. As Fraser had died.

God forgive me! I should destroy the thing. But I daren't. I am too afraid of it. Yet about a fortnight ago, the day I spoke to you in the Upper Hall, I was brave enough to move it out of the bookcase and to lock it away in that safe. You gave me the courage to do that—even though you didn't know you had done so. Now, I am afraid again. I feel it is laughing at me behind that steel door... and biding its time.

You *must* forgive me; but I *had* to tell you all this. One day I, too, may be found strangled. And you, at least, will know the reason why.

As you may imagine, I was not particularly pleased at having this extraordinary burden of knowledge so suddenly thrust upon me. Yet, as I crossed the Quad back to my own room, my thoughts ran in a different vein. "Poor old Allan," I thought. "No wonder he had a breakdown. No wonder he is 'queer'. Fancy living with *that* on your mind all the time. Poor wretch! A victim to his own imagination: with a harmless book locked up in his safe, and fearing it as though it possessed all the malignant power of some genie in the *Arabian Nights*. And mortally afraid to do the one thing which would bring relief."

But I did Allan an injustice.

I had given my lecture next morning, and was talking to a student in my retiring-room, when Wallace, one of the lecturers in the Modern Languages Department, and Allan's next-door neighbour, opened the door and beckoned me outside.

"Did you know Maitland Allan was dead?" he asked.

"Dead?" I repeated.

"Yes. Apparently last night he was all worked up about something. Kept walking up and down his study, saying in a loud voice: 'I *will* do it. I *will* do it'; and generally worrying his housekeeper out of her wits. Then, suddenly, about nine o'clock, she heard him go into the hall. Peeping round her door she saw him put on a cap, his scarf and his overcoat, and literally rush out of the house.

"By this time thoroughly alarmed, she came to us. I did my best to calm her down, but she was so upset that in the end I offered to go back with her and to wait up with her for Allan's return.

"He didn't come in until nearly two o'clock in the morning. We heard him open the front door and then, just when he had shut it again, we heard him give a queer kind of strangled, choking cry. We rushed into the hall and saw him half-hanging from the door and half-sprawled on the rug in the hall. One end of his scarf had caught in the door as he had shut it and, when he had turned away, it had pulled tight round his neck and had trapped him. We opened the door at once and released him, but, when we tried to help him to his feet again, we discovered to our horror that he was dead... I came over to tell you for I believe he had taken quite a liking to you..."

But I was no longer listening. My thoughts were rushing madly towards one word which seemed to loom larger and larger. And the one word was "strangled". Fraser; Inglis; Allan. Could it *all* be coincidence? Or could such things indeed be true?

*

Naturally the Procurator Fiscal conducted an inquiry into Allan's death.

A boatman stated that Allan (whom he identified) had knocked him up about midnight and had asked to be rowed "a full mile out to sea". At first he had demurred, for Allan had seemed "fair demented"; but an offer of five pounds had seemingly settled the matter. He had rowed Allan out to sea and, when he had told him that they were well beyond the full mile for which he had asked, Allan, to his utter surprise, had suddenly plucked a small book from his coat pocket, had raised it with both hands above his head, and had hurled it down into the water with all his force. Then, said the boatman, "he crouched him down in the boat as though he were afraid someone was going to hit him. And he stayed like that till I tied up again, when he jumped out of the boat and fair ran along the quay as if the Devil himself was chasing him."

The doctors were puzzled, but unanimous. Despite the softness and natural elasticity of the scarf, they had been surprised to find a sharp mark around Allan's neck. But they were convinced he had died of shock. His heart, they said, was in poor condition; any shock would probably be too much for it.

And I alone knew what that "shock" would be. I alone knew what would flash through the poor wretch's mind when he felt that sudden, unexpected tightening of his scarf around his neck.

So much I had written yesterday when my mind was free. But how different is today! Today all Allan's fear and dread are now my own. Today, at the close of the Library Committee, our librarian spoke casually, as of a matter of little importance. He had looked over the Rare Book Room, he said, after Allan's death, and there he had found, inside the safe, a book that belonged to the Gowrie Collection but which, to his surprise, *had no entry in the catalogue.*

Dazed and bewildered, I have found my way back to my room. And, as I write this down, I am a prey to every wild imagining. Can it be that Allan, deranged and overwrought on that last fearful night, cast the wrong book away? How could he? It was the only book within the safe. Yet reason recoils from that other thought—that a book can return from the depths of the sea. Reason? How long can reason prevail against this fearful question that is now pulsing through my mind? Already our librarian has handled the book, and opened it.

REVENANT AS TYPEWRITER

Penelope Lively

Dame Penelope Margaret Lively (née Low) was born in 1933 in Cairo, Egypt, to British parents. Her father was a bank manager. When she was twelve she was sent to boarding school in the UK, going from there to St. Anne's College, Oxford, where she studied Modern History. She married Jack Lively, professor of politics at the University of Warwick, in 1957. Initially finding success as a children's author (she won the Carnegie Medal for her 1973 book *The Ghost of Thomas Kempe*), she later started writing for adults too. Her first adult novel, *The Road to Lichfield* (1977), was shortlisted for the Booker Prize, and ten years later she won with *Moon Tiger*. She lives in London.

"Revenant as Typewriter" comes from Lively's second book aimed at an adult audience, the short story collection *Nothing Missing but the Samovar* (1978). It's an interesting play on the traditional antiquarian ghost story, featuring an intellectually snobby female academic who is tormented by a ghost she perceives as distinctly lowbrow.

Muriel Rackham, reaching the penultimate page of her talk, spoke with one eye upon the public library clock. The paper ("Ghosts: an analysis of their fictional and historic function") lasted precisely fifty-one minutes, as she well knew, but the stamina of the Ilmington Literary and Philosophical Society was problematic: an elderly man in the back row had been asleep since page seven, and there was a certain amount of shuffle and fidget in the middle reaches of the thirty-odd seats occupied by the society's membership. Muriel skipped two paragraphs and moved into the concluding phase; it had perhaps been rash (not to say wasteful) to use on this occasion a paper that had a considerable success at the English Studies Conference and with her colleagues at the College Senior Seminar, but she had nothing much else written up at the moment and had felt disinclined to produce a piece especially for the occasion. She paused (nothing like silence to induce attention) and went on: "So, leaving aside for the moment its literary role as vehicle for authorial comment in characters as diverse as Hamlet's father and Peter Quint, let us in conclusion try to summarise the historic function of the ghost—define as far as we can its social purpose, try to see why people needed ghosts and what they used them for. We've already paid tribute to that great source book for the student of the folkloric ghost—Dr. Katharine Briggs' *Dictionary of British Folk-Tales*—of which I think it was Bernard Levin who remarked in a review that a glance down its list of Tale-Types and Motifs disposes once and for all of the notion that the British are a phlegmatic and unfanciful people." (She paused at this point for the ripple of appreciative amusement that should run through the audience, but the Ilmington Lit. and Phil, sat unmoved; there were two sleepers now in the back row.) "... We've looked already at the repetitious nature of Motifs—Ghost follows its own corpse, reading the funeral service silently; Ghost laid when treasure is unearthed: Revenant as hare; Revenant in human form: Wraith appears to person in bedroom; Ghost haunts scene of former crime; Ghost exercises power through possessions of its lifetime—and so on and so forth. The subject-matter of ghostly folklore, in fact, perfectly supports the thesis of Keith Thomas in his book *Religion and the Decline of Magic* that the historic ghost is no random or frivolous character but fulfils a particular social need—in a society where the arm of the law is short it serves to draw attention to the unpunished crime, to seek the rectification of wrongs, to act as a reminder of the past, to..."

She read on, the text familiar enough for the thoughts to wander: Bill Freeman, the chairman, had introduced her appallingly, neglecting to mention her publications and reducing her Senior Lectureship at Ilmington College of Education to a Lectureship—she felt again a flush of irritation, and wondered if it had been deliberate or merely obtuse. They were an undistinguished lot, the audience; surely that woman at the end of the third row was an assistant in W. H. Smith's? Muriel observed them with distaste, as she turned over to the last page; schoolteachers and librarians, for the most part, one was talking right above their heads, in all probability. A somewhat wasted evening—which could have usefully been spent doing things about the house, or going through students' essays, or looking at that article

Paul had given her, in order to have some well-thought-out-comments for the morning.

She concluded, and sat, with a wintry smile towards Bill Freeman at her side who, as one might have expected, rose to thank her with a sequence of remarks as inept as his introduction: "... our appreciation to Dr. Rackham for her fascinating talk and throw the meeting open to discussion."

Discussion could not have been said to flow. There was a man who had been to a production of *Macbeth* in which you actually saw Banquo and did the speaker think that was right or was it better if you just kind of guessed he was there... and a woman who thought *The Turn of the Screw* wasn't awfully good when they made it into an opera, and another who had been interested in the bit about people in historical times believing in ghosts and had the speaker ever visited Hampton Court because if you go there the guide tells you that...

Muriel dealt politely but briefly with the questioners. She glanced again at the clock, and then at Bill Freeman, who would do well to wind things up. There was a pause. Bill Freeman scanned the audience and said, "Well, if no one has anything more to ask Dr. Rackham I think perhaps..."

The small dark woman at the end of the front row leaned forward, looking at Muriel. "I thought what you said was quite interesting and I'd like to tell you about this thing that happened to a friend of mine. She was staying in this house, you see, where apparently..."

It went on for several minutes. It was very tedious, a long rigmarole about inexplicable creakings in the night, objects appearing and disappearing, ghostly footsteps and sounds and so on and so forth, all classifiable according to Tale-Type and Motif if one felt so inclined and hadn't in fact lost interest in the whole subject some time ago, now that one was doing this work on the metaphysical poets with

Paul... Muriel sat back and sighed. She eyed the woman with distaste; the face was vaguely familiar, someone local, presumably. An absurd little person with black, straight, short hair (dyed, by the look of it) fringing her face, those now unfashionable spectacles upswept at the corners and tinted a disagreeable mauve, long ear-rings of some cheap shiny stone. Ear-rings, Muriel noted, more suitable for a younger woman; this creature was her own age, at least. Her skirt was too short, also, and her shirt patterned with what looked like lotus flowers in a discordant pink.

"... and my friend felt that it had come back to see about something, the ghost, something that had annoyed it. I just wondered what the speaker had to say about that, if she'd ever had any experiences of that kind." The woman stared at Muriel, almost aggressively.

Muriel gathered herself. "Well," she said briskly, "of course we've really been concerned this evening with the fictional and historical persona of the ghost, haven't we? As far as I'm concerned I would subscribe to what has been called the intellectual impossibility of ghosts—and of course experiences such as your friend's, if one stops to think about it, are open to all kinds of explanation, aren't they?"—she flashed a quick, placating smile—"And now, I feel perhaps that..."—she half-turned towards the chairman—"if there are no more questions..."

Going home (after coffee and sandwiches in someone's house; the black-haired person, mercifully, had not been there) she shook off the dispiriting atmosphere of the evening with relief: the dingy room, the unresponsive audience. The paper had been far too academic for them, of course. She felt glad that Paul had not come. He had offered to, but she had insisted that he shouldn't. Turning the Mini out of the High Street and past the corner of his road, she allowed herself a glance at the lighted window of his house. The curtains were drawn; Sheila would be watching television, of course. Paul reading (the new Joyce book, probably, or maybe this week's *TLS*). Poor Paul. Poor, dear Paul. It was tragic, such a marriage. That dull, insensitive woman.

"Your friendship is of the greatest value to me, Muriel," he had said, one week ago exactly. He had said it looking out of the window, rather than at her—and she had understood at once. Understood the depth of his feeling, the necessity for understatement, for the avoidance of emotional display. Their position was of extreme delicacy—Paul's position. Head of Department, Vice-Principal of the College. She had nodded and murmured something, and they had gone on to discuss a student, some problems about the syllabus...

At night, she had lain awake, thinking with complacency of their relationship, of its restraint and depth, in such contrast to the stridency of the times. Muriel considered herself—knew herself to be—a tolerant woman, but occasionally she observed her students with disgust; their behaviour was coarse and vulgar, not to put too fine a point upon it. They brandished what should be kept private.

Occasionally, lying there, she was visited by other feelings, which she recognised and suppressed; a mature, balanced person is able to exercise self-control. The satisfaction of love takes more than one form.

She put the car in the garage and let herself into the house, experiencing the usual pleasure. It was delightful; white walls, bare boards sanded and polished, her choice and tasteful possessions—rugs, pictures, the few antique pieces, the comfortable sofa and armchairs, the William Morris curtains. It was so unlike, now, the dirty, cluttered, scruffy place she had bought five months ago as to be almost unrecognisable. Only its early Victorian exterior remembered—and that too was now bright and trim under new paint, with a front door carefully reconstructed in keeping, to replace the appalling twenties porch some previous occupant had built on. The clearing-out process had been gruelling—Muriel blenched even now at the thought of it: cupboards stacked with junk and rubbish that nobody had bothered to remove (there had been an executors' sale, the elderly owner having died some months before), the whole place filthy and in a state of horrid disrepair. She had done the bulk of the work herself, with the help of a local decorator and carpenter for the jobs she felt were beyond her. But alone she had emptied all those cavernous cupboards, carting the stuff down to a skip hired from a local firm. It had been a disagreeable job—not just because of the dirt and physical effort, but because of the nature of the junk, which hinted at an alien and unpleasing way of life. She felt that she wanted to scour the house of its past, make it truly hers, as she heaved bundle after bundle of musty rubbish down the stairs. There had been boxes of old clothes—too old and sour to interest either the salerooms or Oxfam—brash vulgar female clothes, shrill of colour and pattern, in materials like sateen, chenille, and rayon, the feel of which made Muriel shudder. They slithered from her hands, smelling of mould and mouse droppings, their touch so repellent that she took to wearing rubber gloves. And then there were shelves of old magazines and books—not the engrossing treasure-trove that such a hoard ought to be (second-hand bookshops, after all, were an addiction of hers) but dreary and dispiriting in what they suggested of whoever had owned them: pulp romantic fiction, stacks of the cheaper, shriller women's magazines (all sex and crime, not even that limited but wholesome stuff about cooking, children, and health), some tattered booklets with pictures that made Muriel flush—she shovelled the beastly things into a supermarket carton and dumped the lot into the skip. This house had seen little or no literature that could even be called decent during its recent past, that was clear enough; with pleasure she had arranged her own books on the newly-painted shelves at either side of the fireplace. They seemed to clinch her conquest of the place.

There had been other things, too. A dressmaker's dummy that she had found prone at the back of a cupboard (its murky shape had given her a hideous shock); she had scrubbed and kept it, occasionally she made herself a dress or skirt and it might conceivably be useful, though its torso was dumpier than her own. A tangle of hairnets and curlers in a drawer of the kitchen dresser, horribly scented of violets. Bits and pieces of broken and garish jewellery—all fake—that kept appearing from under floorboards or down crevices. Even now she came across things; it was as though the house would never have done with spewing out its tawdry memories. And of course the redecorating had been a major job—stripping away those fearful wallpapers that plastered every room, every conceivable misrepresentation of nature, loud and unnatural roses, poppies and less identifiable flowers that crawled and clustered up and down the walls. Sometimes two or three different ones had fought for survival in the same room; grimly, Muriel, aided by the decorator, tore and soaked and peeled. At last, every wall was crisply white, a background to her prints and lithographs, her Georgian mirror, the Khelim rug.

Now, she felt at last that she had taken possession. There were one or two small things still that jarred—a cupboard in her bedroom from which, scrub as she might, she could not eradicate the sickly smell of some cheap perfume, a hideous art nouveau window (she gathered such things were once again in fashion—*chacun à son goût*) in the hall which she would eventually get around to replacing. Otherwise, all was hers; her quiet but distinctive taste in harmony with the house's original architectural grace.

It was just past nine; time for a look at that article before bed. Muriel went to her desk (which, by day, had a view of the small garden prettily framed in William Morris's "Honeysuckle") and sat reading and taking notes for an hour or so. She remembered that Paul would be away all day tomorrow, at a meeting in London, and she would not be able to see him, so when she had finished reading she pulled her typewriter in front of her and made a résumé of her reflections on the article, to leave in his pigeon-hole. She read them through, satisfied with what she felt to be some neatly put points. Then she got up, locked the back and front doors, checked the windows, and went to bed.

In the night, she woke: the room felt appallingly stuffy—she could even, from her bed, smell that disagreeable cupboard—and she assumed that she must have forgotten to open the window. Getting up to do so, she found the sash raised a couple of inches as usual. She returned to bed, and was visited by unwelcome yearnings which she drove out by a stern concentration on her second-year Shakespeare option.

She had left her page of notes on the article in the typewriter, and almost forgot it in the morning, remembering at the last moment as she was about to leave the house, and going back to twitch it hastily out and put it in her handbag. The day was busy with classes and a lecture, so that it was not until the afternoon that she had time to write a short note for Paul ("I entirely agree with you about the weaknesses in his argument: however, there are one or two points we might discuss, some thoughts on which I enclose. I do hope London was not too exhausting—MCR"), and glance again at the page of typescript.

It was not as satisfactory as Muriel remembered; in fact it was not satisfactory at all. She must have been a great deal more tired than she had realised last night—only in a stupor (and not even, one would have hoped, then) could she have written such muddled sentences, such hideous syntax, such illiteracies of style and spelling. "What I think is that he developped what he said about the character of Tess all wrong so what you ended up feeling was that..." she read in horror "... if Hardy's descriptive passages are not always relivant then personally what I don't see is why..." And what was this note at the bottom—apparently added in haste? "What about meeting for a natter tomorrow—I was thinking about you last night—ssh! you aren't supposed to know that!" I must have been half-asleep, she thought, how could I write such things?

Hot with discomfort (and relief—heavens! she might not have looked again at the thing), she crumpled the paper and threw it into the wastepaper basket. She wrote a second note to Paul saying that she had read the article but unfortunately had not the time now to say more, and hoped to discuss it with him at some point: she then cancelled her late-afternoon class and went home early. I have been overdoing things, she thought—my work, the house—I need rest, a quiet evening.

She settled down to read, but could not concentrate; for almost the first time, she found herself wishing for the anodyne distraction of television. She polished and dusted the sitting-room (finding, in the process, a disgusting matted hank of hairnets and ribbon that had got, quite inexplicably, into her Worcester teapot) and cleaned the windows. Then she did some washing, which led to an inspection of her wardrobe; it seemed sparse. A new dress, perhaps, would lift her spirits. On Saturday, she would buy one, and in the meantime, there was that nice length of tweed her sister had given her and which had lain untouched for months. Perhaps with the aid of the dressmaker's dummy it could be made into a useful skirt. She fetched the dummy and spent an hour or two with scissors and pins—a soothing activity, though the results were not quite as satisfactory as she could have wished. Eventually she left the roughly-fashioned skirt pinned to the dummy and put it away in the spare-room cupboard before going to bed.

A few days later, to her pleasure, Paul accepted an invitation to call in at the house on his way home to pick up a book and have a drink. He had hesitated before accepting, and she understood his difficulties at once; such meetings were rare for them, and the reasons clear enough to her: the pressures of his busy life, Sheila… "Well, yes, how kind, Muriel," he had said. "Yes, fine, then. I'll give Sheila a ring and tell her I'll be a little late."

Poor Paul; the strains of such a marriage did not bear contemplation. Of course they always appeared harmonious enough in public, a further tribute to his wonderful patience and restraint. Nor did he ever hint or complain; one had to be perceptive to realise the tensions that must rise—a man of his intellectual stature fettered to someone without, so far as Muriel understood, so much as an A-level. His tolerance was amazing; Muriel had even heard him, once, join with well-simulated enthusiasm in a discussion of some trashy television series prompted by Sheila at a Staff Club party.

She was delayed at the College and only managed to arrive back at the house a few minutes before he arrived. Pouring the sherry, she heard him say, "What's this, then, Muriel—making a study of popular culture?" and turned round to see him smiling and holding up one of those scabrous women's magazines that—she thought—she had committed to the skip. Disconcerted, she found herself flushing, embarking on a defensive explanation of the rubbish that had been in the house… (But she had cleared all that stuff out, every bit, how could that thing have been, apparently, lying on the little Victorian sewing-table, from which Paul had taken it?)

The incident unnerved her, spoiled what should have been an idyllic hour.

Muriel woke the next day—Saturday—discontented and twitchy. She had slept badly, disturbed by the muffled sound of a woman's shrill laugh, coming presumably from the next house in the terrace; she had not realised before that noise could penetrate the walls.

Remembering her resoluting of a few days before, she went shopping for a new dress. The facilities of Ilmington were hardly metropolitan, but adequate for a woman of her restrained tastes; she found, after some searching, a pleasant enough garment innocent of any of the nastier excesses of modern fashion, in a wholesome colour and fabric, and took it home in a rather calmer frame of mind.

In the evening, there was the Principal's sherry party (Paul would be there; with any luck there would be the opportunity for a few quiet words). She went to take the dress from the wardrobe and indeed was about to put it on before the feel of it in her hands brought her up short; surely there was something wrong? She took it to the window, staring—this was never the dress she had chosen so carefully this morning? The remembered eau-de-nil was now, looked at again, in the light from the street, a harsh and unflattering apple-green; the coarse linen, so pleasant to the touch, a slimy artificial stuff. She had made the most disastrous mistake; tears of frustration and annoyance pricked her eyes. She threw the thing back in the cupboard and put on her old Jaeger print.

Sunday was a day that normally she enjoyed. This one got off to a bad start with the discovery of the *Sunday Mirror* sticking through the front door instead of the *Sunday Times*; after breakfast she rang the shop, knowing that they would be open till eleven, only to be told by a bewildered voice that surely that was what she had asked for, change it, you said on the phone, Thursday it was, for the *Sunday*

Mirror, spicier, you said, good for a laugh. There's been some mistake," said Muriel curtly. "I don't know what you can be thinking of." She slammed down the receiver and set about a massive cleaning of the house; it seemed the proper therapeutic thing to do.

After lunch she sat down at her desk to do some work; her article for *English Today* was coming along nicely. Soon it would be time to show a first draft to Paul. She took the lid off the typewriter and prepared to reread the page she had left in on Friday.

Two minutes later, her heart thumping, she was ripping out the paper, crumpling it into a ball... I never wrote such stuff, she thought, it's impossible, words like that, expressions like—I don't even *know* such expressions.

She sat in horror, staring into the basilisk eye of a thrush on her garden wall. There is something wrong, she thought, I am not myself, am I going mad?

She took a sleeping pill, but even so woke in the depths of the night (again, those muffled peals of laughter), too hot, the room heavy around her so that she had to get up and open the window further; the house creaked. There must be a fault in the heating system, she thought. I'll have to get the man round. She lay in discomfort, her head aching.

In the days that followed it seemed to her that she suffered from continuous headaches. Headaches, and a kind of light-headedness that made her feel sometimes that she had only a tenuous grip on reality: in the house, after work, she heard noises, saw things. There was that laughter again, which must be from next door but when she enquired delicately of the milkman as to who her neighbours were (one didn't want actually to get involved with them) she learned that an elderly man lived there, alone, a retired doctor. And there were things that seemed hallucinatory, there was no other explanation;

going to the cupboard where she had put the dummy, to have another go at that skirt, she had found the thing swathed not in her nice herring-bone tweed but a revolting purple chenille. She slammed the cupboard closed (again, the lurking shape of the dummy had startled her, although she had expected to see it), and sat down on the bed, her chest pounding. I am not well, she thought, I am doing things and then forgetting that I have done them, there is something seriously wrong.

And then there was the wallpaper. She had come into the sitting-room, one bright sunny morning—her spruce, white sitting-room—and, glancing at her Dufy prints, had seen suddenly the shadowy presence of the old, hideous wallpaper behind them, those entwined violets and roses that she and the decorator had so laboriously scraped away. Two walls, she now saw, were scarred all over, behind the new emulsion paint, with the shadowy presence of the old paper; how can we have missed them, she thought angrily—that decorator, I should have kept a sharper eye on him—but surely, I *remember*, we did this room together, every bit was stripped, surely?

Her head spun.

She went to the doctor, unwillingly, disliking her list of neurotic symptoms, envying the bronchitic coughs and bandaged legs in the waiting-room. Stiffly, she submitted to the questions, wanting to say: I am not this kind of person at all, I am balanced, well-adjusted, known for my good sense. With distaste, she listened to the diagnosis: yes, she wanted to say, impatiently, I have heard of menopausal problems but I am not the kind of woman to whom they happen, I keep things under better control than that, overwork is much more likely. She took his prescription and went away, feeling humiliated.

It was the examination season. She was faced, every evening, on returning home, with a stack of scripts and would sit up late marking, grateful for the distraction, though she was even more tired and prone to headaches. The tiredness was leading to confusion, also, she realised. On one occasion, giving a class, she had been aware of covert glances and giggles among her students, apparently prompted by her own appearance; later, in the staff cloakroom, she had looked in a mirror and been appalled to discover herself wearing a frightful low-cut pink blouse with some kind of flower-pattern. It was vaguely familiar—I've seen it before, she thought, and realised it must be a relic of the rubbish in the house, left in the back of her cupboard and put on accidentally this morning, in her bleary awakening from a disturbed night. Condemned to wear it for the rest of the day. she felt taken over by its garishness, as though compelled to behave in character; she found herself joining a group of people at lunch-time with whom she would not normally have associated, the brash set among her colleagues, sharing jokes and conversation that she found distasteful. In Paul's office, later, going over some application forms, she laid her hand on his sleeve, and felt him withdraw his arm; later, the memory of this made her shrivel. It was as though she had betrayed the delicacy of their relationship; never before had they made physical contact.

She decided to take a couple of days off from the College, and mark scripts at home.

The first day passed tranquilly enough; she worked throughout the morning and early afternoon. At around five she felt suddenly moved, against her better judgement, to telephone Paul with what she knew to be a trumped-up query about an exam problem. Talking to him, she was aware of her own voice, with a curious detachment; its tone surprised her, and the shrillness of her laugh. Do I always sound like that? she thought, have I always laughed in that way? It seemed to her that Paul was abrupt, that he deliberately ended the conversation.

She got up the next morning in a curious frame of mind. The scripts she had to mark filled her with irritation; not the irritation stemming from inadequacy in the candidates, but a petulant resentment of the whole thing. Sometimes, she did not seem able to follow the answers to questions. "Don't get you," she scribbled in the margin. "What are you on about?" At the bottom of one script she scrawled a series of doodles: Indeterminate flowers, a face wearing upswept spectacles, a buxom female figure. At last, with the pile of scripts barely eroded, she abandoned her desk and wandered restlessly around the house.

Somehow, it displeased her. It was too stark, too bare, an unlived-in place. I like a bit of life, she thought, a bit of colour, something to pep things up; rummaging in the scullery she found under the sink some gaily patterned curtaining that must have got overlooked when she cleared out those particular shelves. That's nice, she thought, nice and striking. I like that; as she hung it in place of the linen weave in the hall that now seemed so dowdy, it seemed to her that from somewhere in the house came a peal of laughter.

That day merged, somehow, into the next. She did not go to the College. Several times the telephone rang: mostly she ignored it. Once, answering, she heard the departmental secretary's voice, blathering on: "Dr. Rackham?" she kept saying. "Dr. Rackham? Professor Simons has been a bit worried, we wondered if..." Muriel laughed and hung up. The night, the intermediate night (or nights, it might have been, time was a bit confusing, not that it mattered at all) had been most extraordinary. She had had company of some kind; throughout the night, whenever she woke, she had been aware of a low murmuring. A voice. A voice of compulsive intimacy, coarse and insistent: it had repelled but at the same time fascinated her. She had lain there, silent and unresisting.

The house displeased her more and more. It's got no style, she thought, full of dreary old stuff. She took down the Dufy prints, and the Piper cathedral etchings, thinking: I don't like that kind of thing, I like a proper picture, where you can see what's what, don't know where I even picked up these. She made a brief sortie to Boots round the corner and bought a couple of really nice things, not expensive either—a Chinese girl and a lovely painting of horses galloping by the sea. As she hung them in the sitting-room, it seemed to her that someone clutched her arm, and for an instant she shuddered uncontrollably, but the sensation passed, though it left her feeling light-headed, a little hysterical.

Her own appearance dissatisfied her, too. She sat looking at herself in her bedroom mirror and thought: "I've never made the best of myself, a woman's got to make use of what she's got, hasn't she? Where's that nice blouse I found the other day, it's flattering—a bit of décolleté, I'm not past that kind of thing yet." She put it on, and felt pleased. Downstairs, the telephone was ringing again, but she could not be bothered to answer it. Don't want to see anyone, she thought, fed up with people, if it's Paul he can come and find me, can't he? Play hard to get, that's what you should do with men, string them along a bit.

Anyway, she was not alone. She could feel, again, that presence in the room though when she swung round suddenly—with a resurgence of that chill sensation—there was nothing but the dressmaker's dummy, standing in the corner. She must have brought it from the cupboard, and forgotten.

She wandered about the house, muttering to herself; from time to time, a person walked with her, not someone you could see, just a presence, its arm slipped through Muriel's, whispering intimacies, suggestions. All those old books of yours, it said, you don't want those, ring the newsagent, have them send round some mags, a good read, that's what we want. Muriel nodded.

Once, people hammered on the door. She could hear their voices; colleagues from the department. "Muriel?" they called. "Are you there, Muriel?" She went into the kitchen and shut herself in till they had gone. For a moment, sitting there, she felt clearer in her head, free of the confusion that had been dragging her down; something is happening, she thought wildly, something I cannot cope with, can't control...

And then there came again that presence, with its insistent voice, and this time the voice was quite real, and she knew, too, that she had heard it before, somewhere, quite recently, not long ago. Where, where?

... I thought what you said was quite interesting, and I'd like to tell you about this thing that happened to a friend of mine...

Muriel held the banisters, to steady herself (she was on her way upstairs again, in her perpetual edgy drifting up and down the house): the Lit. and Phil., I remember now, that woman.

And it came to her too, with a horrid jolt, that she knew now, remembered suddenly, why, at the time, that evening, the face had been familiar, why she'd felt she'd seen it before.

It had been the face in a yellowed photograph that had tumbled from a tatty book when she had been clearing out the house; Violet Hanson, 1934, in faded ink on the back.

Sale by auction, by order of the Executors of Mrs. Violet Hanson, deceased, No. 27 Clarendon Terrace, a four-bedroomed house with scope for...

Someone was laughing, peals of shrill laughter that rang through the house, and as she reached the top floor, and turned into her bedroom, she knew that it was herself. She went into her bedroom and sat down at her dressing-table and looked in the mirror. The face that looked back at her was haggard. I've got to do something about myself, she thought, I'm turning into an old frump. She groped on the table and found a pair of ear-rings, long, shiny ones that she had forgotten she had. She held them up against her face; yes, that's nice, stylish, and I'll dye my hair, have it cut short and dye it black, take years off me, that would...

There was laughter again, but she no longer knew if it was hers or someone else's.

THE ADVENT VISITOR

C. J. Faraday

Dr. Christina Juliet Faraday (1992–) is a historian of art and ideas, with a special interest in Tudor and Stuart Britain and the wider sixteenth and seventeenth-century world. She is an Affiliated Lecturer in History of Art at the University of Cambridge, a Fellow of the Society of Antiquaries and of the Royal Historical Society, and a Trustee of the Walpole Society for British Art history. She is the author of two books, most recently *The Story of Tudor Art*, the first art history book to encompass the whole of the Tudor century.

Faraday attended St. John's College, Cambridge, both as an undergraduate studying the History of Art and Architecture, and for her PhD, which she was awarded in 2019. This story, inspired by her time in the College, was first published in issue 38 of the small press journal *Ghosts and Scholars*, which celebrates the antiquarian tradition established by M. R. James. The story, and indeed the journal, demonstrate the continuing influence of James's work into the twenty-first century.

"Quis est ille qui venit?"

It was to be my first Christmas vacation in college. As soon as term ended, practically overnight the library emptied and the dining hall was deserted. In the long black evenings the windows—recently bright with the hundred cheerful lights of late-working students—stared dumbly into the empty courts.

I relieved the monotony of my solitary trips to the library with attendance at chapel. Sundays were my favourite, marking the weeks with the progression of Advent. I liked the theme of anticipation that infused the season. I too was waiting: for the start of the next term, the return of my friends, the end of the silence. It wasn't all bad—I enjoyed the peace of college in those weeks when almost everyone, except the night porter, the chaplain and a handful of life fellows, had gone home. In a way I liked having the place to myself, but it was lonely.

It was a couple of weeks into the vacation, and I was now used to seeing the same four or five familiar faces around college and in the stalls opposite mine in the chapel. The life fellows never took much notice of me, except one, Professor John Fanshawe, an ancient scholar of seventeenth-century literature. We would exchange nods when we met in the courts, raising our eyes just enough to recognise each other through the flurries of snow which fell often that December but never settled.

239

On the second Sunday of Advent, as I was leaving Evensong, I overheard hushed voices in the antechapel. Fanshawe had hurried down from his stall as soon as the service ended, and now grasped the chaplain's arm, looking at him intently. The chaplain was saying something—I caught the words "—forgives those who truly repent". But the professor wasn't satisfied: "But are there things he can't forgive?" he asked urgently. Before the chaplain could answer, Fanshawe saw me approaching and turned to leave.

I didn't dwell on what I'd overheard. My work was going badly, and that was all I could think about. Finally my brain stalled completely, and I decided to take a walk by the river to clear my head. The trees were completely bare now, and an icy fog hung low over the water. As I walked a huddled form took shape in front of me. The outline grew stronger as I approached, and I saw that it was Professor Fanshawe. He had stopped next to a willow tree, and was staring into the water.

"Good afternoon," I said, while I was still a few feet away.

The professor started from his reverie, and turned to look at me.

"Ah, good afternoon. Are you also taking a stroll? Would you care to join me?"

I fell into step beside him. We didn't talk much, exchanged a word here or there about the college. He asked me how my work was going.

"I'm meant to be writing a book about witchcraft—or devil worship, really—and church law. But I'm a bit stuck," I confessed.

"A walk can often help with that, you made a good decision coming out," he said.

I nodded. We found ourselves wandering along the back road, towards the old church on the outskirts of the city. The churchyard, long since disused, contained the earthly remains of many a distinguished scholar, and I sometimes thought about the erudite conversations taking place under that quiet earth.

Today in the gloom the place had a sorrowful, neglected air. The tombstones slanted at precarious angles, and ivy and lichen had reclaimed the names of their owners. We threaded ourselves between the graves, walking in parallel lines. The professor stopped and rested his hand on a stone which faced in my direction. I read the name.

PROFESSOR JOHN FANSHAWE

I caught my breath, and looked at the man who stood quietly by the tombstone. Was he... He couldn't be...

"My father's grave," the professor's voice brought me back to earth. My readings on necromancy were getting to me.

"He was a scholar too—of physics, not literature. He was a true scientist: he dealt in facts. It was my mother's idea to bury him in a churchyard: he couldn't stand religion, or superstition of any kind." My companion hesitated, "I'm afraid I was a disappointment to him."

I wanted to ask what he meant, but didn't feel I could probe. He said nothing else. We walked back to college in silence, until finally we found ourselves at the foot of his staircase.

"I enjoyed our walk," he said as he climbed the stairs, "I hope your work picks up."

I thanked him and returned to my set. It was getting dark now, a rare glimpse of moon visible through a chink in the clouds, and snow was starting to fall again.

That night I lay awake listening to the sound of snowflakes hissing in the grate. Around midnight I thought I heard footsteps on the staircase. They seemed to pause on the second landing, before receding again into the night.

In the morning I met with a gruesome sight. Spots of red trailed from the bottom of my staircase to the middle of the court, and last night's snow, thick on the lawn, had been whipped into a frenzy. From a feather-strewn pool of red and pink the prints of a fox led away towards the bridge. I was surprised I hadn't heard the struggle: I thought I had been awake all night. I averted my eyes and turned toward the library with a shudder.

My days in the library continued to be unproductive. The third Sunday of Advent came and went, and I exchanged a friendly nod with Professor Fanshawe across the stalls, but otherwise I saw no-one except my books. Day after day I tried to make sense of my sources, but the words swam before my eyes, playing tricks with their size and depth on the page. I felt distracted and far away, as though floating high above the library, the college, the town. Too much quiet can have that effect on me. Bleary with eye-strain, finally I decided to venture out of the college for an evening, seek out dinner in a local pub—preferably one with a fire—in the hope that the chatter of December revellers would shake me down from my eyrie.

As I crossed the court on my way into town, I bumped into Professor Fanshawe again. He was carrying a book, and as he approached I read the title: *Divination, Witchcraft and Canon Law*. We stopped to speak.

"That looks like something I ought to read," I said, gesturing towards the book.

Fanshawe looked troubled. He took a small step back and glanced around as if looking for an escape route. "I—I'm sorry. I don't lend my books," he said shortly.

I was taken aback by this sudden frost on our conversation. "Oh—of course. That's ok—I didn't mean that. I just thought it looked interesting."

Fanshawe nodded, but I could see he was still troubled. "I'd best be going," he said, and set off again across the court.

I felt puzzled—we'd been getting along so well. I knew I'd just been trying to make conversation, but somehow it felt like my fault, that the professor was for some reason annoyed with me. I shook my head and hurried into town.

Dinner in the pub only compounded my misery. Sitting alone amidst the light and noise made me feel more dislocated than ever. I returned to college having sunk further into gloom; here at least I found some sympathy from the dark and silent buildings, the blind, staring windows.

When I got to my room I found a note wedged under my door.

"Sorry for my gruffness earlier," read the scrawl, "come for a drink in my set, after chapel on Sunday?"

I felt a little better, and not totally alone in this strange place. I would go, of course. And I wouldn't ask to borrow any books.

Sunday came with a dry wind, that howled at the stained glass windows all through Evensong, drowning out the Confession and the Collect and making the candles gutter. After the service I followed Fanshawe into the antechapel, where he deposited his optional college surplice, and out into the biting air of the evening. We fought our way to his set, large and welcoming, a freshly-made fire bubbling in the grate (I supposed the more senior fellows could persuade the college staff to light one for them). Books, of course, lined the room from floor to ceiling, and as I sank into the spacious armchair a sense of calm washed over me for the first time in many weeks.

"Sherry?" Offered Fanshawe, and poured us each a generous glass.

We sat in opposite chairs, next to the fire; apart from a solitary lamp in the corner it was the only source of light in the room. The flames picked out his features as he spoke about his research and the college's history, and I listened in a sleepy haze.

"You said you work on the black arts," he said suddenly, leaning forward in his chair, "I have a story to tell you. It concerns the College, back in the seventeenth century."

I tried to sit up in the armchair but immediately sank back into the cushions. He was looking into the fire, as if he could read the story he was telling amidst the flames.

"It was a winter just like this one: sudden, early snow, and shortly before Christmas a great storm. Howling gales, chunks of tree in the river. A young scholar, Ashbourner they called him, was staying over Christmas, and he was filled with dread over an upcoming disputation—you know the kind, an oral examination—for his degree. In his despair he went to the library, looking for guidance, and came across a very strange book. Full of arcane diagrams, it promised its reader learning and wisdom. Apparently this Ashbourner took it to his room, and followed its instructions. I don't know exactly what it would have involved—you could probably say better than I—but candles, chalk on the ground, incantations, that sort of thing. But— nothing happened."

The professor paused, and took a sip from his glass.

"So Ashbourner ventured out, right out into the storm, more desperate than ever. He hadn't gone much further than the bridge when he was met by a well-dressed man, in the robes of a Master of Arts. The man asked Ashbourner why he was unhappy, and the scholar told him everything, and in particular that he couldn't understand his books. The man offered to help him, and as they walked clarified everything he had been finding difficult. Then the man put forward two new questions: first, whether God was omnipotent, and second, whether God was Good, or simply an absence of evil. They talked about these matters for a while, and then the man offered Ashbourner the chance to study with him. He invited him to Padua, where he was a professor, to study at the ancient university there. Ashbourner willingly accepted, binding himself with the promise: I will give you my soul, if you will teach me learning and wisdom."

"The man was the Devil, then?"

"Summoned by Ashbourner's spells: so it would seem. In any case, when the scholar returned to his room, he grew afraid. The next day his gown was found in the river. The boy was never heard of again."

"Perhaps he was in Padua," I said, wryly.

The fire crackled between us.

"I found his name, you know," he said finally, "in the college records, buttery accounts, that sort of thing. Some of the books in the library belonged to him."

"Did you find out what really happened?" I asked.

"He's quite traceable, until Christmas 1646, and then—" the professor made a gesture with his hand, like letting go of a balloon, "—nothing. He just vanishes."

"How strange," I said, and finished my sherry.

We listened to the clock on the mantelpiece chime 11pm. It was late—we had been talking for hours. But as the chimes died away I noticed the professor seemed to grow tense. He drew back into his chair, like a long, slow flinch.

Then there was a knock at the door.

I glanced in its direction, and waited to see if the professor would answer it, but he continued to stare at the fire. He made no motion to get up.

I started up myself, thinking perhaps it was my job, as the junior partner in the conversation. But as I began to move the professor looked at me, wide-eyed.

"Don't answer it!" he said, urgently.

I looked at him, confused. "But it's late—they must want something. It could be important."

"Don't answer it," he said again. "There's no-one there."

I started to laugh but a sharp look stopped me.

"Stay, won't you?" he said, suddenly small in the large armchair, "just a few more minutes."

"But the door, professor?"

"It won't happen again, tonight," he said, with an air of certainty I couldn't answer.

Eventually, at a quarter to midnight, the professor seemed content to let me go.

"Come again?" he said, as I left, "Thursday?"

Thursday was Christmas Eve, but I had no other plans.

"Yes, I'd be happy to," I said, and turned away down the staircase.

Over the next few days my work finally seemed to be making sense again. It was as if Professor Fanshawe's story had broken the spell over me. Or perhaps I was Ashbourner, and Fanshawe the mysterious Master of Arts who appeared in my hour of need... The college was deadly quiet now. The porters had been given the week off. It seemed as though Fanshawe and I were the only people in the college, save the Chaplain, who I wouldn't see until Christmas morning.

The days slipped by easily enough, and seemingly without any warning at all it was Thursday. I had received another note, inviting me to come at 8pm. When I arrived, the outer of the two doors was open, showing that the Professor was at home to visitors. I knocked.

"It's open," he called from inside, and then, as I entered, "let's sport the oak, we don't want to be disturbed."

I closed the outer door as instructed.

Our conversation was the usual mixture of research and college matters. He seemed genuinely pleased that my work was going well again. The wind, which had not dipped since Sunday, whistled down the chimney as we drank our port. Emboldened by the alcohol inside us and the privacy of the gloom, our talk became more conspiratorial.

"I didn't tell you how I came to know so much about Ashbourner, did I?" said Fanshawe, his eyes half-closed.

"No, please do," I said, sensing another story.

"You see, I wasn't so dissimilar from him in my youth," he said slyly, taking another sip of port. "Always looking for the easy way out—feckless, if you want the truth."

"Come now Professor," I said, "you expect me to believe that!"

"Well, it wasn't just me—there were two of us actually. I had a friend, Alexander. But we all called him Oakeshott. We went everywhere together, and never to the library. Except, that is, on one occasion. Oakeshott was out of town, it was the start of the Christmas vacation, and I was starting to worry about my studies. So I went to have a rummage in the Old Library, see what I could see. And I found this book; a book of spells."

"Like the one Ashbourner found?" I smiled, enjoying this new convergence of fiction and reality.

The professor didn't answer.

"I took it back to my rooms and studied it. I learned a lot, about the black arts. I had this idea that I could use it to jazz up some boring essay on church law or something. But I didn't try any of it out, you know, I was too frightened. When Oakeshott came back, he found the book and wheedled it out of me, everything I'd been reading. I was reluctant to tell him at first, I thought he might laugh at me. But he was interested—much more than I had anticipated. He asked if he could borrow the book.

"I said yes, and we agreed he would return it on Christmas Eve, before he went home. After that I didn't see him for ages. We had exams coming up in January, and neither of us had done a jot of work for them. I sometimes walked past his window and I could see him pacing and gesticulating, as if talking to someone else in the room, just out of sight. One evening he saw me looking, and quickly closed his curtains. This went on for days, then finally it was Christmas Eve. I knew Oakeshott was going home, so I went to his room and knocked—but there was no answer. I looked everywhere, all our usual haunts, but he was nowhere to be found. Actually I was rather annoyed—I wanted the book back. Something about it intrigued me... but it was no good.

"That night I was lying awake in bed, fuming about Oakeshott and wondering what could have happened, when there was a knock at my door. I went to open it, and—"

I leaned forward in my chair, "yes, professor?"

"Nothing."

"Nothing?"

"There was nobody there."

We sat in silence for a few minutes. The professor seemed to be gathering himself for what he had to say next.

"They found him—or rather, his coat, in the river, about a mile downstream, a week later."

I sat back in my chair; just like Ashbourner, I thought.

"His family had been expecting him, but he never arrived home. They said he must have fallen into the river in the dark, found himself unable to climb out," he paused. "But there was unrest in the college after it happened. One of the older fellows took me aside and asked me if I knew about 'Ashbourner's book'. I pretended not to, but my name was on the library slip. No further mention was made of it, but when I tried to find out who Ashbourner was nobody would tell me. It was only by digging around in the archives many years later that I discovered what he meant."

"You mean—it was the same book?" I asked.

"I don't know for sure—*it* was never found either. But I think it must have been," he paused, "and every Sunday in Advent, every year since then, there has been a knock at my door. But when I open it, there is never anyone there."

Silence again, and then the chimes. One, two, three... I counted to eleven.

Knock, knock.

We waited in silence. Neither of us moved.

Knock, knock.

Still we waited. Minutes, five, ten, twenty passed, but we sat there motionless.

Finally, as the clock chimed half past eleven, I rose to go.

"Goodnight, Professor," I said. He had sunk back into his chair, exhausted by his story.

"Do you think—" the professor started, then fell silent.

"Professor?"

He turned towards me. "Do you think—I mean to say, you're religious. Do you think God forgives?"

I realised then that it wasn't fear that afflicted the professor, that made him cower in his chair when the knock came. It was guilt.

"But you couldn't have known he would use the book in that way," I said.

"I should have known," he said, sadly.

I left the professor by the fire and opened his door. No-one there, as he had predicted. But in the dim light from the room I thought I could see an evaporating footprint on the stair.

The next morning I rose early for the Christmas service. The wind had stopped, the clouds were a light but threatening grey. Yet I was surprised to find, when I looked towards his usual stall, that Fanshawe was not in attendance that morning. After the service the chaplain came towards me with a platitudinous smile.

"Sad," he intoned, "but not untimely."

I asked what he meant.

"Professor Fanshawe's absence—I saw you noted it too. I'm afraid to say he died yesterday, but he went peacefully enough."

I started, "Yesterday?"

"Yes, I went to see him shortly before... He was in bed."

"But—what time yesterday?" I asked, my heart thudding.

"In the afternoon, around sundown. This morning I looked in again, all peaceful and secure. Except—," he paused, glancing towards the altar, "it's an odd thing. This morning there was a book on his table, I could have sworn it wasn't there when I left him, last night. And after all, he couldn't have—but perhaps I just didn't notice. My mind was on other things."

"A book?" I encouraged him.

"Yes, from the college library. It was," he hesitated, choosing his words carefully, "about dark things. I was worried he might have been more troubled than I realised." He crossed himself, "but he died at peace. I think he has known that the end was close for some time now. Did you have a chance to say goodbye?"

I muttered something and left. I had to get out of the oppressive gloom of the chapel and into the fresh air. The news had unsettled me deeply.

During the service snow had started to fall again, not settling now, but melting as soon as it touched the cobbles. On the path ahead of me the flakes seemed to transform themselves, for a moment, into a familiar, huddled shape, but dissolved again in an instant.

A headless coachman drives his carriage of lost souls towards a violent fate. A mother's obsession with eugenics spirals into a cruel madness. An adulterous pair are plagued by the suspicion that their dog means to expose their darkest secrets.

In 1911, Violet Hunt published her groundbreaking collection of short stories entitled *Tales of the Uneasy*, which explored a world of psychological and ghostly hauntings, shot through with high tragedy and strange horror. Over time, Hunt's reputation as a literary hostess obscured her important contribution to British weird fiction, and now her uncanny collection—recognised by R. S. Hadji as one of his thirteen "neglected masterpieces of the macabre"—is long overdue its rightful place among the great weird works of the Edwardian era.

At times utterly chilling, startlingly bleak and darkly comic, this new edition also includes Hunt's rare and revised novella version of the beguiling title story, 'The Tiger Skin'.

ALSO AVAILABLE

*Like any other boy I expected ghost stories at Christmas, that
was the time for them. What I had not expected, and now
feared, was that such things should actually become real.*

Strange things happen on the dark wintry nights of December. Welcome
to a new collection of haunting Christmas tales, ranging from traditional
Victorian chillers to weird and uncanny episodes by twentieth-century
horror masters including Daphne du Maurier and Robert Aickman.

Lurking in the blizzard are menacing cat spirits, vengeful trees, malignant
forces on the mountainside and a skater skirting the line between the
mortal and spiritual realms. Wrap up warm—and prepare for the longest
nights of all.

ALSO AVAILABLE

I had been staying just within the shadow of the exit of the great rift. Now, without volition on my part, I drifted out of the semi-darkness and began to move slowly—toward the House.

Amidst the din of roaring water, in a chasm where a house once stood in an isolated corner of Ireland, a manuscript is discovered entitled *The House on the Borderland*. Penned by the enigmatic Recluse, it tells of a revelatory descent into the uncanny. For the Recluse seems to have discovered another land and in it another House; a jade-green double of his own in a realm rife with beasts and cosmic beings without name, encroaching on the bounds of reality itself.

With a new introduction by Ann VanderMeer exploring why Hodgson's tale is the "perfect embodiment of a weird novel", this edition of the 1908 cult classic still thrums with the visionary energy which influenced countless writers including H. P. Lovecraft and Terry Pratchett.

Aeons in the future, Earth's surface faces perpetual night after the failing of the Sun. Humanity is entrenched within the Last Redoubt, a colossal metal pyramid. Beyond the safety of its structure lurk countless unknowable threats.

William Hope Hodgson's strange, visionary novel of humanity's struggle for survival in the eternal darkness of the future was first published in 1912, and is widely acknowledged to be one of the foundation works of the 'Dying Earth' subgenre of Fantasy and Science Fiction. Written in a style composed of strange archaisms which fuel the weird sense of disorientation, this cult classic has won the admiration of writers from Brian Aldiss to C. S. Lewis, who wrote: "*The Night Land* gives, like certain rare dreams, sensations we never had before."

For more Tales of the Weird titles
visit the British Library Shop (shop.bl.uk)

We welcome any suggestions, corrections or feedback you may have, and will
aim to respond to all items addressed to the following:

The Editor (Tales of the Weird), British Library Publishing,
The British Library, 96 Euston Road, London NW1 2DB

We also welcome enquiries through our social media accounts, @BL_Publishing.